were mixed and confused

She knew Jeff was the same person, and yet, he was very different. He was still handsome, in a rugged, totally masculine way. He still had the capability to make her body tingle with an emotion she had never felt with anyone else.

She suspected it was purely sexual. There was a chemistry between them that was as strong now as ever and just as inexplicable. She hadn't understood it then and didn't understand it tonight. The brush of his fingers over hers or his arm against her arm was so innocent, and yet so exciting that her heart would leap every time they accidentally touched. It was something that should have been left behind in her youth....

And she wasn't certain how to handle it.

To my readers,

As the last book in my "Angel" series, *Angel of Mercy* has special meaning for me. It's a story of old loves, unfulfilled dreams, and new beginnings. In the series I tried to include characters that represented every aspect of those who participated in the Vietnam War, including a pilot, an MIA, a nurse who found out good intentions were not enough, a soldier who had to find a reason to live, and all the loved ones that were left behind. These people grew up in an era of turmoil and change and it took until their stories were told for them to accept the past. I lived it with them; now I can let it go.

I am also thrilled that Scott Sanders, the hero of *Kissed by an Angel* (#282, February 1989) won the *Romantic Times* Series WISH Hero award for the best contemporary hero of 1989. I thought he was pretty special, and I'm pleased that others did, too.

Kathy Clark

KATHY CLARK

ANGEL OF MERCY

Harlequin Books

TORONTO • NEW YORK • LONDON
AMSTERDAM • PARIS • SYDNEY • HAMBURG
STOCKHOLM • ATHENS • TOKYO • MILAN

According to the Vietnam Veterans of America, Inc.
Resource Center, over 58,000 men and women lost their
lives in the Vietnam War, 303,704 U.S. personnel were
wounded and recent statistics state that 150,000 vets
committed suicide since their return from the war.

This book is dedicated to all of those courageous men
and women who made the ultimate sacrifice, as well as
to the people whose hearts were broken because of their
deaths.

Special thanks to my dear friends, the Browns and
Garrisons, who live in Montrose, Colorado, and were
invaluable sources of information on sheep ranching
and Western hospitality.

Published November 1990

ISBN 0-373-16366-5

Chapter One

"Yesterday" —The Beatles

The noise from the crowded VFW hall spilled into the parking lot and beckoned late arrivals to hurry inside. It was unseasonably warm for Denver in March, yet still cool enough for a jacket...and too cool to linger outside long.

Yet Angela Greene stayed in her rented car, hiding in the shadows as she watched dozens of people park their vehicles, then funnel in the front door of the huge yellow, metallic building.

She shivered and pulled her rose-colored blazer tighter around her. But she knew it wouldn't warm her. The chill came from within.

Her fingers fumbled for the keys and she clicked the starter into position. No one would miss her if she didn't join the party. In fact, no one knew she had considered attending this reunion, not even her closest friends, back home in Boston. This was a part of her life she had shut off, as if pretending it hadn't existed would make the memories go away.

Then why was she here? Why had she timed her vacation to coincide with this reunion and flown almost two thousand miles to arrive at this place?

The truth of the matter was...she didn't know. When she had first seen the announcement printed in the local newspaper, she hadn't given it more than a passing glance. The last thing she wanted was to get together with other men and women who had served with the military in Vietnam. She had severed those ties with the past and had no desire to become wrapped up in them again. But when she heard about the reunion on *Good Morning America*, then heard it mentioned several times on the radio, Angela's ambivalence had slowly warmed to curiosity.

So why was she still sitting outside?

Because, not for the first time in her life where the war was concerned, she was scared spitless...not of who she might see, but of who she might not. It was the ghosts she couldn't face, the ghosts of all those soldiers she hadn't been able to save. Or those she *had* been able to help, but who had promptly been sent back out to fight again. The confusion of that situation was that she hadn't known whether or not to be pleased with her success rate, because her skill and tender care had often simply postponed a death warrant from the Vietcong. How many faces would she recognize tonight? And how many faces would she never see again? How many men's lives had been irrevocably changed because of their crippling injuries, physical and emotional?

More people were arriving and the parking lot was rapidly filling up. Men dressed in everything from suits to old uniforms and camouflage fatigues passed in front of her car on their way to the hall. Most had brought their wives or girlfriends, but there were quite a few men who were, like Angela, alone.

This is ridiculous, Angela thought. *You've come all this way. Get out of the car and go inside. You might surprise yourself and have a good time.* That thought elicited a skeptical snort. *Okay, okay. If you can't have a good time, then at least confront your fears and get this thing over with as quickly as possible.*

She switched the ignition off, pulled the keys out and dropped them in her purse in a burst of resolve. There was a possibility she wouldn't know a single person inside the building, and their conversations about missing buddies would be about people she had never met. After all, during the war, more than two and a half million Americans had served in South Vietnam. What were the odds that of the five hundred or so who would show up at this reunion there would be veterans she knew?

Feeling much stronger after her little pep talk, Angela flashed a quick look in the rearview mirror to see if her hair was still combed and her lipstick fresh. Satisfied that her appearance was as good as she could make it, she took the critical first step out of her car. Crossing the parking lot was easy. Pulling open the heavy metal door and stepping into the lobby didn't take much nerve. Signing in at the registration table and sticking a name tag on her lapel wasn't difficult. But as she stood in the doorway that led into the large ballroom, a fresh wave of anxiety rooted her to the spot.

HE DIDN'T KNOW WHY he had come. This was the type of social event he usually avoided like the plague. And the timing couldn't have been worse. As he stood near the silent jukebox at the far end of the room, his thoughts kept straying from the people and festivities around him to the activities at his sheep ranch. It had been insanity to consider leaving at the beginning of lambing . . . even if he was gone for only one night. This was the most important time of the year for a sheep rancher, and he knew he shouldn't be shirking his responsibilities. He was trusting Doch Thu and his family to hold the fort until he returned, and while he knew they would do a fine job, he felt guilty that he wasn't there to take his usual sixteen-hour shift.

"Hey, Hawk. What are you doing hanging around way over here?" A friendly, slightly slurred voice interrupted the man's thoughts. "I found a couple of guys from our battalion. We were heading toward the bar for drinks and thought you might like to come along. Lucky's saving us a table."

"Nah, Gopher. You go on without me," the man answered. "I'll probably leave early and head on home tonight, so I'd better stay away from the bar."

Gopher apparently knew his buddy well enough to know it was almost an impossibility to change Hawk's mind. Instead, he squinted a surprisingly perceptive stare at Hawk and asked, "Is she here?"

Hawk's fossilized features didn't betray even a flicker of emotion. "She who?"

"Yeah, right. Pretend like you don't remember," Gopher snorted. "*She*, the babe you wouldn't talk about when you were awake, but whose name you kept muttering over and over in your sleep."

"Your ears and your memory are too damn good," Hawk snapped. "That was a lifetime ago. I haven't thought of that woman in years. I couldn't care less if she showed up here tonight or not."

"Yeah, right," Gopher repeated. Even in his slightly inebriated condition, it was evident he wasn't convinced of Hawk's disinterest. "Well, it probably doesn't matter. She was married, wasn't she?"

Hawk's broad shoulders lifted in a careless shrug.

"I'll bet she wouldn't look anything like you remember, anyway. Eighteen years and fifty pounds can sure change a woman, you know."

Eighteen years...fifty pounds...married. None of it mattered. She was merely a shadow in the darkness of his past. For all Hawk knew or cared, she could have danced by him half a dozen times this evening without him taking the slightest notice.

"You'd better hurry," Hawk encouraged his friend, subtly maneuvering the conversation. "The bar's probably crowded, and you'll lose your place at the table."

"Are you sure you won't come have a drink with us?"

"I'm sure. I've had about as much of this as I can take. Tell Lucky I'll be in touch. I'm working on a few cases now, but I don't have anything solid yet."

"Just give us a call. It's been almost a year since our last trip *in country*." Gopher gave a mirthless chuckle. "When I left there in '73, I couldn't wait to kick the stinking mud off my boots. But now, if I don't get over there every so often, I get antsy. You know what I mean?"

Hawk nodded. "Yeah, I know. It's sort of like a trip to the dentist. You don't really want to go, and yet, for whatever reason, you *have* to."

Gopher slapped Hawk on the shoulder in a companionable gesture. "It's good seeing you again, man. Especially in a place where we don't have to constantly watch our butts."

"I wouldn't let my guard down too soon if I was you. Don't forget, while you're in the bar with your buddies, your wife is out on the dance floor with hundreds of guys to choose from." Hawk's expression sobered as he added, "Not to mention that digging up memories and rehashing old battles can be dangerous in its own way."

Gopher cast a concerned glance in his wife's general direction. "Nah, I don't have to worry about these guys. They're all old, fat and balding."

A hint of a smile touched Hawk's lips. "Don't look now, buddy, but you and I are heading over the same hill."

"Speak for yourself! I'm thirty-nine and holding. And I may have gained a few pounds over the years, but it's all muscle."

Hawk didn't reply. He let the skeptical arch of one dark eyebrow speak in eloquent dispute.

Instead of being insulted by his friend's silent taunt, Gopher chuckled and began weaving his way through the crowd.

Hawk's gaze followed his old friend until the man reached the door that led to the reception area. As Gopher disappeared from his line of vision, Hawk's attention was caught by a person standing just outside the doorway. Almost hidden by the shadows in the hallway, the woman was definitely keeping a safe distance between herself and the surge of humanity inside the ballroom. He couldn't tell whether she was waiting for someone before she joined the party or if she was hiding, hesitant to enter the room.

He couldn't see her features, but even from a distance, there was something very familiar about her. His curiosity aroused, he began strolling through the crowd, slowly working his way closer. Since he had every intention of leaving soon, he figured he might as well head toward the exit.

The disc jockey chose that moment to return to the stage and, with the first chords of a Beach Boys tune, people paired off and began dancing to the old, familiar music. With the mass of moving bodies shifting and swaying, Hawk had to change his course several times to reach the edge of the crowd, encountering one obstacle after another that slowed his progress.

There were dozens of men clustered in groups along the walls. They were deep in individual conversations, oblivious to the dancers and to the man trying to reach the door. Hawk's experienced eye categorized the men as he passed them. He could tell by the way they were dressed, the loudness of their voices and the exaggerations of their stories what kind of soldiers they had been.

But he had to give credit to the people who had showed up tonight, regardless of how they acted. At least they were willing to acknowledge the fact that they were Vietnam veterans. It had been a wasteful, embarrassing war, one most people were desperate to forget. These men and women might not have agreed with the politics, but they weren't ashamed to admit they had served their country.

When Hawk had first heard of the reunion, he'd been skeptical that anyone would come. Even though Vietnam veterans from around the nation had been notified, he hadn't expected many people to participate. He lived on the other side of the Rockies, only six hours from Denver, so the effort and expense were minimal, although he could ill afford the lost time. Which brought him back to the irrationality of his presence in this place on this particular evening.

ANGELA'S GAZE FLICKERED around the room, anxious yet hesitant. There were a few people she recognized, in spite of the years and life experiences that had passed. Most of the attendees were in a festive mood, eagerly partaking of the open bar, well-stocked buffet tables and good fellowship with long-lost friends.

As the moments passed and only good memories swirled through her mind, Angela began to believe she was being silly for not joining the party. She hadn't quite taken that final step into the ballroom when someone stumbled behind her and practically pushed her onto the dance floor.

"I'm sorry, miss . . . Lieutenant Greene!"

Angela turned to see who had bumped into her, and a delighted smile spilled across her face. "Captain Stone, sir," she responded, automatically reverting to her old form of address for the man who had been her superior officer.

"It's just *Dr.* Stone now," he answered with a relaxed cheerfulness she remembered so well. It had been this man's positive, professional, yet almost always joking attitude that had pulled Angela and the other members of the EVAC hospital staff through long, exhausting shifts. "And since I'm no longer your boss, you can call me John," he added.

Angela couldn't resist chuckling at the familiar line of banter they had picked up as if it had been last week instead of more than seventeen years ago that they had teased each other about how she should address him. The overall atmosphere in the hospitals had been so tense, so tragic, that it had seemed silly to refer to each other as captain and lieutenant, and they had long ago lapsed into a less formal relationship when no other officers were around to hear them.

And yet, even though their companionship could have turned into something personal, it never had. They had kept their association on a business level, partly because it would have strained their working relationship, but mainly because the doctor had been happily married, and Angela had been madly in love with a different soldier.

But she didn't want to be reminded of that part of her time in Vietnam, any more than she wanted to think of the blood that had permanently stained her clothes or the men who had died in her arms.

· "My wife's still in the ladies' room, so why don't you dance this one with me?" John Stone asked.

His invitation effectively ended her debate, and Angela took his hand as the mellow voices of the Righteous Brothers flowed through the speakers. It wasn't the first time they had danced together, although the polished wood floor beneath their feet was much smoother than the sheets of plywood that had covered the dirt floor of the officers' club in their medical facility. There, a huge, circular tent had draped over their heads, protecting them from the tropical weather. The canvas walls had been rolled up most of the time, allowing an occasional breeze from the China Sea to provide a natural form of air conditioning. It had been crude and uncomfortable, unlike tonight's facilities.

Angela's gaze was drawn to the acoustic ceiling of the ballroom. Bumping against the tiles were hundreds of red, white and blue helium-filled balloons that trailed curly ribbon tails above the heads of the dancers. Long painted banners listed the names of the divisions and nicknames of fire bases, along with a neatly lettered welcome to the Vietnam veterans.

She knew all too well that it hadn't always been so friendly for the soldiers who had been lucky enough to come home alive. The anger and disgust with America's participation in the war had been wrongly directed toward the men and women in uniform, even those who had been noncombatants such as herself. She had been shocked at the reception she had received when she arrived on American soil. The bitterness and hostility of her native countrymen, combined with the tragedy and pain she had left behind had caused her to drastically change the course of her life.

"So where's your uniform?" John asked, surveying her trim figure with an almost clinical appraisal. "You look like you could still fit into it."

"I have no idea where it is," she answered honestly. She didn't explain that she couldn't have worn her uniform tonight because seventeen years ago, as soon as she was discharged from the Army, she had thrown it into the nearest dumpster. No longer able to witness the suffering in a hospital, she had also tossed aside her nursing career. Anticipating his next question, she said, "I gave up nursing years ago. I went back to school and earned a degree in veterinary medicine."

The quizzical lift of John's bushy eyebrows confirmed her suspicions that he at least partially understood her reasons, yet questioned her abandonment of a worthwhile profession. But he didn't press the subject. Instead he brought up a new one—one that struck an even more distressful chord. "So where is that husband of yours? Did he stay home with the kids?"

She had known it was a question that would come up sooner or later this evening. Perhaps that was why she'd been so reluctant to speak to anyone. Of course, they would wonder where Craig was. Anyone who had known her during the last six months of her duty in the field hospital would remember the impromptu wedding, complete with a white silk Oriental gown and a beautiful bouquet of native orchids.

The ceremony had taken place on the helicopter pad because almost everyone at the EVAC unit had wanted to attend. There had been far too few happy occasions to celebrate, not to mention the fact that the soldiers never let an excuse to party pass without taking advantage of it.

As clearly as if it were yesterday, Angela remembered the golden blessing of the sun and the blissful silence from the skies as no choppers brought in wounded while she and Craig stood in front of the chaplain. But as she turned, in her mind's eye, toward her groom, she saw, not his boyishly handsome face, but the hard, uncompromising features of Craig's best friend, Jeff.

Angela gave herself a mental shake. She refused to think about Jeff. He was one of those ghosts from her past—a ghost she didn't know whether she wanted to confront or forget. He was one of those men whose fate had been decided in those hostile jungles so long ago.

"Angela?" John's voice in her ear reminded her that the conversation had been suspended for several minutes.

"Oh, I'm sorry. I was just thinking about…well, you know how it is. Just a word or a name triggers a whole parade of memories."

"I was asking about Craig," he reminded her with innocent persistence, "and your children."

"No children. Craig and I never got around to starting a family."

"You're speaking of him as if he's in the past tense. The two of you didn't get a divorce, did you?"

Angela took a deep, steadying breath before answering. "Craig died several years ago."

John was clearly shocked. "I hadn't heard. I'm really sorry. You two seemed like such a nice couple. Although I wasn't sure which one of those two fellas you would pick. As I remember, Craig's friend was pretty crazy about you, too.''

"Not really," she denied. "I think it was more of a case of attraction because of the circumstances. If he hadn't been so sick, and if I hadn't been one of the few round-eyed women in the area, and if there hadn't been a daily tango with life and death, he wouldn't have given me a second look. We didn't have anything in common.''

The doctor shrugged, wisely noting, at last, that the mention of Craig and Jeff was upsetting her. Attempting to distract her with an unexpected spin that was followed by a dangerously low dip, he winced. "I haven't done that in years." He gingerly twisted his shoulders, testing the strain on his lower back.

"Do you want me to find you a doctor, Doctor?" she asked, appreciating his effort to lift her sagging spirits.

"Are you kidding? I'm in the hands of the best nurse I've ever had the pleasure of working with. Maybe you could just ease me toward the door. I think I'll sit the next few dances out."

"Your wife should love that."

He chuckled, apparently seeing the danger in becoming a deserter from the dance floor when his wife was ready to take a waltz down memory lane. "Or maybe I'll just grit my teeth and hide the pain...for the sake of peace."

"That's one thing we've all learned the value of," she replied with a wisdom forged from the harshest of realities.

The song ended as they reached the door. Smoothly John guided them toward a woman who was calmly waiting.

"I hope you're not going to tell me you threw your back out again," she commented in a severe tone to her husband, but a friendly wink to Angela took all the sting out of the woman's words.

"Me?" John asked with exaggerated surprise. "I wouldn't dream of using such a lame excuse not to dance with my beautiful wife. Besides, I've got the body of a man twenty years younger."

"Where are you hiding it?" his wife teased.

"Do you see why I volunteered for an extra year in Nam?" he asked Angela, but the glow of affection in his eyes contradicted his words.

Angela felt a twinge of envy for the happily married couple. They had lived through the bad times and the good times—together. Evidently, their relationship had not merely survived, but had grown stronger. It was what Angela had expected to share with her husband. But something had gone wrong.

"Winnie, this is Angela, that gorgeous nurse I was always writing home about." John couldn't seem to leave well enough alone. "And Angela, this is my wife."

"Nice to meet you at last," Angela said and she held out her hand toward the older woman. "I hope you don't mind that I borrowed him for a dance."

"Of course not," Winnie answered cheerfully, as she took Angela's hand in a warm, firm grasp. "If being married to a doctor has taught me anything, it's patience. First, he went off to war when he was barely out of med school, then he worked late every evening and on weekends while he was setting up his practice, and now he's either at the hospital or on the golf course."

"I am not." John leaped to his own defense when it became obvious no one else was going to stand up for him. "I don't play golf that often." His eyes twinkled as he added, "I prefer tennis."

"Then show me some of your moves," Winnie challenged. "This is the first time we've been out of range of your beeper in months."

Angela smiled as they eased onto the dance floor together. She watched until they swirled into the slowly rotating crowd, then she turned, intending to head for the buffet table to get a glass of punch.

She had taken only a few steps when a man moved into her line of vision, separating himself from the mass of humanity that now filled the VFW hall to overflowing. Her gaze traveled up the broad expanse of his chest, over the blunt jut of his chin to the firm set of his lips and the brilliance of his silvery blue eyes. A shock of dark, walnut brown hair fell across his forehead, and he pushed it back with an impatient hand.

"Jeff," she whispered around the pulsing lump that had leaped into her throat, almost cutting off her air supply. Somehow she resisted the urge to reach out and touch him to see if he was really there.

"Angela," he responded, but there was no welcome in his voice or his scrutiny of her. His eyes, cold as crystals, observed her with what appeared to be only remote interest. "You look as if you've just seen a ghost."

Chapter Two

"The First Time Ever I Saw Your Face" —Roberta Flack

He had no idea where he was. Nothing was familiar, not the sounds, not the smells, not the feel of a soft mattress beneath his back ... and especially not the burning pain that seared through his shoulder when he tried to push himself into a sitting position. Weakly, he fell back against the pillow, a real pillow, the first soft, clean-smelling object his head had touched for weeks.

There was a window behind the iron headboard of his bed, and he could hear the steady splatter of rain against the metal awning, a sound much preferable to the drizzle of rain sliding down banana leaves and dripping onto his face. Groans oozed from the darkness. He looked around, noting that there were at least two dozen beds in the room, all filled with patients like himself, and he knew he must be in some sort of hospital. The question was ... whose? American? Or Vietcong?

A surge of panic flashed through him, fully awakening his battle-sharpened senses. His gaze flitted anxiously around the room, searching for something that would identify the facility's nationality. But even as he searched for clues to comfort his fears, his instincts told him this had to be an American field hospital. It was too comfortable and too clean to be a Vietnamese prison.

And, other than the IV tube that was taped to his arm, there was nothing restraining him to the bed. Surely, if he had been captured by the enemy, he would have constraints of some sort discouraging his escape.

Not that he was strong enough to leave even if he had the opportunity, he thought as the throb in his shoulder grew worse. A large, white bandage covered the left side of his upper chest, from his neck to his armpit, so he couldn't see the wound. But he knew from the pain and the spreading bloodstain that was soaking through the gauze that it must be bad. His entire left arm was numb, and no matter how hard he concentrated, he couldn't curl his fingers into a fist. It frightened him to consider the possibilities that might indicate, but from the damage he had witnessed to others, he knew he was lucky to still have his arm attached to his shoulder. Another ripple of pain tore through his chest, and he squeezed his eyes shut and gritted his teeth until the spasm subsided. It hadn't hurt this much when the bullet ripped through his flesh.

Every detail of the attack was clear in his memory. Like a movie, it flickered through his mind, beginning with the scene where he and his squad jumped out of the helicopter just before dawn. A layer of fog clung eerily to the jungle floor, its thick, white moisture swirling around like ghostly warriors in the wind from the chopper's slashing blades. Within seconds, all fourteen soldiers were on the ground and the helicopter lifted off, disappearing into the predawn darkness. For several minutes, the jungle was silent. The men froze, waiting...listening...until the insects resumed their hum, and the chatter of monkeys and the random squawk of birds settling on their roosts reassured the soldiers that all was normal.

They immediately hiked out of the area to lessen their chances of discovery, not stopping until noon. As they sat, eating cold rations out of their packs, they reviewed the map and finalized their plans. They had been sent to locate and provide security for the crew of a chopper that had gone down during a vertical assault in a hot landing zone. A radioed S.O.S. had provided the coordinates. They hoped the crew had moved to a safer hiding place, but Hawk had a point on which to focus.

And even though they were south of the demilitarized zone in the Ashau Valley, an area that was supposed to be under South Vietnamese control, Hawk was aware the danger was very real. The Vietcong had begun to infiltrate the jungles in preparation for an all-out assault on the coastal cities. Not that there was any place in the entire country that was safe anymore.

So Hawk knew it was imperative that he and his men complete this mission as quickly and covertly as possible. More lives than just those of the chopper's crew depended on it.

As they neared the spot, they moved cautiously, slipping in single file through the thickness of the jungle, pausing often to listen for sounds of the crew or the enemy. When they discovered the downed chopper, Hawk signaled his men to remain hidden. There was no sign of activity around the battered helicopter, but Hawk's survival instincts told him to hold back . . . that all was not as it seemed.

He had been ordered to find the chopper and the crew. The gunship's blades were twisted and bent, and there were bullet holes in its green metallic skin, but the landing must have been soft. There were no signs of a fire or a fuel leak, which improved the chances of finding the crew alive. Obviously, at least one member had survived and had had time to send a message.

"Are we going to search the chopper?"

Hawk glanced at the man next to him, who had whispered the question. The man's wide-eyed naiveté was frightening. Hawk had been promoted to sergeant only two months ago, and this was the first squad he had commanded, but he had enough experience to know when a new recruit needed a little extra supervision. Private Greene definitely fell into that category. And yet, there was something about the man's unfailing cheerfulness and enthusiasm for a task, no matter how demeaning or how dangerous, that made his lack of military wisdom forgivable. "In a minute, Greene," Hawk answered. "We'll split up and search the area…"

Before he could complete his plan, his attention was drawn to a man in an American flight suit who was stepping out of the underbrush on the other side of the chopper.

"There's one of the crew members," the private stated unnecessarily, and started to stand.

Hawk reacted by reflex. He reached out and yanked Greene down. "Wait. I don't like the feel of this. Something's not right."

"But, Sarge, that's Joe Cox. He's the gunner on that chopper."

"I know." Hawk rubbed his hand around the back of his neck, wiping away the sweat that trickled down his shirt. So strong was his intuition of danger, he almost expected to feel his hair standing on end, and was surprised it was not.

Joe Cox stopped and glanced into the downed helicopter. He appeared to be listening to someone, then he turned away from the chopper and peered into the underbrush as if he were searching for the rescue team.

Everything seemed to be in order, and Hawk began to wonder if he wasn't being overly cautious. A check of his watch showed he had less than thirty minutes left to get the chopper's crew and his own squad to a prearranged rendezvous point where a large Huey gunship would be touching down just long enough to pick the men up and ferry them to their units. He knew he had to make a move...now.

"Okay, men, let's check it out," he ordered, his hushed voice not reflecting his concern. He had been told that a good leader didn't let his men see his indecisiveness. Uncertainty would be viewed as a weakness, and Hawk didn't want to lose the respect of his squad. However, he couldn't resist adding, "But let's hurry so we can get the hell out of here. I hate the jungle."

The soldiers began easing forward through the bushes, pushing aside the palmetto fronds and tangled vines as they divided their attention between the ground, watching for snakes, and the man standing next to the crippled chopper. The rustle of the plants and leaves drew Joe's attention, and a strange expression froze on his face.

Hawk's squad was just stepping into the clearing when Joe flashed a terrified look behind him, then shouted, "It's a trap! don't come any closer, or they'll . . ." As he called out his warning, Joe threw himself to the ground, but he had sealed his fate by warning the other Americans.

A half dozen Vietcong leaped out of the gunship, their automatic rifles heralding their presence. Joe was the first GI to feel the bite of the bullets, but the shots that were peppering the underbrush were finding other American targets.

Hawk shouted orders, but he couldn't be heard over the earsplitting thunder of weapon fire and the cries of agony when the shiny missiles pierced human flesh. He was lying on his stomach with his rifle resting on a log. The action was too hot and heavy for him to see which of his men had been hit. In the middle of a firefight, a soldier couldn't afford to think. He had to focus on keeping his weapon loaded and hoping it wouldn't jam...and praying that he wouldn't be unlucky enough to be in the wrong place at the same time as an enemy bullet.

In actual time, the small skirmish didn't last long, probably no more than two or three minutes. But to some of the participants, it lasted a lifetime.

The final shot sounded, and a heavy, lifeless silence fell on the small area. No soldier, American or NVA, was left standing. The small troop of Vietcong ambushers lay sprawled in the weeds near the chopper, their deaths evidence of their underestimation of the American rescue team. But Hawk's squad had suffered greatly, too. And Hawk had finally met a bullet with his name on it.

He didn't remember the exact moment he had known he was hit. The wound was to his left shoulder, so he had been able to continue firing his rifle with deadly accuracy. But now that the battle was over, he couldn't help but notice the blood...and the pain.

However, as the squad's leader, he had responsibilities, the first of which was to check the condition of his men. Forcing himself to his knees, he crawled from one soldier to the next...from one body to the next... hoping, praying they would be alive...and bitterly disappointed when they weren't. Tears of sadness, anger, frustration and fear stung his eyelids. This was his squad. These were his men, his friends. How could he have survived when they had all died? How could he have let them all get killed?

During his brief time as a sergeant, he had led his squad on several missions—all dangerous, and all successful. Until this one. He had witnessed more deaths than he ever cared to, but he had never lost one of his own men. It hurt as badly as if he had lost an arm or a leg . . . and multiplied by thirteen made the reality unbearable.

"Hawk . . . help me." A weak voice broke the suffocating silence, and Hawk eagerly scrambled toward the sound.

The only man he hadn't located had been the one he had been most afraid to find. The greenest of green recruits, Craig Greene had desperately needed help in surviving the harshness of war. Although his personality was the exact opposite of Hawk's, the two men had, for some inexplicable reason, immediately hit it off. Hawk had helped Craig through the rough spots, and Craig's lively sense of humor brought laughter to a grim existence.

"Greene, are you hit?"

There was a wry chuckle. "I wouldn't mind getting a hit. It's the strikeouts that I'm worried about."

"Don't joke, buddy. How are you?" Hawk had reached the other man, but the effort cost him. "I hope you're stronger than me, or neither one of us are going to get out of this hellhole."

Craig propped himself up on one elbow and looked at Hawk. "They got me in the leg, and I think it's broken.

I'm not going anywhere unless an angel drops from the sky and carries me out of here."

Hawk blinked his eyes and tried to force them into focus. The jungle was beginning to spin around him, and his lungs couldn't seem to draw in enough air to satisfy his gasping need. "That angel had better hurry," he whispered. "Or the devil's going to get me first."

He must have passed out because he didn't remember anything from that moment until he awoke in this hospital bed. He had no idea how he had gotten from death's door to this place. For that matter, he had no idea where this place was.

Greene! Where was Greene? Had he made it, too? Hawk decided there were too many questions and too few answers . . . a dilemma he could resolve. If only he could get up and find someone to fill him in on the details.

With his right hand supporting his left arm, once again he tried to sit up. He was able to swing his legs over the side of the bed, but bringing his body into an upright position took every ounce of his remaining energy. A layer of cold sweat coated his skin, and the muscles in his arms and legs were quivering as if he had just finished a fifty-mile jog wearing a fully loaded pack.

"What's going on here, Sergeant?" A soft, feminine voice broke through the hazy fog that seemed to be swirling around him. "You don't have anyplace better to be right now. Just lie back," she whispered soothingly.

The slender fingers that lifted his legs onto the bed and guided his shoulders to the mattress were gentle, yet strong. The hand that brushed the damp hair off his forehead and pulled the sheet up to cover his almost nude body was soft and comforting.

He dared not open his eyes until the dizziness stopped, but the simple fact of her presence was reassuring. It was a relief that her voice—her lovely, New England-accented voice—proved he was, indeed, in an American hospital. He had been in the field for so long, it seemed like years since he had heard such a sweet sound.

And her fragrance, light and feminine, caressed his mistreated olfactory senses with tenderness. His nostrils, usually filled with the putrid smell of sweat and death, the rotting greenness of the jungle, the sickening odor of soured mud mixed with human excrement and blood, flared eagerly, wanting to draw in every delightful breath he could before she moved out of his range.

"I'm going to have to change this bandage," she informed him, keeping her voice low so she wouldn't disturb the patients sleeping nearby. "If it hurts too much, tell me. I can give you another shot of morphine for the pain."

Hawk's jaw clenched as the gauze stuck to the wound, but he shook his head against the offer of a shot. She gently freed the bandage, then eased the soiled dressing off and shined a flashlight on his shoulder.

The room had slowed to a lazy revolution, so he dared open his eyes at last, to see if the image of her was in the least bit similar to the picture his mind had conjured. It was too dark to make out any details from the shadows beyond his bed, but as the nurse bent over him, her face was bathed in the soft golden glow of the flashlight, making her appear to be a beautiful, angelic apparition rather than a flesh-and-blood woman. Almost black hair casually styled in a straight pixie cut was striking in its stark simplicity, and served to highlight her delicate features.

But it was her eyes, large, intelligent, compassionate eyes, that dominated her lovely face. In the dim, distorted light, he couldn't determine their exact color. However, he could feel their warmth, their caring, as distinctly as a physical touch. In spite of his injury and the circumstances—or perhaps because of them—his male body, eager from its long period without satisfaction, reacted instinctively.

If she noticed, she didn't give any indication as she applied a fresh bandage to his chest. He appreciated her sensitivity because his natural response was more than a little embarrassing. In her line of work, and considering there weren't that many Caucasian women in this part of the world, she must encounter that sort of reaction with all her patients. He regretted that he couldn't manage a dignified restraint, at least until he got to know her better.

"How bad is it?" he asked, desperate to get his mind off his frustration and on to something of a more paramount importance at the moment.

"Bad enough to get you a couple of months of R and R, but not bad enough to get you a one-way ticket home," she answered, a tired, almost apologetic smile curling her lips.

"How about my men? Did any of them make it, too?"

She lifted her slim, fatigue-covered shoulders. "I'm sorry, but I don't know. People arrive in groups, and I don't know, right off, where they come from or which company they're with." She trimmed the ends of the tape and carefully smoothed them flat on his heated skin. "If you'll give me a few names, I'll check on them for you. This is only one ward out of a half dozen, so they might have survived but not been put here."

"Actually, there w
it." A pain even more
wound twisted deep in his g
hadn't been true until he said
Greene . . . do you recognize the

She shook her head, but tempe
sponse with a qualifying encourage
doesn't mean anything. When things are
notice names. And then there are the really
when I don't even remember my own." Finished
bandage, she reached into her pocket and pulled
thermometer, which she wiped with a clean piece
gauze dipped in alcohol and popped into his mouth.
Lifting his wrist, she positioned her finger on his pulse
and studied her watch as she waited for the mercury to
register his temperature.

"Fo, what'f yourf?" he asked, his question getting
tangled around the piece of glass under his tongue.

She gave him a questioning look, but didn't speak
until she finished the count of his heartbeats and took
the thermometer out.

"So, what's yours?" he repeated persistently.

"My what?"

"Your name."

She turned the beam of the flashlight onto a name
badge that was pinned on the pocket of her jacket.
"Lieutenant Nichols," she answered with just the
slightest accent on the rank.

He sensed it was meant to intimidate him, but, after
all he had been through lately, a silver bar on a very attractive chest wasn't enough to discourage him. "No
first name?"

Even in the semidarkness, he could see her eyes twinkle. "It's Angela."

ddle of the

," she an-
t now, sol-
ky it's been

e conversa-
But he was
to relax be-
his forehead
quickly si-

I'll look for
re I leave in

as only one who could have made
wrenching than his shoulder
ut as he spoke. It was as if it
d it aloud. "Private Craig
name?"
red her negative re-
ment. "But that
busy, I don't
hectic times
with the
out a
of

Another whiff of her perfume drifted through his consciousness and lingered long after she moved away. As his heavy eyelids shut, he could still feel the imprint of her fingers against his skin. Tomorrow he would find out how he had gotten from the bloodied battleground in the jungle to the paradise of this hospital, and where Greene was. And, while he was asking questions, he would ask a few about Lieutenant Angela Nichols.

He awoke to the discomfort of someone removing his bandage. Still feeling the effects of the morphine he had been given, and still weak from the battle and the loss of blood, his sluggish eyelids didn't want to open...not until the memory of last night's encounter with an angel of mercy named Angela penetrated his brain. Looking up at the nurse dabbing antiseptic on his wound, the welcoming smile faded into disappointment. The woman standing next to him was no less attractive, her hands were no less gentle, nor was she any less skilled than Angela. Yet, in Hawk's opinion, this lady was a poor substitute for the one whose face had dominated his dreams. And any woman whose visage could replace the nightmarish reenactments of his tour of duty that usually filled his restless nights was worth her weight in gold.

It was more distressing to think that, to Lieutenant Nichols, he was just another patient. Hawk was amazed at how much that unpleasant realization affected him.

"Hold this under your tongue, please." The nurse thrust a thermometer into his mouth and took his pulse, exactly as Angela had, but Hawk's obedience was unenthusiastic.

"Don't look so glum, soldier," she said in a cheery voice. "You're going to be up and around in no time. The doctor will be here to have a look at that shoulder later this morning. That's when he'll decide if it needs a cast or not."

Dozens of questions tumbled through his mind, but he decided to save them for the doctor. Hawk wasn't in the mood for idle conversation with anyone who couldn't give him exact answers.

"Someone will be bringing your breakfast in just a couple of minutes," the nurse informed him. "I don't know how long you've been in the field, but I'm sure it'll be a nice change for you to have a hot meal." She checked the thermometer, wrote his temperature on his chart, then tidied the sheet over his feet and tucked the corners under the mattress before moving on to the next patient.

Stiff and uncomfortable, Hawk shifted in the bed, then returned to his original position when he felt a strain on his arm. The darkest of black moods settled on him and he would have allowed himself to wallow in a sea of self-pity if he hadn't chosen that moment to look around the room.

The fellow in the bed next to him had half his face and the top of his head swathed in bandages. Breathing tubes were inserted in his mouth, and he lay flat on his back, immobile except for the rise and fall of his chest.

On the other side was a man who appeared to have had both his legs amputated, either by an enemy land mine or a surgeon's knife. Down the line, men with similar afflictions were suffering with injuries much worse than Hawk's, and he began feeling slightly ashamed to have felt sorry for himself when there were so many others who were obviously much worse off.

He had his limbs, and, most importantly, his life, which was more than he could say for the rest of his squad. If he was going to feel bad about anything, that was definitely something worth his anxiety. Those men had been his responsibility. And he had failed them.

He had smelled a trap. Why hadn't he listened to his gut feelings? His head rolled on the pillow, and he stared at the slow drip of medication sliding down the tube that was attached to a needle in his forearm. Resisting the urge to yank it out and suffer the consequences, he bit back a cry of torment. He loved being a soldier. The day he was promoted to sergeant had been one of the happiest of his life. At last he was being given the opportunity to prove his leadership abilities. The United States Army was entrusting an entire squad to him.

And he had blown it. He had proven what his father had always said was true. Jeff Hawkins was a loser.

Chapter Three

"Those Were The Days" —Mary Hopkin

"The bullet missed your vital organs, but it tore some ligaments and cracked your clavicle." The doctor was carefully studying Hawk's injury and comparing it to a new set of X rays. "Because we need to change the bandages on the wound often to avoid infection, we won't be able to set your shoulder in any sort of permanent cast. Instead, I'm going to tape a splint along the top of the clavicle and make you promise to take it easy for a while. I don't suppose you're going to have any problems with that order, are you, Sergeant?"

"No, sir, Captain Stone," Hawk answered, automatically returning the jovial doctor's friendly smile. "I think I can handle a little R and R. How long do you figure it will take..." He hesitated for a nervous second, then added, "To get completely well?"

"Five or six weeks, if we're lucky. And, barring any unforeseen complications, it *should* get completely well." John Stone's tone was calm and reassuring. "Don't push too hard, because we had to do a little stitching inside. It'll take time for your dexterity and sensitivity to return to normal. Since the rest of your company is out in the field, you can choose to stay here in Da Nang or spend your recuperation time in Saigon.''

Hawk shrugged, then grimaced at the pain the simple gesture brought. "Can I think about it and tell you tomorrow?"

"No hurry, son. We've got plenty of beds here and you've arrived at a slow time, if there is such a thing. After we resumed bombing North Vietnam, the number of our casualties has dropped off from appalling to just awful."

"I'll take over from here, Doctor." The physician turned and both men focused on the woman standing at the foot of the bed.

"Nichols, what on earth are you doing here? Didn't you go off duty at six this morning?"

"Yes, sir, but I had a little unfinished business."

"Well, hurry it up so you can get some sleep. Don't think you're going to get by with taking catnaps tonight."

In spite of his rough words, the concern in his tone told Hawk the doctor was as interested in Angela's welfare as he was in his patient's.

"What I have to do won't take long. That is, if I can borrow this patient for a few minutes."

"I have no objections. But you'll have to splint and rebandage his shoulder. And you can remove the IV. I think our patient can be put on a different form of medication."

She nodded and the doctor stepped away, leaving her to complete Hawk's treatment. As she worked, she didn't attempt to make small talk. But the secretive, anticipatory grin that teased the corners of her mouth and the golden lights that danced in her chocolate brown eyes kept Hawk more than entertained.

Now that there was enough light to see, he took advantage of her closeness to study the features that had teased his imagination all night. Not strikingly beautiful in the traditional sense, Angela was still the prettiest sight Hawk's tired eyes had seen in a long time. Her short, sassy hairdo, her full, smiling lips, her soft, flawless complexion, and her large, round eyes all combined to make a very appealing picture.

She had come to see him on her time off. That fact expanded until it was probably all out of proportion with reality. But Hawk needed the reassurance that she thought he was important enough for an off-duty visit. He had enough doubts about his worth in the other avenues of his life. He certainly didn't need the rejection of a woman to whom he was attracted.

Unfortunately, since he was only a sergeant and she was a commissioned officer, she was out of his league. He knew all about the unwritten rules of the military where the nurses were concerned. There were so many more men than nurses, and it was considered bad form for a soldier to make a pass at one unless she initiated it, especially if she outranked him.

Up to this moment, he hadn't considered any of that to be a major concern in his life because he had had no intention of becoming involved with a nurse or anyone else while he was in country. He knew too many guys who had let their minds get messed up with women and buddies, and when the time came for quick, clear thinking, those men had been the ones who got killed.

Hawk didn't want to die. He had discovered that as soon as he made his first foray into the jungles, not knowing if his next step would be his last. There were so many places for the enemy to hide. This was their backyard, and they knew it well. He, on the other hand, was a stranger in a foreign land, unfamiliar with the language, the weather, the food, even the creatures that seemed to be everywhere, including in the food.

The revelation that he wanted to survive this trip to hell had come as quite a shock. There was no one important waiting for him to come home. He had no master plan for his future. He had never quite found his niche in the scheme of things.

But he fit in well with the military system. He didn't mind the discipline or the hard work. He enjoyed the challenge and he knew how to keep his thoughts focused on the job at hand. The first hint of a detour had been when he looked into Angela's face last night.

"There, that should keep your shoulder immobile. But you're going to have to—"

"Take it easy. I know, I know," he interrupted. "The doctor already told me. And, to be honest, it's been so long since I slept on a real bed and ate real food, you aren't going to hear any arguments from me."

"Good. Because if there's one thing I don't like, it's conflict."

"Then Vietnam is definitely the perfect place for you to be," he retorted wryly.

"No sarcasm, or I won't help you."

"Help me do what?"

She returned to the foot of the bed and pushed a wheelchair forward. "I'm going to help you take your first trip to the latrine since your accident."

It was not what he had expected to hear. And definitely not an activity he would have preferred to do with her. But he couldn't deny the practicality of her offer.

Angela cradled his arm in a sling, then pulled the sheet back and helped him ease his legs over the side of the bed. "Don't move too quickly," she cautioned. "You lost a lot of blood, and you're weaker than you think you are. Just put your good arm around my shoulders, and lean on me."

His expression must have been skeptical, because she hurried to add, "I'm stronger than I look. I've developed quite a few muscles since I came over here."

"Mostly from fighting off the men, I'll bet," Hawk couldn't resist commenting, considering how her body felt pressed up against his as she looped his arm around her neck and helped pull him out of bed, then steady him in a standing position.

"Most of the men I come in contact with have had enough fighting to last them a lifetime. They might tease, but they understand the meaning of the word no."

That was not a word Hawk was particularly interested in hearing from Angela, but he knew he was jumping ahead much too quickly. He certainly didn't want to frighten her away. Heck, he didn't want to frighten himself! He didn't understand why this particular woman had fascinated him from the first moment he laid eyes on her. It was a phenomenon he didn't want to think about too deeply. He simply knew he was very attracted to her and wanted to get to know her much better.

A hot breeze, stirred by a fan strategically located at the end of the aisle, tiptoed up the back of the short hospital gown Hawk was wearing. "Do you suppose there's an extra pair of undershorts around here somewhere?"

She chuckled and kept her eyes focused on the part of his body that was decently covered as he settled in the wheelchair. "That would probably be possible. I'll see what I can come up with."

He tugged the insufficient cloth as far down his thighs as possible and tried not to think about the discomfort of his bare behind against the cool plastic of the seat.

Angela wheeled him through the open double doors and into the sunshine. Only a few yards from the hospital, there was a small latrine that was no more than a row of outhouses. With no running water, the facilities were primitive, but as clean as possible.

She locked the wheels and helped Hawk to his feet. "Take your time. I'll wait for you out here."

"You're not going to help me?" His look was all innocence.

"My, aren't we getting sassy! We must be feeling better," she teased.

He flashed her a slow, suggestive wink. "*We* are definitely feeling *much* better," he said, laughing, but added silently, *especially since you came back*. It was amazing how much lighter his spirits had become since her return to the ward. He could allow himself a moment's optimism.

All joking aside, he almost wished she had come into the tiny stall with him when it felt as if all the strength drained from his limbs. For several minutes, he could do nothing more than sit with his head and undamaged shoulder leaning against the rough wooden wall.

"Are you okay in there?" she called through the door.

He mustered his energy to answer that he was doing fine. But the truth was, he couldn't admit that he truly did need her help. It was one thing to laugh about it, but it was another to rely on her for such a simple task. Drawing from an inner resource that had never failed him yet, he pulled himself together and walked out of the latrine under his own power.

Angela had the wheelchair ready, and he gratefully sank into it. She adjusted the sling so his arm was resting comfortably against his chest, and straightened his wrinkled green gown. Then, in a gesture he wasn't quite certain how to interpret, her hand lifted to brush the tumble of dark hair from his forehead. Her fingers combed through its thickness, restoring it to some sort of order.

As if she realized the implied intimacy of her action, she pulled her hand away and murmured, almost in the form of an excuse, "I'll have to find you some personal hygiene items, too." She moved to the back of the chair and pushed it toward the hospital with a sort of reckless speed. It wasn't until she bumped the wheels over the threshold that she slowed down.

But instead of stopping at his bed, she passed it, pushing him through a central area that appeared to be a nurses' station or office. Hawk realized, for the first time, that the room he had been in was merely a wing. The hospital was made up of two buildings, each with three long rooms attached to the central area. Angela explained that one room was used for operations and intensive care, while the other two were for recovery. She turned toward the other recovery ward and they went through a set of double doors. "There's someone here I think you'll be glad to see," she announced, that mysterious gleam returning to her eyes.

Hawk straightened in the chair, his injuries momentarily forgotten. "Greene? You've found him? He's here?"

"Now you're spoiling my surprise." Angela continued down the row of beds, not slowing until she reached one near the end. She pushed the wheelchair forward until Hawk was facing the man lying on the bed. One leg, covered in a cast from foot to hip, was elevated, drastically limiting Craig's mobility. But he managed to scoot up slightly until he was resting on one elbow as he smiled at Hawk.

"I hope you won't order me to stand at attention, Sarge."

"Of course not," Hawk responded in mock seriousness. "A salute will do for now.'

Craig executed a crisp salute. "Yes, sir. It's good to see you, sir," he added, lapsing into sincerity.

"Yes, well, I'm glad you made it out alive and almost well," Hawk replied gruffly. His relief was more than merely a squad leader's concern for his men. Greene had sparked a brotherly response in Hawk that Hawk hadn't been aware existed in himself. He had watched Greene try to adapt to military life, a life for which the new recruit was obviously ill suited. Greene wasn't athletic or overly coordinated. The physical demands required to survive in country were much more difficult for him than for the other men. But the private always tried twice as hard to make up for it. He was the first to volunteer for unpleasant jobs, and he was completely dependable. From the moment he was assigned to Hawk's squad, Greene had tried to follow Hawk's lead, almost to the point of becoming his shadow.

In the beginning, Hawk hadn't known quite how to handle the adoration. Being someone's role model was an unusual situation for him. Greene was a couple years older than Hawk, but many years younger in life experiences. During the long, boring waiting spells on less dangerous patrols, Greene had told his sergeant about his sheltered life as an only child in a Beaver Cleaver-type household. The draft had caught him in his sophomore year of college and, before he knew it, he was on a troop plane bound for Southeast Asia.

Hawk hadn't meant to show partiality, but he couldn't help but respect Greene's eagerness and determination. Besides, Hawk liked hearing stories of a normal, happy childhood. To him, it was all a big fantasy, something he'd longed for when he was a young boy, but of which he had no personal experience. The only loving parents he'd known had been on television. As he grew older, it hadn't mattered so much because he learned to take care of himself. But a peek into that other world was more than he could resist.

"Do you have any idea how we were rescued?" Hawk asked. "I must have passed out after the battle because I don't remember anything until I woke up in my hospital bed." *Looking into the face of an angel,* he added silently, sliding a covert glance at Angela, who was leaning against Greene's bed and listening to the two men's reunion.

"The Huey gunship's crew found us and brought us here," Craig explained simply. "I think they went back for the others later. I'm afraid no one else made it."

"Now, now, you're not telling the whole story," Angela intervened, joining the conversation for the first time. "The way I heard it was that Private Greene crawled, in spite of his broken leg, several yards until he reached the body of the man who had been carrying your squad's radio. After he called in the details of the ambush and gave the exact location, he dragged himself back to you and put a compress on your wound until help arrived. If he hadn't slowed down the bleeding, I'm afraid you might have bled to death before the Huey crew got there. The truth of the matter is, Sergeant Hawkins, this man very likely saved your life."

Hawk was overwhelmed by this revelation. The high color staining Green's cheeks and the suddenly shy look in his eyes confirmed Angela's story. Hawk remembered seeing how much pain the private had been in after the fight, and he knew how difficult it must have been for the green recruit to be in a position where he had to make life-and-death decisions and take command of a combat situation.

He was proud that one of his man had not only survived, but had acted in a brave and expedient manner. It was proof that Greene's instincts were good and that he had learned how to be a soldier. If he hadn't reacted the way he had . . .

Hawk had to swallow the lump in his throat before he could say, "Hey, thanks, buddy. I owe you one.

"I hope I'm never in a position to get paid back." Craig's laugh was self-consciously deprecating. "At least not when gunfire is involved."

"Okay, boys. That's all for now," Angela announced after glancing at her watch. She adjusted Craig's leg on its pile of pillows. "I'll see what I can do about putting you in the same ward if you both promise to get some rest this afternoon."

The men had to force their gazes away from the delicious sight of Angela's feminine curves as they moved within the confines of the green T-shirt and a pair of very short cutoff jeans. Hawk and Craig exchanged a look that clearly stated they shared their appreciation for the welcome change of scenery.

"You would still be our nurse if one of us moves, wouldn't you?" Craig asked, and Hawk silently applauded the question.

Her eyes were friendly but honest. They promised nothing beyond the best professional treatment she could provide for their wounds, and yet both men waited anxiously for her reply. "I have a lot of patients," she said thoughtfully, "but I suppose I could manage to fit one more person into my area." She covered a yawn. "However, if I don't get some sleep before my shift begins, I won't be taking very good care of anyone."

As she pulled Hawk's wheelchair backward, then turned him in the aisle, Craig said his goodbyes, then called out, "Hey, Sarge. Do you suppose you could find an extra pair of underwear for me? These gowns don't cover much."

"I'm already working on that," Hawk answered with a sympathetic chuckle.

From that point on, his recovery became more of a vacation than a misery. Angela managed to move Craig into the bed next to Hawk's as she had promised. She was busy with the constant arrivals of incoming wounded and departures of men so badly injured that they had to be moved to a better equipped hospital or shipped home. But she managed to find time, either during her shift or on her own time to sit in a chair between their beds and keep them company. They would talk, joke and play card games. And, inevitably, their laughter attracted others, until almost all the soldiers who could walk or propel themselves in wheelchairs would gravitate toward the cheerful group.

Craig had the gift of gab and did most of the talking. What he lacked in physical skills, he made up for with his talent for story telling. He seemed to remember every joke he had ever heard in his life, and passed them on to the assembled company with infectious humor. Even the jokes that were only marginally funny or downright stupid got laughs when relayed by Craig's glib tongue.

Hawk sat back and enjoyed himself. For the first time, he was on the fringe of popularity. He wasn't quite sure how to handle it, but he was enjoying the benefits, especially the benefit of having Angela near him often.

As each day passed, his friendship with Craig became more solid and his desire for Angela more intense. He loved the way she looked with her lovely, perpetually smiling lips, her dark, spiky bangs and her expressive eyes. He loved the way her slender, compact body filled out Army-issued outfits so appealingly. He loved the way she smelled, a mixture of flowers and spices, and the way she laughed, like wind chimes in a gentle breeze.

But to Hawk, *love* was a four-letter word, and it scared him to death. He would almost rather face the enemy in the jungle than let the guard around his emotions down. Caring too much would make him vulnerable. And he had learned, the hard way, that people he loved would take advantage of that vulnerability. He couldn't afford to let himself be hurt again.

He stayed in the hospital for almost a month, until the wound healed enough so his shoulder could be set into a cast. Even though he had known he wouldn't be there forever, it was a real disappointment when Captain Stone informed him he was well enough to move out of the ward and into the barracks. The doctor might as well have tossed a bucket of cold water in Hawk's face. It was as if he were being set adrift in an unfriendly sea. There was no denying the fact that he was taking up a bed and that he was in better condition than anyone around him.

But what Hawk feared the most was that by giving up his space in the hospital, he would give up his claim, however imaginary, on Angela. The bed she sat next to wouldn't be his. His brow wouldn't feel the cool caress of her fingers. Her face would no longer be the last sight he would see before falling asleep each night or the first sight each morning. Someone else would take over his position in her schedule. Most of all, he hated that it mattered.

So it was with a notable lack of enthusiasm that he moved his possessions into the barracks. His trunk had been shipped to the hospital, and now it helped make him feel at home in the strange room. He should have been delighted to have a room of his own, as befitted his rank, even though it was small. He should have looked forward to being able to sleep all night without being disturbed by the moans and cries of men in pain or the sudden bustle of activity when new wounded arrived. Instead, he knew he would miss the camaraderie, the activity, the closeness he had felt while staying in the ward.

Because Craig's leg wasn't healing as quickly or cleanly as possible, he was being kept at the hospital. Hawk felt a little better when his friend promised to keep an eye on Angela and protect her from the wolves.

However, Hawk's biggest worries turned out to be unfounded. He had not been reassigned to a new squad and was still under the doctor's care, so he had a lot of free time—time to consider his options as he walked along the beach. The distant rice paddies and bamboo hedgerows could almost be ignored as he relaxed on the white sand dunes and watched the waves of the South China Sea tumble in. With the cast on his shoulder and chest, he couldn't swim, but he enjoyed seeing American soldiers paddle out on their Hobie boards and try to ride in without wiping out. Although the waves weren't monsters, they could be pretty challenging for men who had never tried to balance on a surfboard before.

Hawk settled on a lounge chair, determined to keep his mind absolutely blank as he enjoyed the hot afternoon sun. Now that Vietnam was in the middle of its dry season, it rained only every other day instead of every day, which helped to lift everyone's spirits—everyone except Hawk. He wore shorts and a pair of dark aviator sunglasses to shut out the glare as he reclined and let the sunshine soak into his skin. With the awkward hunk of plaster covering his left shoulder and arm and part of his chest, he knew his tan was going to be a little strange looking, but the draw of the beach was irresistible. It was the only place he could be where, at least for a little while, he could forget he was in a foreign country, fighting for his life in a conflict that the politicians refused to admit was a war.

But he didn't want to think about the fighting, the president or anything else at the moment. Instead, he tried to wipe all conscious thoughts from his mind, leaving it peacefully blank. There were certain things and people he would be better off not thinking about. Soon he would be well enough to return to the field, so he should take advantage of this time.

He sucked a deep, cleansing breath of sea air into his lungs, then stopped as a familiar yet unexpected scent mixed with the breeze. The light floral fragrance of Angela's perfume teased his nostrils, bringing a vivid mental picture of her immediately to mind. Was it a figment of his wishful imagination, or was she somewhere nearby?

"Days like this remind me of home."

The words were spoken in a feminine voice that made all the breath that had been caught in his throat exhale in a ragged sigh. It took every ounce of his self-control not to snap his attention from the smooth rhythm of the waves to the woman who was standing beside him. Of course, he preferred to fill his vision with her beauty rather than Mother Nature's, but he didn't want to let her know how delighted he was to see her.

"Not my home," he responded, and slowly, as if he were in no hurry at all, he turned his head toward her. "They don't have many beaches in Pittsburgh."

"Pittsburgh, huh? No, I don't suppose they do." She let the oversize shirt she had been wearing slide off her shoulders and to the sand, revealing a modestly cut but tantalizing black bikini covering only the most vital spots of her body. "Do you mind if I join you?"

Did he mind? He would have been violently upset if she hadn't. Hawk had spent hours imagining what sort of treasures were hidden beneath the drabness of her Army issue outfits, but the actuality far exceeded his dreams. "No, of course not. There's plenty of sand and sunshine for us both."

She spread a towel next to his chair, then sat, busying herself with applying suntan lotion to her bare skin as she continued. "I grew up in Boston, but my parents had a weekend place on Cape Cod. If I don't look over my shoulder at the shantytown the Army calls a base or at the jungle on top of Monkey Mountain, I can almost pretend this is the strip of beach outside our cottage."

Hawk smiled, noting how close their thoughts were in spite of their different roots. "I've never been to Boston, but I've heard it's a nice city."

Surprisingly, her eyes filled with tears. "It's a terrific city. Some days I feel like I'm doing something really important by working in the hospital here, but some days I miss my home and my family so much I can hardly stand it. Don't you?"

Hawk didn't even have to consider the question. "No, no, I don't. There's nothing in Pittsburgh for me."

Her hazel eyes warmed sympathetically. "You don't have a family there?"

"I didn't say that," he replied, not really wanting to go into greater detail.

"Oh." She nodded, apparently understanding his reluctance. It was probably not the first time she had met a soldier who was less than eager to discuss his past. Thoughtfully, she changed the subject. "We've missed you in the ward."

We? Did that include Angela in a large group of people, or was she telling him that *she* missed him? "I've been by to see Greene almost every day this week," he commented, hoping to draw a more definite response from her.

"I guess it must have been after my shift." She smoothed lotion on her shapely legs in slow, sensual strokes. "It hasn't been the same since you left."

"I didn't add that much to the conversation when I was there."

"I always enjoyed our conversations. You don't say much, but when you speak, everyone listens." She held out the bottle. "Would you mind putting some lotion on my back?"

Would I mind letting my fingers feel the softness of your skin? Silently, because his mouth had suddenly gone bone dry, he took the bottle and squeezed a curling line of white lotion above the thin strap of her top. Even before his hand touched her flesh, it began to tingle in anticipation.

Her skin was warm and smooth as velvet. There wasn't much space to cover, and his large hand accomplished the task all too quickly, if somewhat awkwardly. Resisting the urge to let his fingers wander to forbidden places, he dropped the bottle into her lap.

"Thanks." She stretched out on her stomach and cradled her head on her arms. "I'm not on duty tonight. I know you guys have some sort of code about not fraternizing with the nurses, but maybe we could go somewhere for dinner."

Her invitation was presented so casually, Hawk hesitated. He wanted to read between the lines, but he couldn't be sure. *We?* There was that word again. How did she mean it this time? "You and me?" he asked, deciding not to get his hopes up too much until she was more specific.

She twisted her head and squinted against the blazing sun as she looked at Hawk. "I suppose we could bring Craig along. He can get around fairly well in a wheelchair."

Hawk knew he could be generous and share his time with Angela, or he could hoard it selfishly. In spite of his closeness to Craig, he decided to go with the latter. Friendship was one thing, but the chance to spend the evening alone with a gorgeous woman was something else entirely.

"Maybe we could bring Greene next time, but I'd like to go somewhere without the whole gang. I've heard there's a fairly decent restaurant in Da Nang that serves French food. I could borrow a jeep from the motor pool, but either you'll have to do the driving or help me with the gear shift." He decided he might as well take a chance, and see if she was willing to spend some time with him away from the hospital. In the uncertainties of war, time was not something to waste.

She met his gaze, and even though she had the disadvantage of not being able to read his eyes through the mirrored lenses of his glasses, a long, silent moment passed as they considered the implications of her response. Both knew that her acceptance of the two of them going alone would change the complexion of their relationship. It could go either way, locked for an eternity into friendship or swirled into the passion of an affair. They also knew the fleetingness of their situation. Soon he would be gone, back to the heat of the action. Her tour of duty would be over in a few months, and she would be flying home. But that very sense of impermanence heightened emotions and made tomorrow seem very far away.

"I'd like that," she answered simply. "It will be nice to get away for a while."

Hawk couldn't agree more, but the prospect struck him dumb. He could only watch, with heated anticipation, as she jumped to her feet and jogged across the sand and into the surf. Even when he could barely make out her dark head bobbing on the crest of the waves as she swam, he continued watching her, wanting her, needing her.

He didn't remember what he ate that evening. All he could see or smell or think about was Angela. They didn't talk much, but the looks that passed between them were filled with the desire that had sparked almost from the first moment they met. Idle conversation wasn't necessary.

No mention was made, but it was as if they knew how the evening would end. They dropped the jeep off at the motor pool and walked across the almost deserted helicopter pad to the nurses' barracks, a series of small rooms connected in a long double row. A huge orange moon hung over the China Sea, bathing the coastline in a romantic glow, which perfectly suited their mood.

Reality was the farthest thing from their minds as they paused outside her door.

"I had a terrific time," Angela said, leaning against the wooden wall. "I feel comfortable around you, as if we've known each other for years."

They were standing so close to each other he could feel the warmth of her body. He braced his good arm over her shoulder and stepped even closer until only inches separated them. "You're very special, Angie," he whispered, gazing into the dark glow of her eyes. "I know you probably hear this from a lot of men, but I can promise I don't say it often." Her face was tilted upward, tempting, inviting him to kiss her...an offer he couldn't resist. His head lowered until he felt the moistness of her lips beneath his. She trembled...or was it him? He couldn't tell who was affected more as a rush of emotions swept through him, centering his strength in his maleness and leaving his knees weak.

"Jeff...Jeff," she breathed, her words quickly swallowed by his hungry mouth. She had insisted on calling him by his first name, even though everyone else used his nickname, and her usage made it sound like an endearment. "I don't usually do this," she went on, her sentence broken by their fevered kisses, "but...you can...come inside my room...if you want to."

He never wanted anything more in his life.

Their lovemaking was wild and wonderful, as they each reached their own pleasure quickly. It left the rest of the night for tenderness, long, sensual kisses and exploratory caresses. Because of the awkwardness of his cast, they had to be creative, but it added to the uniqueness of the moment.

He spent the night in her single bed, sharing the narrow space. Their bodies were pressed together as if they were one.

It was a luxury they couldn't enjoy often during the next few weeks, but whenever possible, they would slip away and spend a few hours in her room. A small air conditioner in the window cooled their sated bodies and hummed a monotonous tune that lulled them to sleep. It became their haven, a place to escape to for peace and passion. They spoke only of unimportant things, not plans for the future or sins of the past.

Hawk knew he was in love with her, but he couldn't find the words to tell her. What could he offer? He had no prospects, no life outside the Army. And, with more than six months left to serve in Vietnam, he had no promise he would survive.

Two months after his injury, the doctors removed his cast. Another month of rehabilitation followed until, except for a little weakness, his arm was as good as new. It felt wonderful to be able to hold Angela against him, to feel the softness of her skin against his without the cold plaster of his cast separating them. He wished it could last forever. He began to believe it could. When he received orders that he would be shipping out in a week, he tried to think of some way he and Angela could be together.

He considered telling her how much he loved her. He even toyed with the idea of asking her to wait for him. Like a schoolboy rehearsing a play, he wrote down what he would say, and repeated it in the privacy of his room, until he had built up his nerve. Not only did he plan his words, but he imagined every possible reaction she could have and tried to think of how he should respond.

On the evening before he was to leave, he made plans for them to go to their favorite restaurant. He was nervous, barely touching his meal as he waited until the right moment to begin his speech. She, too, seemed uneasy, and finally, after pushing her food around on her plate for half an hour, she set down her fork and met his troubled gaze.

"Jeff, I've got something..."

"Angie, I want to ask you..."

They began speaking together, then stopped at the same time. He smiled and she gave a weak laugh.

"You go first," she said.

"No, you go ahead."

She wiped her mouth on her napkin and placed it on the table. For a long, anxious moment, she meticulously arranged her silverware on her plate, then lifted her gaze.

Hawk waited, more worried about what he would be saying than what she had to tell him. But as she began again, he sat up with a jerk, giving her his undivided attention. Of all the words she could have spoken, all the responses she could have given, all the things she could have done, even in a worst case scenario, he had never expected to hear her say the words that crushed all his hopes and dreams.

"Jeff, I don't know how to tell you this. I wanted you to be the first to know, and I wanted you to hear it from me." She paused and nervously cleared her throat, but her brown eyes were steady and calm as she met his look. "Craig and I are getting married."

Chapter Four

"It Don't Matter To Me" —Bread

"I thought you were dead!" Angela exclaimed, her eyes rounded with disbelief.

"So did I, once or twice, but I eventually made it out alive." A cynical grin twisted his lips. "I guess I was one of the lucky ones."

His words were heavy with double meaning. Even though she understood his sarcasm, she wasn't certain how to interrupt his response. Was he glad he had made it out? His devil-may-care attitude had given her the impression he didn't value his life very much. That was what had frightened her the most about him. When a man played Russian roulette with the grim reaper, the man was usually the loser.

However, that dangerous edge combined with his aggressively confident attitude had been a major part of his attraction. With death and depression constantly surrounding her, it had been a pleasant relief to be with a man who was as anxious to make the most of every moment as she was. He had shared her eagerness to pretend there wasn't a war going on around them. Because they had to keep their relationship secret, it had been easy to slip into a land of make-believe once she stepped outside the doors of the hospital and into his arms.

After Jeff left camp and Angela began her life as Craig's wife, she had almost convinced herself that the brief, passionate but futureless interlude with Jeff had never existed. By the time she returned home, Jeff Hawkins had faded into a misty dream she had conjured up out of desperation to escape the grim reality of the situation.

But now, facing him, standing so close she could see the black spikes highlighting the crystal blue irises of his eyes and smell the tangy, masculine scent of his aftershave, it was impossible to deny his existence. And it was even more difficult to ignore the flashes of memory of their heated afternoons together. Like the flickering scenes of a silent movie reeling through her brain, she saw him as he lay on the gurney the night he had arrived at the hospital. The images continued with a close-up of his attractively crooked grin as they talked of having dinner together alone for the first time, his tanned, muscular body as they sunbathed then made love on a deserted section of the beach, his large, eager hands as they teased her body to incredible peaks of arousal and his gentle, hungry lips as they tasted almost every inch of her sweat-slickened skin.

Angela was delighted he had survived the jungles, and yet the fact shook her to the very depths of her soul. She didn't want to be reminded of any part of that time in her life. It had been another world, another time, and she had been a different person.

She wanted to turn away and disappear into the crowd, but the piercing force of his gaze impaled her as if she were a butterfly pinned to a board.

"How's Greene?" Jeff asked. His voice was polite, but his indifference made the question seem obligatory.

His total lack of emotion disturbed her even more than his presence. He and Craig had been close once, and even though they had not corresponded since the wedding, he should feel at least a minor interest in the fate of his friend.

Apparently, he didn't know. But then, so few people from their past did. Angela had realized she would have to address the issue if she came to the reunion. And she had prepared a suitable response, one that would encourage a minimum of sympathy for her, but a great deal of empathy for Craig.

"Craig never quite recovered from his wounds," she answered in a studiedly calm voice. "He died several years ago."

It was Jeff's turn to look startled. He tried to keep his expression stern, but it was obvious the news had caught him off guard. "I'm sorry. I hadn't heard..."

"He talked about you often, especially toward the end. He was very upset when he heard you had been killed." She knew it was a low blow, but after his frigid greeting, she felt he more than deserved it.

"Toward the end? But he seemed to be almost well the last time I saw him. He still had the cast on his leg, but he was getting around on his crutches."

"There was more damage to his knee than originally diagnosed. He had to have a couple more operations after we returned to the States, but it never was normal. He couldn't get around as easily as he would have liked, and he was in a lot of pain."

A thoughtful frown creased Jeff's tanned forehead. "But people don't die because of a knee operation. What else was wrong?"

Angela hesitated. This was the question she had been expecting, but the answer caught in her throat. She would have liked to be able to tell the truth. But she couldn't. It had been almost twelve years since Craig's death, but the wound—*her* wound—was still too fresh for her to discuss it.

But Jeff was waiting for an answer, and she was finally able to respond, "It was just one thing after another. He couldn't build his strength up enough to fight off illness."

"I suppose the two of you had a houseful of kids before Craig got too sick."

"No children. We never quite got around to starting a family," she informed him with obvious regret.

It was not at all what he had expected to hear. He had tried not to think of Angela and Craig during the past eighteen years, an effort that had been mostly unsuccessful. But whenever they had managed to sneak through his carefully erected defenses, Jeff had always assumed the couple had lived happily ever after. At Christmas he imagined them opening presents with half a dozen beautiful, dark-haired, brown-eyed children. During the winter months, he visualized the whole clan gathering in the front yard of their home, building a plumply perfect snowman, and in the summer, he could see them spending long, hot days on the beach at Cape Cod. He had tried to block the images from his mind, but they had haunted him, angered him and made him grow bitter with envy.

It was not something he was proud of. Especially now, when he found his self-torture had been so far from the truth. And it left him strangely relieved—something that shamed him even more.

A commotion near the entrance caught Angela's attention, and Jeff was glad for the distraction. Her revelation and his reaction to it had left him so flustered he was unable to respond. There were many questions he wanted to ask, answers he needed to know.

A man walking backward and carrying a video camera on his shoulder led a procession. The call letters of a local television station were embroidered on the man's jacket and printed on the microphone held in a female reporter's hand.

"Captain Dayton, do you remember any part of your military service prior to when your airplane was shot down?" she asked a tall, blond man who appeared to be the center of attention.

"No, ma'am," the man answered with a politeness that didn't reflect how many hundreds of times he had heard that question in the past few months.

The reporter gestured toward the room's occupants. "Isn't there anyone here you recognize?" she persisted, searching for the scoop.

Indulgently, Captain Dayton let his gaze travel around the room even though it was obvious he didn't expect to see any familiar faces. But suddenly, his affable scrutiny halted and a wide, genuine grin broke through his military poise. "Well, yes, ma'am. As a matter of fact, there is. Will you excuse me?" Wrapping his arm protectively around a tall, strikingly attractive woman, he hurried forward until he reached the spot where Jeff and Angela were standing.

"Hawk, it's good to see you," the blond man exclaimed with obvious delight. "I was hoping you'd be here, but I wasn't really expecting it."

A smile, the first of the evening, stretched across Jeff's face. "Bo. You're looking great, man." The two men clasped hands in an enthusiastic handshake. "*Captain* Dayton, huh? Last time I saw you, you were a lowly lieutenant."

"I got a promotion, a job and a wife all in the same month," Bo replied with a look at the woman next to him that clearly illustrated which of these accomplishments most pleased him.

"You're a lucky man," Jeff said sincerely as he turned his attention to Bo's wife. With her red hair tumbling loose around her shoulders and her sea-green eyes sparkling happily, she was prettier than he remembered. But his respect for her went much deeper than her physical appearance. She was an incredible woman—intelligent, persistent and loyal. One in a million, Jeff thought, casting a quick glance in Angela's direction. "Yes, you're damn lucky," he repeated, looking at Bo.

"That's very true." Bo's solemn reply was a profound understatement, and it reminded Jeff that Angela didn't have a clue what was going on behind the conversation. He noticed she had begun to edge away, obviously planning on melting into the crowd.

Perversely, he wished he hadn't seen her that evening, and at the same time he was struck by a feeling of devastation if she should disappear before they had had time to finish their conversation. Moving so quickly it startled them both, Jeff reached out and grabbed her arm, effectively stopping her escape.

She glanced at the fingers circling her wrist, and an unexpected shiver shook her. How well she remembered those fingers, so strong, so tender, so very exciting. And dangerous.

Slowly her gaze lifted until she was looking directly into his eyes. No longer cold and condemning, they registered the same unwelcome confusion she was feeling. She hated the way his touch affected her. She knew she should pull away, break his hold and leave.

But she didn't. It wasn't his hand that was holding her; it was the past. She had run away once before, leaving behind many loose ends. Now, for whatever reasons, he didn't want her to go. And she, for whatever reasons, didn't want him to let her go.

After several long moments, he spoke, his voice calm but compelling. "Angela, I want you to meet some friends of mine."

She hesitated. Why was he insisting on prolonging this awkward situation? After the way he had been treating her, first giving her the big freeze, then pointedly ignoring her, she had no clue as to why he had stopped her or why he wanted to introduce her to the other couple. And from the odd way he was staring at her, neither did he.

Angela took a step forward, and the pressure on her wrist eased. The captain and his wife seemed like nice enough people, and the bits and pieces of the conversation she had heard intrigued her. It wouldn't hurt for her to stay a little longer. After all, she had no plans for the evening.

Jeff didn't release his hold, but continued to pull her forward until she was standing next to him. Somehow his hand had slid down so that his fingers were wrapped securely around hers. His grip wasn't so tight that she couldn't have pulled away, but there was something gentle and comfortable about the feeling of her hand cradled in his. Angela's fingers closed around his in an automatic response.

A curious look washed over Jeff's face, taking with it much of the hardness that had masked his features, but leaving a shadow of bewilderment. Angela suspected that look of confusion was probably part of her expression, too. It was brought on by her unexpected reunion with that particular part of her past.

"Bo and Melora, I'd like you to meet Angela." Jeff dragged his gaze away from Angela and began a belated introduction. "She was the nurse who helped get me on my feet and back into combat in Nam after I was wounded. Angela, this is Captain Bo Dayton, also known as Kahuna, and his wife, Melora."

The woman's lips curved into a friendly smile. "Hello, Angela. I owe you a huge debt of gratitude."

Angela blinked. "Me? How could you owe me anything? We've just met."

"If you're the one responsible for helping Hawk get well, then I owe you a great deal. You see, it was Hawk who introduced Bo to me, in a manner of speaking. And I can't tell you how much my life improved after that."

Angela turned a questioning look at Jeff.

Jeff's nod was modest, and he seemed hesitant to explain, so Melora continued.

"You might have heard about the discovery of a man in Vietnam who had been missing in action for seventeen years. Well—" she paused and glanced at the man standing next to her "—my Bo is that man."

Of course Angela had heard about it. Every television station, newspaper and radio station had carried the story. There had been a ticker-tape parade for him, and the president had honored him with a special dinner at the White House.

She vaguely remembered hearing how the man's plane had been shot down over North Vietnam. He and his buddy had ejected from the plane. The buddy had crawled out of the jungle, but Bo had been badly injured during the dogfight or when he hit the ground. Suffering from amnesia, he had been taken in by a pair of elderly Vietnamese sisters who kept him alive so he could work their farm. The rest of their family had been killed during the war.

Melora had put together a search party for her missing brother and discovered Bo instead. Because Melora was a psychologist, she had taken Bo home to California where she caught him up on all the years and events he had missed. She also tried to help him adjust to the changes. The navy had been able to track down his family, and there had been an emotional reunion, all of which had been played up by the press until Angela had begun to believe it was a gimmick to boost the military's image.

But now, standing in front of Captain Dayton, seeing a man who appeared to be every good thing that had been said about him and hearing the story verified by his adoring wife, Angela was happy it had turned out to be true. She had seen too many unhappy endings while she had been overseas, and it was nice to see some people could survive the hard times and find true love.

And there was no doubt Bo and Melora were wildly in love. Their faces shone with it, their eyes overflowed with it, and the affectionate way they held on to each other clearly reflected what they were feeling. Angela didn't begrudge their happiness in the least. But just as she had been skeptical of the media blitz, she didn't truly believe in love. Soon enough the glow would be gone and the reality would set in. She would like to see Bo and Melora then. No, she wouldn't. She had already seen the sadness and tragedy of human relationships.

"But how did Jeff fit into all this?" Angela asked.

After a quick glance in Jeff's direction, Melora explained, "Hawk put me in contact with the person who eventually coordinated the journey into the jungle where

I found Bo. Then he offered his advice on Bo's recovery program."

It seemed like a tenuous link at best, but if Melora wanted to give Jeff credit for her happiness, then Angela was certainly not going to scoff. It shouldn't come as that much of a surprise. It wasn't the first time that Jeff had played matchmaker. In a roundabout way, he had brought her and Craig together.

The irony was not lost on Jeff, either. He, too, was thinking of how quickly love could happen and how quickly it could disappear. He hoped Bo and Melora would somehow be the exception to the rule.

However, the conversation was taking a dangerous turn. His involvement in Bo's escape from Vietnam was something he would rather not discuss, especially in front of Angela.

Melora must have sensed his concern, and he breathed a sigh of relief as she subtly changed the subject. "So you're a nurse? I planned on becoming a nurse until I saw what a desperate need there was for psychologists who specialized in veterans and their families."

"I'm not a nurse anymore. I gave that up when I came back from Nam." A movement very much like a shudder shook her, telegraphing itself to Jeff through their connected hands. "I handled enough human injuries to last the rest of my life, so I decided to diversify by treating a different kind of patient. I own a veterinary clinic in Boston, and I really enjoy working with the animals."

"I'll have to get your advice later," Bo commented. "There's a cow at Gramps's dairy that's been off her feed and we can't figure out why."

"Unfortunately, I specialize in small animals. I've never treated a cow in my life." Angela chuckled. "There aren't too many cows in the Boston area."

"How about sheep?" Jeff asked. "I've got more than seven hundred, and that number is going to be tripling in the next few weeks."

For not the first time that evening Angela stared at him in shock. "You raise sheep?" she asked with as much incredulity as if he had said he robbed banks for a living.

"Why not? Don't I look like a rancher?"

Her gaze swept his tall, muscular body, from the tips of his gray ostrich-leather boots, up the straight line of his black slacks and across the heather-blue wool sweater he was wearing over a white dress shirt.

"I don't suppose I've ever met a sheep rancher before," she admitted. "It's just that of all the occupations I would have expected you to have..."

Jeff couldn't resist a sardonic smile. "Such a tame lifestyle for someone as wild and irresponsible as me, huh?"

A splash of pink highlighted her cheekbones. He had spoken the truth. "I didn't mean that, exactly. I just can't imagine you settling for something so calm as raising sheep."

"Calm? Ha!" He snorted. "There's nothing calm about lambing. Someone has to be there the instant those lambs hit the ground so the mother and babies can be isolated before they forget who they belong to. For three weeks, I play midwife, nursemaid, and mother to orphans, as well as feeding and watering them. Needless to say, I don't get much sleep."

Angela shook her head, unable to picture him doing those things. "It sounds like fun," she joked. "It also sounds like you need help."

"I sure do. But everyone in my area is going through the same thing, so there's no one to spare."

"Too bad I don't know anything about sheep, or I could help you." Her suggestion was more offhand than serious.

"All it takes is someone who can carry lambs, haul buckets of food and water and go for long periods of time without sleep. But I don't suppose Boston veterinarians would have much experience with any of those things, would they?"

It was Angela's turn to snort. She pulled her hand out of his and glared at him. "I've delivered my share of baby animals, and even a few baby humans. And it took quite a few muscles to get you heavy soldiers on and off gurneys and hospital beds, so I don't believe I would have any trouble with a few little lambs or buckets."

"Speaking of lambs," Bo interrupted, attempting to defuse a volatile situation, "Melora and I just found out some interesting news."

Jeff and Angela continued to eye each other in silent challenge for several seconds before turning their attention to the patiently waiting couple.

Bo tightened his arm around Melora's shoulders, pulling her against him as he proudly announced, "The doctor told us we're going to become parents in about seven months."

"No kidding? Congratulations!" Jeff reached out and pounded Bo on the back. "You'll make great parents."

"We're getting a late start, but this baby couldn't find parents that want him or her more than we do."

"What baby?" A new voice burst into the celebration, causing all four people to look around to see who the intruder was.

"Scott! Kristi! It's about time you got here." Bo greeted the couple, pulling them into the group. "Hawk, I don't think you've met my friend, Commander Scott Sanders. He was the pilot of the plane I was in that crashed in North Vietnam. He's been with the Blue Angels for the past four years, first as one of the performers and now in public relations."

Bo conducted introductions before sharing the news of his and Melora's baby.

"So where's your little girl?" Melora asked Kristi. "I was hoping you would bring her with you. I haven't seen her since Christmas."

"My mother is taking care of her while we're here. This is the first time Scott and I have left Shelley home while we travel. We thought it would be nice to have a sort of second honeymoon, but we already miss her so much that we've called twice to see how she's doing," Kristi moaned.

"Can you believe she's almost nine months old?" Scott marveled. "If I had known fatherhood was this much fun, I wouldn't have waited until I was so old to get started."

Kristi punched him in the arm. "You would have started without me, since I didn't meet you until two years ago."

A mischievous sparkle brightened his blue eyes. "You have no idea how much time I spent on that beach waiting for the right woman to walk by."

Kristi punched him again, a little harder this time. But there was laughter in her voice as she commented, "Thank goodness you and Maverick were selective enough to be patient."

"Maverick is my dog," Scott explained. "He fell in love with Kristi almost as quickly as I did. She was the first woman in my life he liked."

"And with a handsome pilot for his master, you can just imagine how many women Maverick had an opportunity to meet!" Kristi teased.

"Hey, don't forget that my nickname is the Saint," Scott remarked in his own defense.

"Which could have been a clever play on words," Bo commented. "Of course, I don't personally remember, but Scott could have been quite a ladies' man in his heyday."

"Which would mean that *you* probably were, too," Melora pointed out. "And, frankly, I'd rather not know about that particular part of your past."

Jeff was beginning to feel a little overwhelmed and very left out. All this talk of babies and love reminded him how far out of the mainstream he was. He looked at Angela and saw she was watching the interchange with as much detachment as he was. He realized that, in the scheme of things, she was no farther along than he was. It was too bad he had no feelings for her anymore, because at the moment they had a lot in common.

He had once believed they had a chance for happiness together. The stolen hours away from the hospital, whether they had been spent talking or making love, had been the first real happiness he had ever known. She had given him hope for the future—*their* future.

What had made her change her mind? Had she ever truly cared for him? Or had it been a self-serving search for pleasure? Had she used him to get through the lonely days and nights while she was waiting for Mr. Right to come along? And why was Mr. Right Craig instead of him?

For years he had called her every kind of name for sleeping with him, then marrying his best friend. Some men thought it was acceptable behavior for a man to seek gratification from one woman but marry another. But everyone thought it was intolerable for a woman to do the same thing—particularly if Jeff was the man who wasn't good enough.

Why had she chosen Craig over him? The question had haunted him since the moment she first told him she was getting married. It sounded silly, and he would never have admitted it to anyone, but Angela had broken his heart. When she spoke her vows to Craig instead of to him, his dreams had been shattered. From that moment he no longer cared if he lived or died. He volunteered for dangerous missions and signed up for a second tour of duty. He'd been promoted to an officer in Special Services and became a deadly efficient Green Beret.

When he returned home alive, he'd almost been disappointed. What did he have to look forward to? Certainly not a happy home with a loving wife and children. He hadn't even had parents who welcomed him back.

Jeff dragged his fingers through his hair. He was tired of being alone. If love was possible, he wanted to experience it.

At that moment Angela lifted her head and their eyes met. Hers were dark with a seemingly unreachable sadness. Was she satisfied with the choices she had made in her life?

It always came back to that one question. Had she loved him, even a little? He wished it didn't matter so much that he know the answer, but it did. Within hours the party would end and he would be driving over the Rockies to his ranch. She would be flying to Boston. This was his opportunity to know the truth because fate wouldn't bring them together again. This time Angela would truly be out of his life forever. He would never see her again.

He felt an inexplicable constriction around his heart. Reminding himself he felt no love for her didn't help. It might be totally illogical, but Jeff felt he could never find true happiness unless the question was answered. He couldn't hope to be a good husband until he found out why Angela had tossed him aside. If only he had a little more time to spend with her, he believed the issue could be discussed and resolved.

A warning bell went off in his head. She was an attractive woman, someone he had known intimately, someone for whom he had had very strong feelings. Being around her again, even after all those years and without the passion, would it be dangerous to put himself into such a situation?

She had hurt him once. Surely he wouldn't be foolish enough to let her do it again.

"The Blues are flying in an air show at eleven tomorrow morning." Scott's voice abruptly brought Jeff back to the conversation. "I'll be narrating the show, and I have to get there about an hour early, but Kristi and I could meet you guys for breakfast somewhere."

"Sounds great to me," Bo agreed. "I try to never miss a meal, especially when we're away from home. Melora and I have been taking cooking lessons, but neither of us have progressed much past spaghetti or broiled steaks. Where are you staying tonight, Hawk?"

"I'm not," Jeff replied. "I'm driving to the ranch. I've got seven hundred pregnant ewes waiting for me to get home."

"Oh, come on, Hawk," Bo prompted. "You can spare a couple of days. There's still lots of things I'd like to talk over with you."

"I'd love to, man, but I really can't. I time the breeding in the fall so that lambing will start on April fifth, which is later this week. There's probably already a couple of them delivering today. My sheepherder and his wife are watching them while I'm gone, but I've got to get back before the heavy action starts." Hawk was apologetic, but it was clear the point was not negotiable. "Maybe the two of you can stop by for a visit this summer when things quiet down."

Bo had no choice but to accept the decision. "Yes, maybe we can do that. Or you could come to San Diego. We've got a great view of the Pacific Ocean from our deck. It's only a flight of stairs down the cliff to the beach."

"First, I've got to make it through April," Jeff said with a chuckle. "Then I'll make plans for the summer."

"So how about you, Angela?" Bo asked, looking expectantly at the woman who was standing quietly next to Hawk.

Angela seemed startled to hear her name. She, too, had obviously been thinking about something far removed from the activities. "I'm not sure what time I'll leave tomorrow."

"You don't have a plane reservation?" Melora joined in to question.

"I'd never been west of the Mississippi River, so when I decided to come to the reunion, it seemed like a perfect opportunity to take some time off and relax." Angela's smile was a weary conformation to her need for a vacation. "I rented a car and I'm going to wander around the mountains for a few weeks. I'll do a little hiking and catch up on my reading."

"All by yourself?" Melora's lovely green eyes were filled with concern. "What if you get lost or hurt? No one would miss you for days. And it gets below freezing in the mountains at night, doesn't it, Hawk?"

He nodded. "Yes, there's still quite a lot of snow at the higher elevations."

"And she shouldn't be wandering around alone, should she?" Melora persisted.

This time he answered with a shrug. "Angela has survived worse conditions. She's a pretty tough lady." Even though his words were not an obvious compliment, his tone lacked any trace of sarcasm.

"I probably won't be alone long." Angela spoke up as if compelled to explain. "I've checked on a couple of guest ranches and they have plenty of openings at this time of year. I'll probably spend a few days at one of those. There will be horses to ride, and I'll have a chance to see how a ranch operates."

"If you wanted to *really* experience ranch life, you should come help me with the lambing," Jeff suggested wryly.

It would be the ideal way to buy a little extra time away from the real world, and to get Angela to tell him what he needed to know. Surely after a few days filled with exhausting work and a few nights without sleep, her resistance would be low enough for her to be absolutely honest about everything.

Angela's gaze was questioning and unsure as she studied Jeff's face. Apparently she wasn't totally averse to the idea, but it had obviously taken her by surprise.

"I'm sure you wouldn't want to spend your vacation working with animals." Jeff tried to allow for her objections before she had time to voice them. "After all, you're surrounded by them all day long at your clinic."

"I like animals," she responded defensively. "I wouldn't mind spending my vacation working with your sheep. It would be a refreshing change from being indoors all the time."

He sensed she was considering it, and he knew he'd better take his best shot. "It would be a lot of work ... *hard* work," he emphasized with a glance, as if he was measuring her stamina and found it questionable. The Angela he used to know would never avoid a direct challenge, especially when it concerned her abilities. He had seen her accept—and win—some of the most ridiculous bets imaginable. If this didn't capture her interest, nothing would.

Silently she stared at him. He could almost see her analyzing the whys and why nots of the offer. As the seconds stretched into a minute, he began to get a little angry. The meaning of her hesitation was becoming painfully obvious. Angela didn't care what he thought. She wasn't interested in spending any more time than was absolutely necessary with him. She had always been able to walk away from him without the slightest qualm.

Well, he wasn't going to be the one left behind again. This time he wouldn't give her the satisfaction. He didn't need her. He didn't want her. And he could darn well live without her. Just as he opened his mouth to joke away his invitation, she spoke.

"I read an article about lambing just a few weeks ago, and it sounded fascinating. It might be a good experience for a city girl like me, and I could certainly use the exercise." She shrugged as if it really didn't matter one way or the other to her. "I don't have any definite plans for the next couple of weeks. Sure, why not?"

Chapter Five

"Yesterday's Gone" —Chad & Jeremy

She changed her mind at least a dozen times as she followed Jeff's taillights through the thick darkness of the night. But she decided it was not the ideal time to strike out on her own. Besides, it wouldn't be fair to Jeff. He had certainly not pressured her into agreeing to this trip. In fact, he had given her every opportunity to back out. She had agreed to lend a hand and it would be pretty chickenhearted of her to turn around and head back to civilization without even discussing it with him. Perhaps when they stopped for gasoline, she would be able to talk to him about it.

Angela sighed. Once they were face to face, she knew she wouldn't say anything about her indecision. As much as she hated to admit it, there was still something compelling about him that attracted her. Perhaps *attracted* was not accurate. It was more like *fascinated*, like watching a snake charmer tease a deadly cobra.

Back in 1972, when she looked into his sparkling blue eyes and felt herself being held against the solid warmth of his body, the last word she had wanted to say to him was no. She was older and wiser now, but standing next to him all evening, feeling the heat of his gaze and the strength of his hand, an emotion long buried had stirred within her. For years she had told herself the insatiable desire she had felt for him had been the result of immaturity and desperate hormones. It was extremely disturbing to discover his presence still had the ability to make her knees weak and her resistance weaker. The truth was, some unfathomable part of her wanted to feel that thrill again.

Now, alone in her rental car, Angela could be more objective. During the five-hour drive to Montrose, a small town on the west slope of the Rockies, she would have plenty of time to think about what on earth had caused her to agree to postpone her vacation to work side by side with a man who both tempted and frightened her. A man she barely knew.

Angela realized it was debatable that she barely knew a man with whom she had shared so much. He had been her lover and her confidant at a time when she desperately needed a pair of strong arms to hold her and sympathetic ears to listen to her. But it had been she who had done most of the talking, a fact she hadn't noted until later. It wasn't until she tried to remember their conversations that she discovered how very little she knew about Jeff Hawkins.

Oh, sure, she could even to this day visualize the magnificence of his body, whether it was filling out the Army-issue T-shirts and shorts or reclining in naked splendor on her bed. She remembered the story of his injury, but mainly because she had heard it from Craig. Jeff had had little to say about anything that had happened to him in the field. He had had even less to say about his life before he joined the Army. She couldn't recall hearing anything about his plans after his tour of duty was over. Something about the way he adapted to military life had caused her to assume he would be a career soldier.

All Jeff had talked about during their secret hours together had been subjects like his favorite movies and rock groups, his appreciation of the beautiful sunrises that splashed their colors over the China Sea or the sunsets that melted into the emerald green of the jungles. She had known of his love for animals, although she had never imagined it would demonstrate itself in such a dramatic fashion as owning and operating a sheep ranch. During his months of recuperation and rehabilitation, he had adopted dozens of puppies, kittens, birds, monkeys and even a baby sun bear. Somehow he had always been able to find good homes for his creatures.

He had an ability to attract children. It was an unlikely camaraderie. He never fawned over them or played with them. But the children must have sensed some sort of mutual ground, an understanding, a kinship. They followed him around and, in a curious role reversal, they brought him presents. Nothing fancy or expensive, just a pretty rock, a seashell, a bottle of beer they had somehow gotten their hands on. Occasionally, they had passed on a piece of personal property some dead G.I. had left behind in the jungle. In return, Jeff would always find a coin or some extra food in his jacket pocket for them.

Angela discovered she was smiling. She hadn't thought about Jeff's relationship with the children for years. It had been a softer side of his personality he had shown no one other than the kids . . . and her.

Angela rubbed her hands across her tired eyes and stretched her tense shoulders. She was exhausted from the emotional turmoil of the evening, as well as the jet lag that was finally catching up to her from the flight.

She wished she hadn't agreed to drive through the night. When he asked her, she had thought she could make it, but the hypnotic flicker of white stripes and red tail-lights was putting her to sleep.

She fought it by rolling down her window to let the frigid mountain air splash against her face, and she turned the volume of the radio up, hoping the loud sound would help. A few minutes later, her face chapped and her eardrums throbbing, she again wondered why she was giving up the safe anonymity of a guest ranch for a situation that could prove volatile.

What did she hope to accomplish by this excursion? Was she truly challenged by viewing and experiencing a different side of the animal-care industry? Or was there unfinished business from her past that should be resolved? Or could it be that she was approaching some sort of midlife crisis and thought a change would be good for her?

Actually, she couldn't explain her decision because she didn't understand it. It was sort of like volunteering for nursing duty in Vietnam. There were dozens of reasons she shouldn't.

Not usually impulsive, Angela had shocked everyone with her decision to join the Army. Her friends and family thought she was crazy to give up a good job at Boston's finest hospital to travel thousands of miles to take care of mortally wounded men. Not men in the sense of age, because most of them were barely old enough to vote and too young to buy beer in the States, but men because they had earned the right to the title by risking their lives for their country.

It had been bad—worse than she could possibly have imagined. Nothing in her nursing experience had pre-pared her for the tragic sight of men with parts of their bodies blown away, their limbs paralyzed, their skin melted in napalm flash fires. Even during the worst natural disaster, multicar collision or mass murder, no emergency room in America had ever seen such a devastating number and variety of serious injuries.

At first, her work in the field hospital had torn her apart. She had let herself care too much about her patients. When one died, she cried. When one got well and went out to fight some more, she cried. When one was injured so badly he had to be sent home, she cried. But after a few months, the tears had been used up. There were none left to shed for the men or for herself. In order to survive, her heart had had to grow callused, and she stopped looking too closely at the men's faces or trying to remember their names.

She had succeeded. She remained emotionally detached while competently assisting in surgery and follow-up care, until a man with sad blue-gray eyes had looked at her one night. She sensed his physical wounds were the least of his pain. It had almost been a challenge to make him smile. And after that first slow, sexy grin had transformed his expression, she had been fascinated. Yes, fascinated was definitely the word she would choose to describe her feelings for Jeff Hawkins.

A yawn reminded her how very tired she was. If she hadn't insisted on keeping her rental car, she could be dozing in the front seat of Jeff's pickup truck right now. But somehow, having personal transportation available, even though Jeff had told her he had an extra car she could use and even though the rental car was costing her money—made her feel less locked in. She was free to leave the moment she felt threatened.

Threatened. She never had felt physically threatened by Jeff. He had always been a gentleman. Their situa-

tion had been complicated by military protocol. Angela
was an officer, Jeff an enlisted man, so their activities
together should have been restricted to necessary en-
counters. Angela's commanding officer would have been
upset to know she was fraternizing with a sergeant. The
secrecy had pushed what might have been only a temporary friendship into intimacy. If they had been able to
sit in the officers' club and listen to the jukebox, they
would not have spent so much time in her room listening to the record player she had brought from home.
They could have danced in public instead of dancing
much too closely in her small room.

Even with the window rolled down a couple of inches,
Angela felt a rush of heat flow through her as she remembered all the things she and Jeff had done while listening to those records. They had had a special song,
with neither of them tiring of hearing the romantic, yet
wistful words of "Hold Me, Thrill Me, Kiss Me." All
too well, they had understood the immediacy and ur-
gency the song implied.

Angela followed Jeff's truck into a large tunnel, and
the sudden brightness hurt her eyes. The radio blared
static, and she hurriedly turned it off. More than a minute later, when they exited from the illuminated corri-
dor into the blackness of the night, she felt disoriented.
She had no idea where they were. Tall, jagged mountains surrounded her, their shapes several shades darker
than the star-studded sky. The scenery was very different from the harbor lights, the church steeples, and col-
umnar skyscrapers she was accustomed to seeing around
her Boston brownstone. An impulse had taken her to
Vietnam, a decision that had changed her life. And an
impulse was taking her to yet another strange land where
the unknown awaited her.

She yawned again and stretched her eyes wide in an effort to force them to stay open. A glance at the clock told her they had been on the road only about two hours. Angela knew she wasn't going to make it for three more hours. If she stopped for a cup of coffee or to catch a nap, she would never catch up with Jeff. Of course, she could continue to Montrose alone, and it shouldn't be impossible to find him. But she knew she wouldn't go that far. If the connection was broken tonight, she wouldn't follow him and he wouldn't contact her.

Perhaps it was because she was exhausted, or because her nerves had been stretched until she could no longer think clearly. She was struck by a disappointment that was as devastating as it was illogical. She had long accepted that this man would be out of her life forever. Why then did it matter that once his taillights disappeared into the darkness, she would truly never see him again?

The blink of one of those taillights caught her attention, but her sluggish brain took several seconds to calculate that he was turning off the highway. Mechanically, she followed as he exited down the ramp and circled under the overpass and into a small town. He pulled into an all-night restaurant, and Angela parked next to his truck. For several seconds, she sat, trying to collect enough energy to get out of the car. When her door opened, she automatically stepped out, almost bumping into Jeff as he stood next to her car. She must have swayed, because he reached out and took hold of her arms. Her gaze leveled on the soft knit of his sweater as it stretched across the expanse of his broad chest, and at that moment, she wanted more than anything to rest her head against it, close her eyes and feel the strength of his arms holding her.

A hint of her thoughts must have been evident in her expression because Jeff's voice was husky as he said, "I could use a cup of coffee. How about you?"

"Coffee?" she echoed, then gave herself a mental shake. "Yes, coffee. That sounds good."

They sat across from each other and he filled her in on a little of the history of the area.

A half hour later they left the restaurant. Jeff stretched and pointed to a motel sign across the street. "I think we should call it a night. We both need some sleep and if we leave by nine in the morning, we can make it home by noon."

Angela wanted to assure him she could make it all the way tonight. She knew how anxious he was to check on his sheep, and it was clear that he was not nearly as tired as she was. But she knew it would be dangerous for her to continue. Wearily, she nodded. Fleetingly, the question of whether he would rent one room or two flashed through her mind. But she was not really surprised when he carried her suitcase into a room, then handed her the key and left her alone. He was a curious mix of gentleman and aggressor—unpredictable, dangerous.

By the time he knocked on her door at nine o'clock, she had showered and dressed and was packing her suitcase. He seemed surprised that she was up and ready to go, and he managed a smile. "I'd forgotten what an early riser you are," he commented, then seemed to immediately regret that little memory.

"This isn't so early when you consider it's two hours later in Boston. But, yes, I still like to watch the sun rise over the ocean."

"They say old habits are hard to break," he commented, "but people can change a lot in eighteen years."

"Unfortunately, everything changes in eighteen years."

He had his shaving kit in one hand and picked up her suitcase with his other hand. "Some things never change," he disputed firmly, but he didn't explain.

After a quick breakfast, they were again on the road. Angela felt much better. She was able to enjoy the beauty of the mountains and relax while she drove. The time passed quickly, and she was surprised when she saw the sign marking the city limits of Montrose.

Modern stores blended well with old-fashioned shops to give the town a comfortable Western flavor. Jeff continued down the wide main street until they had left the commercial buildings behind. There were no apartment complexes or sprawling subdivisions on the outskirts of the city. Instead the land appeared to be cut into small farms with houses that were dwarfed by huge barns or oversize sheds. Horses and cattle grazed on the winter-dried grasses in the front yards or dozed beneath tall cottonwood trees.

Jeff turned into a driveway and parked his truck next to the back porch, then motioned for Angela to park in the carport. Leaving her suitcases, she stepped out and stretched while looking at the empty pasture behind the house. A shaggy black and white dog came charging around the side of the house, but his barks became excited yaps when he realized his master had come home. Jeff bent and rubbed the dog's ears in an affectionate greeting.

"Where are all your sheep?" Angela asked, beginning to wonder if maybe she had been too gullible. What if he had been lying to her about the ranch, the sheep, the lambing?

His amused grin did nothing to relieve her concerns. "City girl," he scoffed. "Can you imagine stuffing seven hundred pregnant sheep onto five acres? It would look like a sardine can filled with cotton balls." He unlocked the back door and held it open for her, then followed her into a partially modernized kitchen. "I keep the sheep in a pasture about five miles from here. During the winter I rent it from a farmer who grows corn on it during the summer."

Angela thought about the small setup and tried not to let him see her disappointment. "I thought your ranch would be . . . well, bigger."

"But this isn't my ranch," he explained. He led her to a large picture window that took up almost a whole wall of the dining room. "Do you see that mountain on the right?"

She followed the imaginary line projected by his index finger. "The tall, pointy one?" she asked, trying to single out one from a jagged ridge of mountain peaks.

"No, not the tallest one. The one next to it that's sort of flat on top." She nodded, so he continued, "That's where my ranch is. It's covered with grass in the summer and provides plenty of food for my sheep. But in the winter, the snow is three to six feet deep up there, so I have to bring my sheep to a lower elevation. The road up there is usually closed from December to late March or early April."

"Do you live there during the summer, or here?"

"At the ranch, except for a night here once or twice a week when I go grocery shopping or on a date. As soon as the lambing slows down, I'll try to get up there and see how well my cabin and the fences made it through the winter. But this time of year, the only creatures that can live at that elevation are elk and coyotes." He stepped away from the window. "I'll show you which room you can use. There's only one bath, so we'll have to take turns, but I don't think that'll be a problem."

He gave her a tour of the house that didn't take long considering there were only five main rooms. Although it had been built more than fifty years ago, it had been well taken care of, and it had a comfortable, homey feeling. Slightly frayed braided rugs covered parts of the oak plank floors, and antique brass lighting fixtures hung from the high ceilings. The house was surprisingly neat considering a bachelor lived there, but the decorating definitely lacked a feminine touch. There were no knickknacks sitting next to the books on the shelves. There were no flower arrangements in the dining room or frilly curtains in the kitchen or bathroom. Everything looked well-used, and appeared to be chosen because of its practicality.

Jeff indicated his bedroom, but didn't open the door on his way to the room she would be using. More books were stacked on shelves, and a pile of magazines filled one corner. Odd pieces of furniture lined the walls, and a saddle was draped over an old bow-topped trunk.

"Sorry it's so crowded in here, but I use it mostly for storage." He began moving things around so there was more space around the bed. "There are empty drawers in that chest and space to hang clothes in the closet. Feel free to rearrange anything you want. I'm afraid I spend most of my time outside, and I don't pay much attention to this house."

"I'll be fine," she assured him. "After all, I won't be here but for a week or two."

He nodded. "Well, just make yourself at home. The kitchen is not overstocked, but we'll pick up some groceries later. I'll bring in your suitcases now. Do you want to stay here and unpack or go with me to check on the sheep?''

She smiled and answered, ''Give me a minute to change into jeans and I'll go with you. We might as well get right to work.''

That proved to be an understatement. As soon as the truck stopped, Angela was almost ashamed she had ever had a moment's doubt about the existence of Jeff's sheep. Even through the closed windows and doors of the vehicle, she could hear the drawled bleat of the animals that was surprisingly loud. Well rounded bodies in various shades of white and black were clumped in sociable groups in a large pasture. About a dozen rams were isolated in a small adjoining pasture, along with a brown and white spotted llama.

As she and Jeff crossed the short distance from the truck to the pens, she pointed toward the tall, aristocratic-looking animal and asked, ''Is that yours, too?''

''That's Lambert.''

''Named after the Disney cartoon about a sheepish lion?''

''Yes, I have to admit that that's one of my all-time favorite cartoons. But this Lambert is very brave. He's actually my guard llama.'' At her slightly bewildered expression, he chuckled. ''I used to lose several dozen sheep to predators every year. But since I got Lambert, I haven't lost but one or two. I'm not sure why, but he's very protective of the flock. He grew up around sheep, so maybe he thinks he is one. I've seen him chase down and kill a coyote with a single kick from his hind leg. He's not so bold around mountain lions and bears, but he's smart enough to get the sheepherder and the dogs to scare the bigger animals away.''

''That's the craziest thing I've ever heard.''

"I wouldn't have believed it if I hadn't seen it, either," Jeff admitted. "But since Lambert's been so much more successful than dogs at protecting the sheep, several other ranchers are buying llamas for their flocks. You should see the prices they're getting for llamas now. I've seen them go for as high as thirty thousand dollars."

"I suppose that when you consider how much the losses add up to, it's worth it," Angela commented. "Is he gentle?"

"Usually, but he's very choosy about who he likes, so you should be careful around him. He's not too crazy about women. One bad experience can ruin something forever, I guess."

Angela looked at Jeff sharply, but there was nothing in his expression to keep her from believing he was still talking about the llama.

They were met at the gate by a man with a lamb in his arms. The tiny, fuzzy creature was so cute it immediately caught Angela's attention, and it wasn't until Jeff spoke that she glanced at the man holding the animal.

"Doch Thu, how's it going? They started without me, didn't they?"

"Yes, Mr. Jeff, they did. This is the tenth one today. But everything is very good."

Angela froze. The sound of the man's voice sent chills down her spine. His accent was thick and hard to understand, but she recognized it immediately. The war was over. She knew it shouldn't bother her after all these years, but he stood for so many things she found disturbing and unforgivable. Seeing his flat Oriental features brought back a rush of anger and hostility... and painful memories. Without knowing anything about the man, she hated him. He was Vietnamese.

Chapter Six

"Mary Had a Little Lamb" —Paul McCartney

Stiffly, she pivoted and headed toward the truck. She had to put some distance between her and that man. Her fingers had just closed around the door handle when she felt a pair of strong hands grip her arms and whirl her around.

"What the hell was that all about?" Jeff demanded, keeping his voice low.

Her expression was incredulous. "Does that man work for you?"

"Yes, he and his family have taken care of my sheep for several years."

She shook her head in disbelief. "For several years? How can you stand being around him every day? Doesn't it bother you that you are supporting the enemy?"

"The enemy?" Jeff echoed. "Doch Thu isn't the enemy He never was. He and his family lost everything during the war. When the North Vietnamese took over the country, Doch Thu was classified as a traitor, and he would have been arrested had he been caught. Fortunately, he and his family were able to escape before the NVA found them."

Angela studied Jeff's eyes for a few seconds before she stated with disgust, "Why do I have a feeling that you had something to do with that man's escape? Frankly, I'm not sure just who the real traitor is in this situation."

All color drained from Jeff's face except for an angry flush that splashed across his cheekbones. His eyes became colorless until they looked like shards of sooty glass.

"I fought for my country," he informed her in a deadly calm voice. "I wasn't one of those draft dodgers who ran off to Canada or hid behind their college professor. In fact, I didn't even wait to be drafted. I went to Vietnam of my own free will, and I returned for a second tour of duty because I thought I could make a difference. I was wrong about that. What the South Vietnamese needed couldn't be given to them by one man or even a whole army."

He released his hold on her arms abruptly, and she took an awkward step back. The door of the truck braced her back. Only the flare of his nostrils and the glitter of his eyes betrayed the intensity of Jeff's feelings.

"But damn it, I tried. I did everything I could do. I was one of the last GIs to leave Vietnam in 1973. I'm not proud of everything I've done in my life, but there's nothing I would apologize for. Certainly not my sponsorship of Doch Thu. And if you can't accept that . . . well, that's your problem."

A plaintive cry drew Jeff's attention. "I've got to get out there. Doch Thu and his son have been working around the clock since I left, and they need to get some sleep." Without another look in her direction, he turned and walked away.

Angela watched his broad, rigidly set back for several seconds before she realized the conversation was over. Her opinion about the Vietnamese man hadn't changed a bit, but she did regret her thoughtless challenge of Jeff's loyalty. She didn't for a minute doubt that he was a true-blue American and had been an excellent soldier. But she couldn't understand how he could have any sympathy for the people from Southeast Asia. Jeff had seen his buddies ambushed and slaughtered. Surely he had heard the stories of torture and cruelty at the hands of the Vietnamese. And the acts of inhumanity hadn't been performed only by the Vietcong soldiers. There had been traitors everywhere. Even the women and children had set booby traps and tricked Americans to their deaths.

Angela had seen the results. She had tried to save the limbs that had been partially blown away, the organs that had been damaged, the lives of the GIs who were in the hospital because of the Vietnamese. After a while, it hadn't mattered to her that it was the Communist-controlled Vietcong causing the damage. She resented the South Vietnamese because they couldn't handle their own problems, which had caused thousands of American lives to be lost. She didn't believe the sacrifice was worth the few years of freedom the United States involvement had bought.

The longer she stayed in Vietnam, the more she hated the Vietnamese—*all* the Vietnamese, regardless of which side of the demilitarized zone they lived in or where their loyalties were. She was certain that, if it had served their cause, the South Vietnamese would have turned their guns on their American protectors. And she felt more than enough had been done to help them in their own country. There was no reason to bring them to the States, to give them jobs that could be held by unemployed Americans, to add their families to the already over-crowded welfare rolls.

Angela watched Jeff carry on an animated conversation with Doch Thu, who kept shaking his head. But Jeff must have finally been convincing because Doch Thu called his son and they walked to their ancient but clean Toyota pickup truck and drove away.

When she looked back, Jeff had dropped out of sight. She scanned the flock of sheep until she saw him kneeling next to one ewe. Angela knew he was angry, justifiably so. After not seeing a person for so many years, especially a man with whom she had shared so much, she had definitely been out of line in calling him a traitor. It wasn't the best way to begin a vacation.

As she gathered her courage to face him, she studied the setup of the wintering area. Several large fenced pastures were tilled into rows with dried corn husks scattered around. They surrounded a much smaller pasture where most of the sheep were confined. In the center of the small pasture was a horseshoe-shaped arrangement of small wooden pens about four feet wide by four feet deep. Each pen contained a bucket of water and a wooden box for food. In the middle of the horseshoe were two large bins that Angela guessed were used to store feed. There were three small, wooden-fenced corrals behind the pens and a round-roofed trailer next to the corrals.

Hesitantly, she returned to the gate. Jeff's back was to her, so she was able to observe him freely for several minutes. He was too busy to pay her any attention as the ewe delivered not one, but two wet, shaky little lambs. When the mother stood up, Jeff gathered one of the babies in his arms and headed toward the back row of isolation pens. The other sheep began crowding around the remaining twin, and the mother seemed confused as she became separated from her babies.

Angela opened the gate and stepped inside the corral, carefully closing the gate behind her. She hurried to the lamb and, following Jeff's lead, picked up the bleating baby. He was so tiny she was able to lift him easily. He didn't struggle, but seemed to welcome her warmth as she carried him to his mother. As she bent down, letting the mother lick the lamb's fuzzy head, Angela noticed Jeff had returned.

"What should I do?" she asked.

The seconds stretched out as he seemed to consider his answer. "I can't leave right now. You can wait in the truck . . . or you can give me a hand." He glanced at another ewe who was circling a bed of straw. "It looks like I'm going to be pretty busy for awhile."

From her position, he looked very tall and intimidating. With the sun at his back his face was in shadow, making his expression unreadable. The silhouetted outline of his body reminded her how sturdy and strong it was, and how unmistakably masculine. The wound that had kept him in the hospital for so many weeks had surely left external scars. But there seemed to be no lasting emotional effects from the war. In fact, Jeff appeared to have recovered amazingly well considering all he had seen and done. Too well. It was as if he had shut out the experience, pretending it had never happened.

She stood and moved so she could look into his eyes. Instead of being cold and remote as she expected, they were filled with a melancholy sadness and a longing that went beyond sexual desire. It surprised her so much that she reached out, her fingers lightly gripping his shoulder. She could feel the warmth of his skin through the soft cotton shirt. He lifted his hand and covered hers as if to pull it away. Instead, his fingers entwined with hers and he moved her hand until it rested against his chest.

"Angie," he began, using her nickname from long ago, "I shouldn't have asked you to come here." He shook his head and sighed. "I don't know why I did. This is no place for you to spend a vacation."

The irregular rhythm of his heartbeat beneath her open palm told her he was not as coolly neutral as he was trying to appear. With a gentle smile, she confessed, "I don't know why I agreed, either. This is certainly not how I planned to spend my vacation."

"I won't hold you to it. As soon as Doch Thu comes back this evening, I'll take you to your car. It was a mistake—"

The frightened cries of a lamb intruded. Jeff and Angela looked around and saw that the mother and baby had been separated, and a pregnant ewe was trying to steal the newborn.

"Jeff, I'm sorry about what I said earlier," Angela began, but he interrupted.

"I've got to get that ewe and her baby into the pen with the other twin before she forgets he's hers. We'll finish this conversation later." For a second longer, his hand remained wrapped around hers, then he released it and stepped away.

Angela sighed. There was so much left unsaid that she doubted they would ever be able to finish the conversation. Especially if she left that night.

Jeff picked up the lamb and lured the mother into following along by letting her see and smell her baby. Angela looked around at the mass of newly shorn, very pregnant ewes and could imagine how busy it would be when a half dozen or more of them went into labor at the same time. Jeff definitely needed another set of hands. And her hands were experienced with animal birthings, even if the animals she usually assisted were of a different species. Without waiting for instructions, she went to the ewe who had been circling. She was lying down, panting and straining as two incredibly tiny hooves inched their way out of her womb.

As soon as the lamb was born, Angela followed Jeff's lead and carried the baby to a pen. She passed Jeff, who was carrying another set of twins, and he flashed her a rueful grin. "We may be too tired to have that conversation tonight," he said.

Angela responded with a casual shrug. "Then I suppose I'll have to stay another day."

His dark eyebrows arched in silent query, but they were both too busy to pursue the matter.

It was almost ten o'clock before Doch Thu and his son returned. Twenty-seven of the small pens were occupied by newly delivered lambs and their mothers. Between births, Angela had helped Jeff carry buckets of water from the pump to the pails inside the pens, as well as a generous measure of corn and hay.

Every muscle in Angela's body ached as she slouched on the seat during the short trip to Jeff's house.

"What would you like for dinner?" he asked as they parked in the driveway. "I could broil us a steak or open a can of chili."

Angela shook her head. "I'm too tired to eat. I think I'll just take a quick shower and fall into bed." She yawned and pushed her tangled hair off her forehead. "Unless you'd like to take your shower first."

"No, go ahead. You worked hard today. Thanks."

She managed a tired smile. "No problem. I enjoyed it. And if I can get a few hours of sleep, I'll be ready to go back tomorrow."

"You don't have to, you know."

She stopped in the hall and looked back. "I don't mind helping. Honestly." She observed his reaction, then added, "If you want me to stay, I will."

Steadily, he met her gaze. His silvery blue eyes gave away nothing, but his voice was lower, huskier as he answered, "I want you . . . to stay."

The hesitation was so slight she could have imagined it. But a shiver raced through her at the implication. She knew she was playing with fire. How many men could look so incredibly attractive dressed in clothes that were spotted with mud and manure? How many men could have captured such a prominent place in her thoughts and held it for all those years? She couldn't keep from wondering if she had blown her memories of Jeff all out of proportion, and if he could possibly be as excitingly satisfying as she remembered.

The shiver turned into a heated flush that left her weakened limbs shaky. She decided it would be wise of her to escape to the shower. "Good, then it's all settled," she exclaimed before hurrying to her bedroom to get her nightclothes.

The shower washed away the layer of dirt and much of her exhaustion. When she left the bathroom, the smell of bacon and eggs changed her mind about her hunger. After leaving her dirty clothes in her room, she went to the kitchen.

"Um, something smells good," she said as she drew in a deep breath. "Is there enough for one more person? If there is, I think I'll change my mind about dinner. Or would you call this breakfast?"

Jeff chuckled. "I figured the smell would get to you, so I made enough for both of us. But I'm not sure what meal this is. Our schedule is all messed up because we ate breakfast so late and skipped lunch. Actually, I've always thought eggs and bacon tasted better at night than in the morning."

"So do I," she agreed, moving down the row of cabinets until she found the one containing plates. "There's something sort of nauseating about looking at two eggs that seem to be looking back at you first thing in the morning.'

"Speaking of eggs, what do you like in your omelet?"

"Anything but onions and jalapeños."

He sprinkled a mixture of ingredients onto the fluffy yellow eggs, then deftly folded the omelet in half. "My sheep love onions."

"I thought I detected that odor on their breaths." Angela laughed.

"You think I'm kidding, but I'm not. About ten days before lambing starts, a crew arrives from New Zealand and goes from ranch to ranch shearing the sheep. But to get rid of parasites that would lower the value of the wool, I start feeding the sheep onions a few weeks before they're sheared."

"I'm sure the shearers appreciate that. No wonder they work so quickly." Jeff lifted her omelet out, placed it on a plate and set it on the table in front of her. While his omelet was cooking, he poured himself a glass of milk and offered her some, but she declined. "I'd rather have coffee, but since it's so late, I'll settle for water."

As soon as his food was done, Jeff sat down across from her. "It's too bad you missed the shearing. It's sort of fun to watch. Fourteen or so people make up the crew. They have a portable shed with a dozen stalls and they herd the sheep in one by one. A good hand can shear about two hundred sheep a day, so it didn't take them long to get through with my flock."

"Two hundred a day," she repeated in disbelief. "What do you do with all the wool?"

"A couple of women in the crew roll the wool, and another person packs it into big bags and sews them shut. The lanolin in the wool keeps their skin really soft."

Angela's dark eyebrows arched suggestively at the implication that Jeff might know exactly how soft the women's skin was, but he didn't appear to notice as he continued.

"They're experimenting with a new drug in New Zealand that will cause the sheep's wool to become brittle at the root. Then it can actually be pulled off the sheep's back quickly and painlessly, and the wool is in perfect condition. The only problem is that the sheep are totally naked and have to be kept indoors for several days to avoid sunburn or injury to their unprotected skin."

"Is the wool from the black or spotted sheep worth less than the white ones?"

"No, it all sells for the same amount. I guess the people who buy it can dye it any color they want. But the black sheep come in handy for me. I keep enough black sheep to help me get a quick count of the flocks when they're separated to different areas. I run one black sheep with every ninety-nine white ones, so I can tell at a glance the total number that should be in each group, which makes it easier to know if some have wandered off."

"But what would happen if a black one wandered off?" she asked.

He chuckled. "Then I'd have to take off my shoes and start counting."

She smiled at the image before inquiring, "They're only sheared once a year?"

"Yes, just in spring so they'll be cool all summer. They have time to grow a new coat before winter. Every year each sheep produces enough wool to make a three-piece suit."

"Multiply that by seven hundred and that's quite a few bags of wool." Angela was fascinated by the unfamiliar process. She had never been around farm animals of any kind.

For several minutes, they ate in silence. Then she spoke again. "This is delicious. I never would have guessed that cooking was one of your talents."

"It wasn't until I discovered I'd rather cook than starve to death. Especially when I'm staying at the ranch. Down here I can run into town for a meal, but that gets old after a while, not to mention expensive. So I had the wife of a friend of mine teach me the basics." He didn't seem to be the least bit embarrassed by admitting, "Actually, I realized I sort of like it. I experiment a lot. Sometimes it works and sometimes the dog won't eat it." As if reminded of the dog's presence at his feet, Jeff handed the black and white border collie the last bite of his omelet.

"What's his name?" Angela offered the dog a piece of her food, which he licked from her fingers. She noticed the animal's eyes were cloudy with cataracts and his muzzle was white with age. "He's pretty old, isn't he?"

"Pepper was just a puppy when I came to work on the ranch, which was about 1975. That would make him at least sixteen. He wasn't raised to be a pet, but he's almost blind and too old to work the sheep anymore." Absently, he tousled the dog's long, soft hair. "I know he'd rather be out there with the flock, but he's accepted living with me now in semiretirement. His children and grandchildren have taken over his job. They live with Doch Thu during the winter because he needs to keep a bond between himself and the dogs all year long."

Angela picked up the dishes and walked to the sink. "You cooked, so I'll clean up."

"No, I'll help. This is your first night here and I know you're tired. With the two of us, it'll go more quickly. Do you want to wash or dry?"

She chose to wash since she wasn't sure where the dishes belonged once they were dry. But as they stood shoulder to shoulder at the sink, she wished she had been able to do the job alone. It was such a deceptively domestic scene that it reminded her of things she'd rather not think of. She and Craig had never shared kitchen chores. His leg injury had made it difficult for him to stand for long periods of time. Besides, she and he had both come from wealthy families, and they had been able to afford full-time help with the cooking and cleaning. After Jeff's admission about enjoying cooking, Angela dared not admit that he was probably a much better cook than she since her experience in the kitchen was extremely limited.

While she had been taking her shower, Jeff had exchanged his dirty jeans for a clean pair and had taken off his long-sleeved shirt. The white T-shirt that covered his torso emphasized his build, bringing on a disturbing comparison of how much his chest had filled out and his shoulders widened since she had seen him last. But, of course, then he had still been a kid. He was only eighteen when she first met him. She was almost three years older than he. Age had been irrelevant because the war had made everyone grow up quickly. Their age was never a topic of discussion. She'd known his only because she'd had access to his file while he was in the hospital.

Even then, however, he had seemed older. There was a maturity, an independence about him that she suspected must have been brought on by his background. But that was another topic they barely touched during their talks.

Angela was reminded how little she knew about this man. And to complicate the issue, each time she found out something, it didn't match what she thought she already knew. The Jeff she'd known then was a rough-edged, impulsive, angry young man. He'd been on a mission to save the world and make a mark for himself in the process. It was as if he had been determined to prove something to the world and to himself.

All of that was in sharp contrast to the man standing next to her. Quiet, calm and confident, he seemed capable of handling any situation. All the rough edges had been smoothed out, but now that the personal insecurities were gone, so, too, was the vulnerability. There were moments when she caught a glimpse of the sadness that had often filled his eyes when he first came to the hospital. But now she had the impression there was an invisible wall surrounding him, insulating and cushioning him from the world. Perhaps it was his way of dealing with the memories of the war and his reentry into real life. Or maybe that wall had always been there, but it had been less solid and impenetrable because of the circumstances that had thrown them together.

As she stood next to him, she was confused. She knew he was the same person, and yet he was very different. He was still handsome, in a rugged, totally masculine way. He still had the ability to make her body tingle with an emotion she had never felt about anyone else.

She suspected it was purely sexual. There was a chemistry between them that was as strong now as ever, and just as inexplicable. She hadn't understood it then and she didn't understand it tonight. The brush of his fingers over hers or his arm against her arm was so innocent and yet so exciting that her heart would leap in her chest every time they accidentally touched. It was something that should have been left behind in her youth. And she wasn't certain how to handle it.

A little voice deep within her whispered a warning. It reminded her how much she had enjoyed making love with this man. It also reminded her how very long she had gone without feeling the satisfaction and security of being loved. She knew what she was feeling for Jeff had nothing to do with love, but everything to do with sex, just as it had eighteen years ago. But it was a powerful emotion, so powerful that she was considering the consequences if she and Jeff should just happen to...

"Angie, are you trying to wash the pattern off that plate?"

His voice broke into her thoughts, and she jerked around so abruptly the plate slipped from her soapy fingers. Jeff reacted automatically, trying to catch the falling plate in midair. It bounced off one hand and slid through the other before he was able to get a secure grip on it when it was just inches from the floor. He looked at her, a crooked grin lifting one corner of his mouth.

Something in his expression told her he knew exactly where her thoughts had been wandering, and a heated flush rushed across her cheeks. Slowly he stood, his eyes never leaving hers. He was standing so close she could feel the warmth of his breath as it traveled the length of her body. The silk gown and matching robe covered her adequately, but she suddenly wished she was wearing something thicker. She dared not look to see how obvious her physical reaction was, but she could feel the swell of her nipples pushing against the soft material when his breath caressed them.

Only the width of the plate separated her from Jeff. It would be so easy for him to reach out and pull her to him. To capture her lips with his. To crush her breasts against the hardness of his chest. To make her forget all the bad times and remember only the good ones. She felt herself swaying toward him as if pulled by invisible strings.

"We'd better go to bed," he suggested.

Angela blinked. His voice was much calmer than the whirlwind of confusion that was raging within her. Her body said *yes*, her mind said *no*, and her heart said *leave me out of this*.

The amused sparkle in his eyes slowly hardened to a brittle gleam. "We both need the sleep," he continued in the same flat tone. "I usually relieve Doch Thu at about eight o'clock. We could pick up some doughnuts on the way."

Nonchalantly he turned to the sink and washed the plate.

He couldn't have rejected her more obviously if he had physically pushed her away. Her face burned, but his actions had been as effective as a slap in the face. Stiffening her spine and pulling in her emotions, she forced her voice to be as steady as his. "I hope they have apple fritters." She wiped her hands on the dish towel and tossed it onto the countertop. "See you in the morning."

Chapter Seven

"All Day And All Of The Night" —Kinks

In a rare moment of rest, Angela stood next to the fence, her arms crossed on top of a post and her chin resting on the back of her hand as she watched the lambs become acquainted with each other. Shy at first, they would approach each other cautiously. But soon they were all running and leaping around like playful children until they returned to their mother for a meal or a nap.

Angela's smile was tired. She could sure use a nap. The nights were all too short, and once she was in bed, she slept so deeply that she woke up groggy. But she didn't sleep late or complain about the long hours. It had become a matter of principle. Angela was determined to survive the physical and emotional challenge of her *vacation.* For seven days she had forced her aching body to get up as soon as Jeff's alarm went off. She worked for twelve to sixteen hours delivering lambs, segregating them in the pens and hauling countless buckets of water and feed. Then she had fallen into bed around midnight. If she had had time to think about the craziness of the situation, she might have packed her suitcases and driven to the airport.

Actually, she was enjoying herself except for the fact that she had no idea what game Jeff was playing. Apparently only he knew the rules. Sometimes he was charming, witty and friendly, and other times he was so remote he seemed to have forgotten she was there.

But she loved working with the sheep. Every time she held a newborn lamb in her arms, felt the warm, fuzzy little body lean against hers and heard it utter a first shaky bleat, she was filled with a sense of accomplishment. She was glad she had been there to witness the birth. And she was glad that she wouldn't be around to see the fate of the lambs. She'd seen too many deaths and too few births. It was nice to be involved with the positive side of life's cycle.

Right on schedule, the majority of the ewes had begun going into labor. Angela and Jeff worked side by side, too busy to talk, too tired to resolve any unfinished business, too wary to start anything new. When all one hundred of the small pens were full, Jeff had gone to the first row and released the mothers and babies into a corral. As she participated in each step, Angela began to understand why the birthing area had been divided into so many small units. Since sheep weren't very intelligent and would forget they had given birth, it was important that the mothers spend about a week isolated with their babies so they would bond before being turned out into the corral. By that time, the lambs were stronger and more independent.

"They look like they're having a lot of fun." Jeff had walked up behind her and joined her to watch the lambs' clumsy cavorting.

"They're just like kids. They all have their own personalities," Angela commented. "Look at that big one over there. He's a bully and likes to butt the others and push them around. And that spotted one is so shy she barely ventures out from behind her mother."

"She's a day younger than the others, and at that age every day makes a big difference. In another week, she'll be right out there in the middle of things."

"How long do you keep them in this corral?" Angela asked.

"About another week," he replied. "Then they have their tails cropped, their ears clipped, and if they're bucks, they're castrated."

Angela grimaced. "Poor little things."

"It has to be done. They're sore for a couple of days, then they're out there playing as hard as before."

"You probably cut their tails for cleanliness and castrate them to keep them from fighting, but why do you clip their ears?"

"That's how they're marked to show ownership, since we can't use hot brands like cattle ranchers—we'd damage the wool," he explained. "To show they belong to me, I cut two splits in their left ear and a swallow fork in their right ear. As a temporary identification so I can keep up with which lambs go with which mothers and who had twins or triplets, I spray washable paint brands on them before I let them loose in the big pastures, then again in the fall when I'm dividing them up for sale."

"I'm glad I won't be here when you do the clipping and castrating. Surgery is my least favorite part of being a veterinarian. What sort of tools do you use?"

"Sharp knives and rubber bands. Some of the old-timers still use their teeth, but I didn't think I could handle that."

Angela's nose wrinkled in distaste. "I'm *really* glad I won't see that. How on earth did you learn all these things? You're a city boy from Pittsburgh. I'll bet you hadn't even seen a lamb before you joined the Army."

"I was lucky to stumble onto a man who was an excellent teacher. He was the kindest, most patient person I've ever known." Jeff was silent for a moment, his gaze lifted to focus on some point in the distant mountains. "He died four years ago. I wish you could have met him. You would have liked him . . . and he would have liked you. He admired courage and perseverance—" Jeff managed a wry chuckle "—both of which you've shown for the last week, not to mention the two years you were in Vietnam."

She could tell he had been very close to the man and that he truly missed his friend. "He must have been a good influence. You seem to have mellowed quite a bit since I knew you back then."

He shrugged. "I learned how to fight in Pittsburgh, I learned how to survive in Vietnam, but I didn't learn how to live until I moved here. The minute I arrived in the Rockies I felt like I had come home at last."

"So you plan on staying here and being a gentleman rancher the rest of your life?"

"Sounds like a perfect idea to me," he confirmed with a nod. "I've built up the flock and with the two new purebred Rambouillet bucks I bought last year, the quality of the lambs should be better than ever."

"Why do you call them bucks? I have always heard male sheep referred to as rams."

"You'll hear it both ways, but since most of the sheep ranchers around here call them bucks, I've fallen into the habit."

Angela let her gaze wander over the flock of fluffy babies as they cavorted around the corral. "It looks like you're going to at least double your flock with all the multiple births. Is it unusual to have so many twins?"

"There's a higher percentage of triplets, but we usually have about a ninety percent twin rate."

"How many will you keep?"

"I'll keep enough lambs to replace the older sheep that I'll sell. After they're about eight years old, their wool starts getting shorter. And I'll probably bring my total flock up to about seven hundred and fifty to allow for loss."

"So, in the fall, you'll have about twelve to fourteen hundred lambs to sell?"

"About that, if Lambert does a good job protecting the flock from predators and if we don't have a late snow or some other kind of catastrophic weather. Sheep aren't the brightest creatures in the world. They have been known to drown during a rainstorm or freeze to death mere feet from shelter. A rancher can't count his money until it's in the bank." He turned and directed his disturbingly steady gaze on her. With his hip leaning against the fence post and his arm draped across its top, he changed the course of the conversation. "So what about you? Are you going to take care of neurotic poodles and overweight tabbies the rest of your life? What about the motherhood thing? The biological clock? The midlife crisis? The almost-forty-something syndrome?"

Angela snorted and gave him an exaggerated glare. "Thank you very much for reminding me. Every day I make it a point to think about the delightful fact that forty is only months away."

He refused to be sidetracked. "You didn't answer my questions."

"Is this a belated employee interview?" Her attitude had changed from joking to defensive as he pressed an issue she felt was too personal and painful to discuss.

"I remember hearing you say that you wanted half a dozen kids. What happened?"

"Real life got in the way," she answered brusquely.

"Just because Craig died you can't stop living, too. You're not too old to start a family."

Her sigh was doubtful. "I've been dating a colleague for a couple of years. Lately, he's been talking about marriage, but even if we should actually go through with it, I don't think children are likely." A cool breeze lifted her hair and swirled it around her face. Grateful for the diversion, her fingers slowly pushed the dark strands of hair into some semblance of order. She couldn't tell him that it wasn't possible for her to have children. It was a disappointment she had shared with no one but her mother. Not even Craig had known. And why would it matter to Jeff anyway?

"Besides, you're one to talk," she retorted as the irony of the conversation hit her. "You're about the same age as me. Why aren't you married? Where are your children?"

"I've been doing a little dating, too. But I'm in no hurry. I've still got a few years of prime time left."

"Sure. And you can play baseball with your son using your cane for a bat." Her head tilted as she listened to the sheep. "I hear one calling us."

He straightened. But before he could take a step, she continued, "I'll take this one." She didn't wait for his answer, but walked away, tossing over her shoulder a parting gibe. "I think the sheep in the last ten pens need water."

Jeff didn't want to smile. But he did. And he didn't want her to fit into his life so well. But she did.

He leaned against the post and watched her walk away. The sheep would just have to wait a few more minutes. When he had asked her if she wanted to help, he had had several reasons for hoping she would accept. One was that he hoped to settle the past with her. He wanted to be able to put her out of his mind forever, but he knew that wouldn't happen until he found out why she had led him on, and why she had chosen Craig.

But it wasn't until he had spent a few days with her in this new environment—*his* turf—that he realized he had wanted to overwhelm her, to exhaust her, to beat her down until she admitted she couldn't handle the situation. In a juvenile, masculine way, he had wanted to find something she wasn't good at, something that he happened to be very good at. He had wanted to show her up. And he had wanted her to leave in defeat.

Once he recognized his motives, he was ashamed of himself. It was not very admirable to break someone down to build himself up. The fact that she was helping so much and learning so quickly, all without a word of complaint, made him feel even worse. Every minute he spent with her and every night she slept in a bed only a few feet away from his with just a thin wall separating them served as a reminder of how much he wanted her and how good things had been for them.

She looked great in jeans and an oversize sweatshirt he had loaned her. But then he had never had any complaints about her appearance. Whether she had been dressed in drab green fatigues or barely covered with the casual drape of a sheet, he had always thought she was beautiful. A compact five foot two, she was almost a foot shorter than he, but she was so physically strong and her personality was so powerful that he didn't realize how small she was unless he was standing next to her or holding her in his arms.

Which reminded him of another part of his plan that wasn't working out quite like he had expected. The time he had spent with her in Vietnam, the intimate, peaceful time in her room or away from the base, had lived in his memory as the best hours of his life. But had that been because he had so desperately needed an oasis in the midst of the battle? Or had the memories grown sweeter with age? As soon as he'd seen her at the reunion, he had known he would have to either reduce the memories to their true level or get rid of them entirely. It had seemed the easiest way was to be around Angela long enough to remember her flaws and magnify them until they overpowered the good attributes so he could rid himself, once and for all, of this woman who had haunted his dreams, both waking and sleeping, for so long.

Unfortunately, the more time he spent with her, the less her flaws mattered. He kept reminding himself how she had led him on, then dropped him flat. Every time he remembered hearing her say she was going to marry Craig, a bitter taste rose in his throat, and he was able to push any tinges of romantic feelings aside. It was all that was saving him from making a total fool of himself.

That first night in his kitchen, it had taken every ounce of resistance he had not to grab her and kiss her when she was standing so close to him that he could smell the fragrance of her skin and see the enticing outline of her breasts encased in the softest of silk. Since then he had been careful not to let himself be put into such a tempting position.

But it was almost as bad seeing her every morning with her hair deliciously tousled and her eyes liquid and dark with sleep. And late at night, after a hard day with the sheep, she looked so feminine and vulnerable, he wanted to kiss the dark circles from under her eyes, massage the aches from her shoulders and feel her nestled drowsily in his arms.

He groaned and shifted uncomfortably as his intimate thoughts brought an immediate physical response. It was obvious that his plan was backfiring. Angela was probably counting the days until she would be leaving to return to her busy, lucrative practice—and her boyfriend.

Jeff didn't know why it hadn't occurred to him that she might have a boyfriend. It had been a shock to hear that Craig had died, making her a young widow. He hadn't considered the possibility she might have fallen in love with someone else.

Not that it mattered. There was no place in her life for a man like Jeff. She had made that obvious eighteen years ago, and she had given no indication that things were any different now. She came from a wealthy, privileged background. Even though her parents had divorced when she was young, they had both loved her and vied for her affections. She had grown up with servants and summers in a beach house on Cape Cod. The man she was dating was probably in the same social sphere as she, and would provide her with a life of luxury and ease.

Jeff couldn't offer her that. Every penny he made went into the ranch. Raising sheep was profitable, but he wanted to build and improve his stock in order to secure his future. Gradually, during the four years he had owned the ranch, he had replaced the Suffolk sheep with a newer, better breed. His Rambouillet purebred and Rambouillet Columbian crossbreeds were producing more lambs and a finer, longer wool. He had purchased a small bulldozer to use on his ranch, and had replaced much of the patched-together fencing. All the improvements were costing money, but they would pay off. But for the present, Jeff's financial situation had no room for luxuries.

Don't be a fool, he chided. Angela wasn't the least bit interested in anything he had to offer. And, he reminded himself with a mental kick, he wasn't interested in offering her anything, anyway. He had a few more days to uncover those flaws, and by the time she left, he wouldn't care if he never saw her again.

Actually, he *had* discovered a flaw of sorts. Angela had made her feelings about Doch Thu and his family very clear at their first meeting. Nothing else had been said, but since then she had managed to avoid any contact with them. Each morning at the sheep pens, she stayed around the truck while Jeff talked to his hired help, getting updates on the night's activities. It wasn't until Doch Thu had driven off that she would join Jeff in the lambing area.

While Jeff wished she would make an effort to get to know Doch Thu better before she formed an opinion, it was not difficult to understand why she was so negatively affected by the Vietnamese man's presence. When they were in Vietnam, they had been programmed not to trust any of the natives because the most innocent-looking child could be holding a live grenade. She had seen the destruction caused by Vietcong booby traps and Communist-provided weapons. She had tried to be with the American soldiers when they died so their last image would be of a friendly, familiar face instead of an Oriental one. She had tried to correct some of the damage, both physical and mental, that the soldiers had received at the hands of the enemy.

No, he couldn't really condemn her for any resentment that was left over from the war. Jeff, too, had flashbacks—moments when the terror was so real he could almost feel the cold stare of a Vietcong soldier slicing through him or hear the cries of a buddy who fell, mortally wounded by a sniper's bullet. But when Jeff put the military behind him, he had resolved to overcome the anger and the fear. Most of the time, he succeeded. However, he certainly couldn't criticize someone who had not been able to put enough distance between herself and the horror of the war.

THE NEEDLE SCRATCHED against the record, distorting the sound of the music. Still drowsy from an afternoon nap, Angela made a mental note to ask her mother to send some new needles with the next care package, along with several bars of soft fragrant soap, a couple of bottles of cream rinse and a box of fudge. The Army provided her with the basics. But there were so many simple things she had taken for granted that she now considered luxuries.

Raindrops splattered against the windows and drummed noisily on the roof, further diluting the song's melody. She knew the shower would stop soon, leaving the air hot and heavy. Inside the air was cool, and Angela was in no hurry to get up and dress for her late duty at the hospital.

The man lying on the bed beside her stirred, his arms automatically tightening around her. He was another reason she wasn't anxious to leave her room. While she was with him, she felt safe, protected from the outside world. It was possible to pretend that nothing beyond her room existed. There was no war, no blood, no death, and there were no other people.

Angela had made it a nonnegotiable policy not to get involved with *any* man while she was in the Army. It didn't matter if they were officers or enlisted men; both were off limits. And she had stuck to her promise until she met Jeff.

She often tried to analyze why he had been different, and the only solution was just that—he was different. From the first moment she assisted in his surgery, she had known he would eventually be well enough to be sent into action. That had been an insurance against any sort of serious relationship. Neither she nor any of the soldiers had the time, the energy or the inclination to make plans or commitments.

And yet, she had never met anyone quite like him, so independent, so detached. He had made it clear he didn't need anyone, and hadn't for a very long time. The impression he gave was that he had practically raised himself, although he rarely mentioned his family. It was apparent he was not anxious to go home.

But most disturbing was that he was strong, brave and a loner, which was a very dangerous combination. That was the type of soldier who usually earned a Purple Heart, a Congressional Medal of Honor and an escorted, flag-draped casket home.

It quickly became apparent that Angela and Jeff had no mutual experiences from their past to bond them. Nor did they have any hope for a future together. It all added up to making him a very low risk for temptation. It should have been easy to resist his sad, lonely eyes and his hesitant but charmingly crooked grin. But some things can't be predicted.

Angela never thought she would invite Jeff into her room that first evening. Nor would she have guessed she would chance military reprimand and public embarrassment by continuing to meet him clandestinely. Their relationship was comfortable, satisfying and nonthreatening. He didn't press her for promises, and the word "love" was never mentioned.

Not that it was never in her thoughts. As she rubbed her head against the tanned skin of his chest, she carefully avoided putting pressure on his left arm. The cast had been removed yesterday, and she knew the arm would still be tender and sore. She should move away, but she loved the feel of his body next to hers, the warmth of his skin and the possessiveness of his legs around hers. She knew she shouldn't let these meetings continue. But as much as her common sense told her to break it off, she hesitated. Soon enough he would be leaving and the decision would be taken out of her hands. She would smile and kiss him goodbye. And it would be over. The dreaded word they both seemed to be desperately avoiding would never be spoken.

She would certainly not try to force him to say he loved her. The last thing she needed was empty declarations. If he didn't care enough to say it of his own accord, she didn't want to hear it. Her feelings didn't matter. She had been foolish to let herself fall in love with him. But if he never knew, it wouldn't hurt so much when she had to let him go.

Thank goodness she had her friendship with Craig to fall back on. She and Craig had similar backgrounds and childhoods. They understood each other, and joked that they belonged at a country club sipping cool drinks, not in a jungle swatting mosquitoes and dodging bullets. With a sense of humor that kept her and the other patients laughing, he provided a diversion from the depressing atmosphere.

Angela admitted that she didn't have the same feelings for Craig as she had for Jeff, but then what she felt for Jeff would never last. If his death at the hands of the Vietnamese didn't sever whatever ties he and she had, then reality would.

But, as she listened to the steady thump of his heartbeat beneath her ear and breathed in his masculine scent, a mixture of sweat and after-shave, she was in no hurry for him to get well. Her life, which had seemed full and worthwhile before he entered it, would feel emptier without him. She could only hope that something or someone would come along to take his place. Quickly, before she had time to miss him.

The last record on the stack dropped, and the needle slid through the grooves, sending the music to the built-in speaker of the portable hi-fi. Soon the song would end. Soon Jeff would be gone, and Angela would have to forget him and get on with her life. Soon there would be silence.

Chapter Eight

"Rocky Mountain High" —*John Denver*

"Angie, it's time to wake up."

The voice interrupted her dream and she tried to ignore it. Burrowing deeper into her pillow, she reached for the elusive threads of the misty image that had not quite faded. She wasn't ready for Jeff to leave.

She felt his hand on her shoulder and bent her head until her cheek rubbed against his knuckles. "I'm not ready to get up," she mumbled, her voice unintentionally sexy. She patted the pillow next to her and added, "Come on back to bed."

The hand beneath her cheek stiffened, then abruptly withdrew. "The coffee's ready. I'm leaving in thirty minutes, and you can go with me or sleep in."

Through the fog of disturbed sleep, she heard him leave the room and shut the door firmly behind him. Slowly, the haze began to dissipate. The war was over. She was no longer in Vietnam. Craig was dead and Jeff had survived—an ending to the dream that was opposite what she had expected. The only thing that hadn't changed was her irrational attraction to a man whose only interest in her was as a mutton midwife.

She rolled onto her back and stared sightlessly at the ceiling. Day after tomorrow she would be leaving, returning to a world where she felt confident and in charge of the situation. It was difficult to believe almost two weeks had passed since she had bumped into Jeff at the reunion—two weeks of hard, but satisfying work, two weeks of riding an emotional merry-go-round with no brass ring in sight.

By Jeff's meticulous count last night, Angela knew that of six hundred eighty-nine pregnant ewes, four hundred seventy-three had given birth. Eight hundred and six lambs were now frolicking in the holding corrals or nuzzling up to their mothers in the small post-birthing pens. It was an incredible adventure, and Angela didn't regret having changed her vacation plans. Her Colorado getaway had taken on a different twist, but she couldn't imagine she would have had a better time going on trail rides, roasting marshmallows or whatever she would have done at a guest ranch. She would much rather keep busy than sit around doing nothing for two weeks.

There were certain similarities to this and her last impulsive venture. Vietnam had been a unique experience. She was glad she had gone and even more glad to have come back. But during her two years of duty, she felt she had done all she could to make a difference. If just one man had survived and come home because of her nursing abilities, it had been worth the sacrifice.

Putting in twelve to eighteen hour days in a pasture had the same physical effect of pulling two shifts in a field hospital. It left her exhausted, but she didn't have to suffer through nights of insomnia like she often did at home. Of course, forcing a tiny lamb to breath after it was born with the umbilical cord wrapped around its throat was not on the same level as saving a human life.

But it was more fulfilling than treating an Akita with allergies or cleaning tartar off a Shar Pei's teeth.

Angela glanced at her watch and jumped out of bed. Jeff left promptly at eight, and it was already five minutes to. If she didn't hurry, he would leave her. Hastily, she pulled on a clean pair of jeans and tossed her nightgown aside in exchange for her bra and a red shaker knit sweater. She combed the tangles out of her shoulder-length hair as she raced to the bathroom and called out to Jeff, "I'm almost ready. Just give me a minute to brush my teeth." She didn't wait to hear his response, but quickly finished her business in the bathroom.

"Okay, let's go," she said a little breathlessly when she walked into the kitchen at exactly one minute after eight.

But the kitchen was empty. She walked to the window and looked out, noting with exasperation that his truck was gone. He hadn't waited for her. Her exasperation turned into anger, then disappointment. After all the hours she had put in, he hadn't felt her contribution was important enough to give her an extra minute.

She poured herself a cup of coffee and slumped onto one of the padded chrome chairs at the kitchen table. Tears of frustration stung her eyelids. She had hoped to put her relationship with Jeff into perspective, and to understand why it still mattered so much after almost twenty years. But nothing had been resolved. In fact, she was more confused than ever.

Well, there was no reason she should stick around when it was obvious she wasn't needed. She pushed to her feet, stalked to the sink, rinsed out her coffee cup and went to the bedroom. With her suitcase open on the bed, she began packing her clothes and planning her itinerary. She would head toward Denver. But because she had an extra day and a half, she could take her time, stopping for a night in Aspen or Glenwood Springs. Or maybe she would make the loop through Rocky Mountain National Park and Estes Park, if Trailridge Road was open.

A drop of water splashed on the top of the suitcase as she latched it shut, followed by another before Angela could brush away the flow of tears trickling down her cheeks. She was annoyed with Jeff for being so unreachable, and she was annoyed with herself for caring. It was a waste of time. Her emotions would be better spent on someone who might reciprocate her feelings and offer her a future, which certainly eliminated the man his buddies had called Hawk.

She pulled her suitcase to the floor, then turned to the bed and stripped off the sheets. By the time Jeff returned at midnight, she would be gone, along with any evidence that she had been there.

"What are you doing?"

She whirled, clutching the sheets to her chest as her heart leaped into her throat. She hadn't heard him enter the house, and his voice from the doorway startled her.

"Going somewhere?" he asked.

"I figured you didn't need my help anymore," she retorted. "I was only a minute late and you left me."

"I thought you might want to lay in bed and keep dreaming about Craig or your new boyfriend, or whoever it was you were inviting to come back to bed."

Angela's cheeks flushed a bright red. Apparently he hadn't guessed he had had the starring role in her dream, for which she was grateful. But there was a note of vulnerability in his accusations that caused her to admit, "It was a crazy sort of dream about when I was in Vietnam." Hoping he wouldn't notice, she brushed her face across the sheet, trying to erase any evidence that she had been crying.

But Jeff must have noticed because his expression softened and he crossed the room in a few long strides. Curling his finger under her chin, he lifted her face until he could look directly into her eyes. "What's wrong, Angie? Are you having trouble letting it go?"

"Not really. Well, how can anyone ever completely let it go?" But that wasn't what had been on her mind. She shook her head, unable to tell him the cause of her tears because she wasn't sure herself.

He didn't release his gentle hold on her chin. For several long, silent moments, he searched her eyes as if hoping to find the answer to some unspoken question. Unconsciously, the tip of her tongue slipped out and raced around the circle of her lips, moistening them and drawing his attention. His gaze lowered, and his tongue moved against his upper lip as if it longed to touch hers instead. "Were you going to leave me again, Angie?" His whisper was ragged.

She blinked in surprise. *Again?* She wondered if he realized he had said that. And she wondered what he meant by it. There was an insecurity, an undisguised pain lingering in his eyes that touched her. She had never seen any hint of weakness in him before, and she wasn't sure how to react. To her dismay, she felt another plump, wet tear escape from her eye and wind its way around the curve of her cheekbone.

Jeff reacted by drawing her into his arms and holding her against the solidness of his chest. The sheets dropped to the floor and her hands automatically moved to grip his back. "You're just tired," he murmured, his breath stirring the top of her hair. "It's all my fault. I've been working you too hard, without enough rest or regular meals." He rubbed his chin against her head. "Angie, I think it's time we both took a day off."

"A day off?" She sniffled, trying to control her emotions. His gentleness had increased the tears instead of stopping them. "But how can you afford it? Who'll take care of the sheep today?"

"Doch Thu's son is home from college on spring break. I went to their house to see if he'd like to earn a little extra money while he's here. He said he really needed the money for next term's tuition and books, so he and his mother are going to take the day shift. The majority of the flock has delivered, so the action should be slowing way down from here on out."

"Why didn't you say something instead of just leaving like that?"

He shrugged, and the movement lifted her head from his shoulder. "I thought you were asleep. Besides, I wanted to work out the details first."

She leaned back and looked up at him. Already her spirits had risen considerably. "What did you have in mind for the rest of the day?"

"I need to get up to the ranch and see how it fared during the winter. And I thought you would like to see the place. We could combine the two into a quick trip."

She nodded, her spirits rising. "Yes, I'd love to see it. How long will it take us to get there?"

"If the county road is open and has been plowed, only about forty-five minutes." As if he just realized he was still holding her in a rather intimate position, he took a step back and broke the physical contact. "I'm sure the road from the highway onto the property won't be clear, so we'll have to ride snowmobiles from the gate to the cabin. Be sure and dress warmly. I'll see if I can find an insulated suit and some boots that will fit you."

Angela put a long-sleeved turtleneck shirt on under her sweater and packed a lunch while Jeff loaded two snowmobiles on the trailer he had hitched to his truck. She sensed he was very proud of his ranch, and his eagerness to show it to her added to the sense of excitement and anticipation she was feeling at the prospect of a day with Jeff not surrounded by noisy sheep. The fact that he had rearranged his schedule to give her a sort of farewell tour was very touching. She knew how important his time was during lambing. It proved he was glad she had come and that her help had been appreciated, which somehow made it more worthwhile.

It was a beautiful drive along the curving, narrow road up the mountain. Several times, they negotiated hairpin turns around deep, shadowy draws. Miniature waterfalls cascaded over rocks and down crevices as the rapidly melting snow raced down the mountain to join the frothy, swollen streams that tumbled through the shallow canyons. The pipe gate that closed the road off for the season was open, so they continued to the top of the ridge. There had been only patches of snow hiding in the shadows in the valley around the sheep pasture, but the higher they got, the deeper the snow was packed.

Several miles farther on, Jeff parked his truck off the main road in a spot where the snow drifts were relatively shallow. Angela pulled on the one-piece insulated snowmobile suit while he unloaded the machines. The outfit was several sizes too large for her, but she snapped the bottoms of the legs around her ankles and tucked them into the large boots. She was struggling to roll up the sleeves when he rounded the truck and walked over to her.

"I'd forgotten what a tiny thing you are," he remarked, but the hint of a smile that twinkled in his blue-gray eyes made the comment sound almost like a compliment. "Here, let me help you with those sleeves." He pulled off his gloves and stuck them in his pocket as he reached toward her.

She held out one arm at a time while he folded the thick material over until her gloved hands were visible. After pushing her hair from her face, she pulled a stocking cap over her head and securely covered her ears. She hadn't ridden on a snowmobile since she was a teenager. Remembering how much she had enjoyed it then, she was looking forward to the last leg of their journey onto his ranch.

"Ready?" he asked after zipping his jacket up to his chin, replacing his gloves and putting a stocking cap on his head.

She nodded and flashed him an enthusiastic smile. He patted the seat of one of the machines, identifying it as the one she would be using, so she swung her leg over the elongated cushion and sat down. He showed her how to start the engine, use the brakes and steer the vehicle before settling himself on the seat of his machine.

He led the way to a wide, metal gate, and while he unfastened the lock, Angela studied the arched sign that proclaimed this to be the Second Chance Ranch.

"Where did you get that name?" she asked when he returned to his machine.

"It was named that when I arrived. It fit, so I didn't change it." His explanation was brief and while it barely answered her question, Angela suspected he was leaving out the most important details. But the roar of the engines discouraged discussion.

Her driving was jerky at first, but as she followed Jeff along an invisible road, she quickly mastered the basics. She felt confident enough to pull up alongside him.

"Are you having fun?" He mouthed the words in broad pantomime, and she nodded. His answering grin was carefree and cheerful, two characteristics Angela hadn't seen often during this reunion visit. It reminded her what a quick, dry sense of humor he had, and how he had been able to make the most ordinary afternoon pleasant at the military compound.

They flashed past stands of tall, slender aspens and clumps of evergreens. Startled birds crisscrossed in front of them, and squirrels, disturbed from their spring foraging, scurried to the end of nearby branches and chattered their disapproval.

At one point, Jeff pulled into a small clearing and stopped his machine. He motioned for Angela to turn off her engine and follow him, and she obeyed without question, trusting his directions.

They walked through knee-deep snow for several hundred yards. It wasn't a long way on flat, dry ground at sea level, but the terrain and high elevation made it difficult. Angela was panting when they finally reached the edge of a cliff. Jeff put his index finger to his lips, urging silence. The lack of oxygen combined with the deafening thunder of her heart. Angela couldn't have uttered a word if she had wanted to.

Dropping to the ground, Jeff pointed toward the valley below them. Angela collapsed next to him, and had to force her eyes to focus on the objects he was indicating. But as soon as she saw them, she forgot her burning lungs and shaky legs.

At least a hundred elk filled the large area. Some were pawing through the snow, searching for leftover grass, while others stripped pieces of bark off the aspen trees. Most of the animals were females, their bellies swollen with unborn calves. Angela could see about two dozen bulls with the herd, the buds that would soon become huge, heavy antlers coated with a thick padding of velvet.

"I can't believe there are so many," she whispered. "Do they live here all year?"

"A few of them do. But most of them only come here in the winter and will move on to the top of the San Juans as soon as the snow melts a little more. They like their privacy, so they pick the most isolated spots they can find."

"They're beautiful. And so big. I didn't realize they were quite that large."

"The bulls can be as tall as five feet at their shoulders and weigh almost half a ton." He seemed inordinately pleased that she was awed at the spectacle. "The herd has really built up in the past few years because we've had several mild winters in a row."

One of the bulls stretched his neck and issued a piercing squeal that echoed through the valley. Angela shivered, not from cold or fear, but from the thrill of the moment. "What an incredible sound! Is that what they call a bugle?"

"That was a sort of halfhearted bugle. They talk to each other all year, but in late October and early November during mating season, you should hear the noise they make. It's so shrill yet powerful, it's almost eerie. Everyone should watch the courting ritual and hear the bugling at least once. Maybe you could plan your next vacation for that time of year."

Angela glanced at him, wondering if she was reading more into the suggestion than he intended, or if his words held some sort of veiled invitation. His gaze didn't move from the grazing herd, so she couldn't check his expression.

"I suppose that one is the boss?" she prompted, referring to the elk who had made the fascinating noise.

"From the darkness of hair down his back and around his neck and the size of his body, I'd say he's one of the older bulls. But until mating season, they peacefully coexist in large groups. The bulls will often leave the cows and congregate on their own. But right now, the only competition is for food."

"Why aren't they running away from us?"

"We're downwind of them, so they can't smell us," he answered, leaning toward her so he was only a fraction of an inch away from her ear. "And the sound of our snowmobiles was muffled so they probably couldn't tell exactly where we were. Usually, they're very spooky, but at this time of year, they don't see or smell humans for months at a time and they're not as wary."

"How did you know they'd be here?"

"I didn't. Not for sure. But every year I've seen signs that a lot of them winter here, and I've caught them in this spot several times. So I figured it was worth a little walk."

Angela eyed the trail they had broken through the snow and didn't comment on how his definition of "a little walk" and her definition contradicted each other. However, it had been worth it. She doubted she would ever see such a sight again in her life.

He stood and they made their way to the snowmobiles. The only other stops they made were at downed fences that Jeff assessed with a quick look before continuing. Angela could tell he was making mental notes of work that would need to be done before the sheep were moved up to the ranch in the middle of May, and again she was impressed with his efficiency and knowledge of rural life.

Jeff followed a road that was completely hidden by snow and skirted hazards she wouldn't have noticed. They circled several fence lines, taking their time. Whenever they stopped, he would ask if she was cold or ready to go to the cabin, but Angela was having such fun, she didn't realize how cold she was until the quaint building came into sight. It was longer than it was wide, and larger than she had expected a log cabin would be. A covered porch stretched across most of the front, but had offered very little defense from the blowing snow that lay piled in window-high drifts under the roof.

They parked their machines in an open shed next to the house and blazed a trail across the yard to the door. The surface of the snow was almost perfectly undisturbed, except for a couple of pock-marked trails left by deer, coyotes or foxes. Angela turned to look at the way they had come, and involuntarily gasped at the beauty of the mountains in the distance, towering over the forest of evergreens in the foreground.

"This is a spectacular view. I can see why you prefer to stay up here." Her voice was softened by the majesty of the scene before her.

"It's the most beautiful place on earth," he agreed. "I'm sure you've heard the song about the guy who was born when he was twenty-seven and came home to a place he'd never been before. I was only twenty-two, but that's exactly how I felt when I first saw the place."

He turned and opened the door, which Angela noticed wasn't locked, and held it open for her. "Welcome to my home, Angie," he stated proudly.

The cabin consisted of only three rooms—two bedrooms on one end and a very large open area that was kitchen, dining room and living room combined. The tall cathedral ceiling had heavy log beams, and a natural rock fireplace dominated the back wall. Oversize windows were cut into every wall to take advantage of the incredible view that surrounded the cabin. The furniture was mismatched pieces that somehow fit together to look comfortable and inviting. Deer and elk heads with heavy antler formations were mounted and hung over the fireplace and along the walls, and a black bearskin rug was draped over the back of the couch.

Angela took her time circling the room, studying each trophy before commenting. "My uncle was a big game hunter and he had quite a few very nice heads mounted in his study. But I'll bet he'd be impressed with these. Did you shoot them all?"

Jeff shook his head. "No, some were in the old cabin that was built on this ranch in the early 1900s. I have no idea when or how they were killed. And some were killed by George and his sons. But by the time I arrived here, I had seen enough killing and had no interest in hunting as a sport. I have shot a few to put meat in my freezer to save money on groceries. Beef's too expensive and I get tired of mutton."

"You mean the meat we've been eating is venison?"

"Most of it. I've learned how to live off the land as much as possible to cut expenses. What did you think of it?"

"It cooked differently, with a lot less fat, but it tasted fine," she was surprised to admit. "What about the bear? He wasn't on our menu, too, was he?"

"Absolutely not." Jeff chuckled. "I've heard there are people who like bear meat, but I'm not one of them. I shot him last fall after he had hit my flock two nights in a row. Bears don't come in and kill one or two animals. They rampage through the flock, slashing and killing dozens of sheep just for fun, I guess. Or maybe they do it because they're cranky and the sheep got in their way." Jeff's broad shoulders lifted unapologetically. "But whatever his reasons, I couldn't let him keep it up or he'd put me out of business. He'd already hit a couple of the other ranches around here and killed almost a hundred animals."

"He reminds me of that little sun bear you had for a pet. After you rescued him, I think he thought of you as his father and would follow you around everywhere. His name was Misha, wasn't it?"

"Misha," Jeff echoed. "I haven't thought of him in years. I saw a Russian circus once and they had black bears with white ruffs around their necks like he did. Remember how happy he was when we took him into the jungle and let him go?"

"I remember how he used to lie on the floor by my bed like a big dog and snore so loud we couldn't sleep. I hate to think what kind of trouble I'd have gotten into if the major had found out I had a bear in my room."

"More trouble than if he had found out you had a sergeant in there?"

"No, probably not. He was adamant against the nurses fraternizing with you lowly grunts," she teased. She had completed her tour of the cabin without discovering one very important room. "I realize this is probably a stupid question, but there's no bathroom inside, is there?"

This time his shrug *was* apologetic. "No running water, no electricity, no indoor plumbing. But the outdoor facilities are as nice as I could make them. A little cold, maybe."

She rolled her eyes, but she accepted the news with good humor. "I thought I'd seen the last latrine the day I shipped out of Da Nang."

"It's right out the back door and to the left. But I'd better check it out first. Last winter a family of skunks took up residence there, and I almost couldn't convince them to move out. I've also known of porcupines that hide in places you'd rather not sit on."

"Good idea," she quickly agreed. "I'll get lunch ready while you exterminate the outhouse."

He handed her the sack with their lunch in it, which he had strapped on the back of his snowmobile, picked up a flashlight and left the room. He returned in a few minutes with a cheerful, "All clear."

"I hope you aren't hungry," Angela informed him as she dropped one of the sandwiches on a plate with a clatter. "Our lunch is frozen solid, and it could take a while before it thaws out enough so we won't break our teeth."

He took the news with amazing nonchalance for a man who hadn't eaten since early morning. "No problem. I'll turn on the propane bottle so we can use the stove. I take the perishable food down with me in the winter, but I always leave some cans of chili, stew or other quick meals in the cabinet for emergencies like this."

By the time Angela returned from the outhouse, Jeff was stirring a pot of bubbling hot chili. "There are some crackers in one of those metal canisters. They might be a little stale, but they'll taste okay," he informed her as she took off her coat, boots and hat.

Jeff started a fire in the fireplace and Angela set their meal on the coffee table instead of the dining room table. It was easy to understand why the living areas had been left open. The large fireplace soon had taken the chill from the air and was working to make the whole house cozy and snug. After they had eaten, they were feeling comfortably lazy, and neither Jeff nor Angela wanted to leave the warmth and return to the outside for the snowmobile ride to the truck.

"This is nice," she murmured, sitting on the floor with her feet stretched toward the fire, leaning against the couch with her head propped on a plump pillow.

"It's going to start to get dark soon," he commented, his position exactly like hers, but several feet away.

"I wouldn't have minded staying up here for a couple of days."

He rolled his head on his pillow until he was looking at her. She didn't turn her head, but she could feel his gaze. But whatever was on his mind, he didn't speak it aloud.

For several more minutes, they sat there, enjoying the fire and the quiet feeling of companionship, a feeling they had once shared that had been conspicuously absent since her arrival in Montrose. "How on earth did you ever find this place?" she asked. "This is light years away from the jungles of Nam."

He was silent for so long she began to doubt he would answer. In fact, her thoughts had begun to drift off when he finally heaved a weighty sigh and said, "I was lucky. Damn lucky."

"Lucky to have made it out of Nam?"

"No . . . lucky to have found a reason to live."

Chapter Nine

"Only The Good Die Young" —Billy Joel

"No one was more surprised than me that I survived the jungle. Not even serving with the Green Berets got me killed."

"You sound like you were disappointed," Angela remarked. She turned so she was sitting on her hip, facing him.

"In a way, I suppose I was. It threw me into a position of deciding what to do with the rest of my life. During that last year, I discovered I didn't want to stay in the military as I had originally planned. There was too much politics, too many deals and favors."

"What about Pittsburgh? Didn't your parents live there?"

Involuntarily, his hands clenched into tense fists. "I would never go back there. My parents couldn't have cared less whether I lived or died, so there was no reason for me to go back and give them the good news that I had survived."

"You mean you haven't seen or talked to your parents since you went into the Army?"

The shake of his head showed how inconsequential he considered the issue.

"They don't know if you're alive or dead?"

Again he responded negatively. "They weren't like your parents. They honestly wouldn't care. Besides, I'm not even sure where they live anymore."

If it hadn't been for the haunted, pained expression in his eyes and the memories of what he *hadn't* told her about his childhood, Angela would have thought he had overreacted. Her childhood had been upset by divorce, but it was still difficult for her to imagine parents who wouldn't care about their child's welfare.

"People change. Maybe you should call them and..." she began.

But he interrupted her with a low but firm, "No! As far as I'm concerned, I have no parents."

The subject appeared to be closed, but she was curious about his life after the Army. "So how did you end up in Colorado?"

As his thoughts turned to one of his favorite subjects, he visibly relaxed. "I drifted for a couple of years after I was discharged, trying my hand at a few different jobs and visiting places I'd always wanted to see. I had been in California for a few months and was heading up to Montana. But I took a detour to see Aspen and never made it past Montrose. I don't know why the town hit me like it did, but I didn't want to leave."

He smiled and stared into the crackling flames as he thought back to that first day. "When I stopped for lunch, someone had left a newspaper on the table, so I picked it up and flipped to the want-ads section. There weren't many jobs, none I was qualified for, and I was really disappointed because it didn't look like I would be able to stay.

"I finished lunch and was about to leave when an old man came up to me and asked if I was looking for work. This guy was dressed in filthy jeans and a filthier shirt, and didn't look like he had two nickels to rub together. Yet there was something in his eyes . . . They were warm and friendly, but so perceptive I felt he could see right through me to the depths of my empty soul. I told him that I was just passing through, but I wouldn't mind staying for a while if I could find a good job and a place to live.''

Angela listened without comment, delighted he had chosen to share part of his past with her. Her interested look must have encouraged him, because he continued.

"Anyway, this man asked me how much I knew about ranching, and I told him I didn't know much about anything except fighting. And he said that was just the type of employee he was looking for. He took me to the field where we've been lambing and put me to work delivering lambs, just as you've been doing. I had never worked harder in my life, and by the end of the week, I was ready to move on.

"But the old man offered to give me the bum lambs to bottle feed and raise so I could start my own flock. I hired on full time as his sheepherder."

"Bum lambs?" she interrupted.

"Lambs whose mothers either died or wouldn't accept them," he patiently explained. "He even talked to his fellow sheep ranchers and they said they'd give me their bum lambs, too. Well, I sort of had to stay then. I had a dozen little mouths to feed. I was up every four hours, warming their bottles or finding them an overproductive ewe who would let them get a free meal. I stayed all that year, and the next, and the next. My flock multiplied until I had almost a hundred sheep, and I was learning the basics from a master."

He paused, pushing himself to his feet. "Do you want something to drink?" She nodded and he took their coffee cups to the counter where he refilled them. After handing her her cup, he didn't sit down, but walked to one of the windows and looked outside as he went on with his story.

"What I couldn't figure out was why this man had such an interest in me, taking me under his wing and being so patient with my city-bred stupidity. We got to be good friends...more than that, actually. George treated me like a son, and I suppose he did become a sort of father figure to me. It wasn't until he was on his deathbed that he told me he had had two sons, both of whom had been killed in Vietnam.

"He also explained how he, as a young man coming home from World War II, had met a man with a ranch— this ranch. Even though the outcome of that war was different than the one I had been in, George said he had felt the same sadness and disillusionment I was experiencing when I returned. The rancher took George in, taught him the business and gave George a second chance to do something with his life. The rancher had eventually sold the place, lock, stock and barrel, to George, who built it up to be one of the best in the area."

Jeff combed his fingers through his dark hair, letting his hand rest on the base of his neck, massaging his tired muscles. "George had big plans for his sons. When neither of them made it home, he let the place go downhill. I suppose he just lost his enthusiasm for it since he had no one to share it with. His wife had died a few years earlier, and he had no relatives he cared about."

Jeff's chuckle was wry and humorless. "He thought I was helping him get through a tough situation, but he probably saved my life. I was heading for trouble because there wasn't a thing...or a person...I cared about when I rolled into town. You can't imagine how shocked

I was to find out he had left me the ranch in his will. I didn't expect it. And oddly enough, while the ranch had the greatest material worth, it was the least valuable thing he gave me.

"Because, you see, he gave me back my confidence and helped me focus on something positive. He showed me how deaths and births are a natural part of life's cycle. George had suffered some major losses. He could have let them crush him, but he didn't. Until the day he died, he had a terrific, upbeat attitude that he tried his best to pass on to me." Jeff drew in a deep, shaky breath. "He was a great guy..." His voice trailed off, and he let his head tilt forward until his forehead rested against the fogged glass.

There was something about the slump of his shoulders and the way his voice had wavered that touched Angela. Setting down her coffee cup, she crossed the room until she was standing behind him. In a gesture meant to comfort him, she ran her hand up his back and squeezed the tense ridge of muscles across his shoulder blades. "You must have meant a lot to him. It was nice that you came into his life when you did."

Jeff didn't respond, but she knew he was listening. She knew this was something he needed to hear.

"You took the place of his sons, and he obviously cared about you very much. He must have seen what a good man you are."

Jeff's shoulders seemed to droop even more as he shook his head slowly. "That's the point. I'm *not* a good man. If it hadn't been for George Randall, I would never have made anything of myself. God only knows where I would have ended up."

"You're being too hard on yourself," Angela protested softly. "You were just a kid when you were drafted. You spent two years in hell witnessing all sorts of atrocities and living with death every day. Then when you got back on *friendly* American soil, they spit on you and called you a baby killer.'' Angela realized she was voicing her own personal experiences and feelings. But she knew Jeff must have gone through the same thing. ''Of course you were a little confused and ungrounded. It was certainly not a hero's welcome, but at least you made it home in one piece.''

A shudder shook his body. His voice was raw and filled with pain as he cried, ''But that's just it. George's sons should have come home. Those men in my squad should have come home. They were all good men.'' He hesitated before adding in a tone so low she could barely hear him, ''It should have been me. Nobody would have cared if I hadn't come home.''

Angela's heart twisted in her chest. She was reminded of all the nights she had slept next to Craig, wishing he was Jeff. She remembered how many days she had cried when Craig told her he had heard Jeff had been killed. Now that she knew that wasn't the truth, she wondered if Craig had gotten incorrect news, or if he hadn't somehow suspected that she would never love him as much as she had loved Jeff. They'd certainly never spoken of it, and Angela had tried very hard to keep her true feelings to herself. But the fact remained, she'd loved Jeff eighteen years ago, and while her emotions had undergone many changes since then, there would always be a special place in her heart reserved for him.

As if she could transfer some of her genuine concern and empathy to him, she leaned against his back, resting her head against the hard planes of his shoulder blades. ''Jeff, you're wrong about no one caring. I did.''

At first he didn't react other than to issue a mirthless chuckle. Then abruptly he pivoted, and Angela found herself caught in a painful grip. "Sure you did," he drawled, the sarcasm dripping from his words.

"Jeff, you're hurting me."

"I'll bet you barely got any sleep at all on your honeymoon while you were thinking about me."

"That's not fair."

"How could you sleep with me one day and with Craig the next? Or was that going on the whole time I was with you?"

She had never slapped a man in her life, but she would have at that moment if she had been able to free her hands from his grasp. Instead, she tried to defend herself with words. "How could you cheapen what we had together by saying something like that?"

"I wasn't dating someone else while I was dating you."

Angela sighed and let her head fall forward. He would never understand, not when his ego was involved. She had wounded his pride, and even if he hadn't been in love with her, he hadn't wanted anyone else to have her. It was probably futile to try to convince him things were not as he believed, but as she raised her head and stared boldly into his eyes, she was compelled to say, "Since you have such a low opinion of me, I'm sure you'll think I'm lying, but you were the only man I ever let so much as kiss me while I was in Vietnam. Craig and I never did more than hold hands until after we were married."

"How touching."

"You can believe what you want, but I *did* care for you."

A hint of confusion diffused the chill of his glittering gaze. "Then why did you marry him? What made you choose him over me?"

The hurt was so sincere and deep that Angela was able to forgive Jeff his earlier accusations. More than wounding his pride, she realized she had unintentionally added to the low self-esteem he had developed because of his unhappy childhood. Although he had never told her he loved her, he must have felt some sort of attachment for her, so that when she accepted Craig's proposal, Jeff felt betrayed. He had had plenty of time to mull it over and blow everything out of proportion. His lashing out at her was merely a way to settle an old score. Unfortunately, the answers she had to give him wouldn't help him forgive her.

There were things in her life she would change if she had the chance, but marrying Craig would not be one of them. He had needed her then, and even more later. How could she make Jeff understand?

"What you and I had together was exciting and wonderful. You made my last few months in Vietnam bearable. But you knew you had to go out there and fight, and I had had enough. I wanted to go home. I wanted to wash the blood off my hands and forget the war. I wanted to get back to Boston and see people who were doing normal things like going to work or spending the afternoon shopping for frivolous things or going to a play. I wanted to sleep on a comfortable bed and eat real food."

She felt his hands loosen their hold, but he didn't release her. Nor did his expression of skepticism and disapproval change.

"Craig wanted the same things out of life as I did," she went on. "He had plans to attend law school and he knew where he was going and what he wanted out of life." She gave a mirthless chuckle. "Which is funny, because I thought I did, too."

"Did your life turn out like you planned?"

"Does anyone's?"

"Mine didn't."

"Yours turned out better," she pointed out.

"I was lucky," he repeated. "I got a second chance when I needed it the most."

"Your guardian angel must have had to work awfully hard. Who would have guessed you'd end up here, at the top of the world as a country rancher?"

"There are a few things I wish that angel would have done differently," he commented with a tinge of regret. His hands slid up and down her arms in an unconsciously sensual caress.

The emotionally charged atmosphere in the room had undergone a subtle change. Angela noticed the nearness of her body to Jeff's had become intimate rather than comforting. From the blue flames that leaped to life in his eyes, she could tell that Jeff had suddenly realized the same thing. But he didn't move away.

"You and I had some good times together. I'll never forget the first time I saw you, rushing over and pushing me back into bed. I couldn't see your eyes, but I heard your voice and I smelled your perfume." He breathed an almost wistful sigh. "From then on, I didn't even have to open my eyes to know when you were standing next to me. To this day, I can walk past a perfume counter and pick it out." He leaned closer, and drew in an experimental breath. "You don't wear it anymore."

Angela was caught off guard by his confession. "No, I've changed perfumes several times since then. It was sort of an extravagance to wear perfume to the hospital, but the men told me they liked to smell something fresh and feminine for a change. Wind Song was very popular in the sixties, but I haven't worn it in years. I didn't even realize they still sold it. I'm surprised that you remembered."

"I remembered," he confirmed, his voice growing husky. Threading his fingers through her hair, he added, "I also remember how soft your hair was and how it used to tickle my chin when we danced." He lifted a thick strand and let it trickle into place. "You've let it grow. I like it longer."

Angela wasn't certain how the conversation had turned in such a disturbing direction. She hadn't been comfortable with the previous discussion, but it hadn't caused her heart to race. Her hands curved around the back of his neck, her fingers tunneling through the hair that curled over the collar of his shirt. "Thanks. Yours is longer, too," she commented. "The last time I saw you, you barely had enough hair to comb."

"You know what else I remember?" he persisted, letting the palm of one of his hands cup her cheek, drawing her face closer to his.

"No, what?" she answered in a breathy whisper, knowing he was going to kiss her. The words "second chance" kept repeating themselves in her mind, keeping rhythm with the increased tempo of her heartbeat.

His lips were so near, she could feel the gentle brush of them against hers as he said, "I remember how sweet you tasted, and the little sounds you made when we made love. And I remember thinking my luck had changed when that VC bullet sent me to the hospital and into the tender loving care of a beautiful angel of mercy."

Angela repeated weakly, "We were both just kids..."
His mouth moved across hers tenderly, teasingly. "And
we were living with life and death every day..." The tip
of his tongue outlined her lips, leaving a moist, heated
trail. "Things weren't real..."

One hand still curled around the back of her head,
offering it the support her neck seemed strangely incap-
able of providing at the moment, while his other hand
slid to the small of her back, pulling her against him.

"Tell me again that you cared about me," he murmured, his breath hot against her mouth.

Her body was pressed to his, intimately molding the
softness of her curves against his hard contours from
thigh to chest. His desire was evident, and its boldness
intensified the ache that was building within her. For
several seconds, his lips silenced hers with a kiss so urgent and hungry that her legs almost buckled beneath
her.

"Tell me you thought about me at least a couple of
times in the past few years," he insisted in a low, almost
taunting tone. But the slight tremble in his voice told her
that in spite of his attempt to minimize her response, her
answer was very important to him. It was almost as if he
was holding his breath, waiting, wanting, needing to
know that at least one person would have been sorry if
he had died.

"Yes," she breathed, anxious for him to kiss her
again. "You were very special to me. I wanted you to get
well, but I hated that you would recover and be sent out
again instead of going home to safety." His face was so
close she couldn't see him clearly, but his sexy, masculine scent filled the parts of her senses that weren't already drugged by his provocative barrage. His tactics

had broken down her defenses, leaving her eagerly waiting for the final charge.

"But did you forget me the minute you left Nam?" he inquired with urgent persistence.

Her arms tightened around his neck and she heard him groan at the pleasure of her breasts rubbing against him. "I could never forget you," she assured him. "Even after Craig told me you were dead, you were always in my thoughts."

"Well, I, for one, am glad he was wrong."

She glanced over his shoulder at the lengthening shadows outside the windows. Unable to hide her disappointment and regret, she sighed. "It's getting dark. I suppose we're going to have to leave soon or we won't make it back tonight."

"We could stay."

He stated it simply, but Angela knew there was more involved than just spending the night in the cabin. If she should agree to stay, she would be agreeing to much more. It was evident that if they remained at the cabin, they would be using only one of the bedrooms. The prospect was not an unpleasant one, but she felt she must be sure he had considered all the issues.

"But what about the sheep? Won't you be missed?" she asked, leaning back so she could watch his expressions.

"I trust Doch Thu and his family. Between the four of them, they can cover both shifts."

"Are you sure you can stay away from them and not spend all your time thinking about the lambs?"

His chuckle rumbled through her body. "Are you joking? If you think I could hold you in my arms and make mad, passionate love with you all night and still be

thinking about sheep, then you're drastically underesti-
mating yourself.''

"So if we stay, we will definitely be making mad,
passionate love?" she echoed weakly, anxiously, wanting to know this meant as much to him as it did to her.

The corner of his mouth lifted in an endearingly
crooked grin. "Hold that thought for just a minute."
Gently disengaging himself from their embrace, he
walked to an antique oak sideboard and pulled a cassette tape out of one of the drawers. Popping it into the
battery-operated cassette player on the top of the cabinet, he punched the play button and returned to her side
before the music began.

"Lieutenant Nichols, may I have this dance?" he
asked, dipping into a courtly bow and holding out his
arms.

Angela smiled and moved into his arms. She had always found him irresistible when he was in a playful
mood. As the opening chords sent the familiar song
swirling into the room, she shoved aside thoughts of tomorrow.

They had no more chance of a future together today
than they had yesterday or eighteen years ago. They had
both changed, but they were the same people with the
same likes and dislikes. It would make a difference when
the sun came up, but for right now, being with him,
feeling his kisses and knowing she was somehow healing old wounds was enough for her.

Tonight he needed her . . . and she needed him.

Chapter Ten

"Hold Me, Thrill Me, Kiss Me" —Mel Carter

"You remembered." Angela's voice was muffled against the curve of his neck where her face was nestled.

How could he have forgotten? One of his first purchases when he returned to the States was a copy of the song they had listened to over and over in her room, the song that would always remind him of the only good thing that had happened to him during the war. But he couldn't tell her that. Nor could he tell her how many times he had listened to it while he was at the house in Montrose, riding around in the truck or staying alone in the cabin. That song has been his link, however tenuous, with a woman from his past—a woman who could have been very important to him, a woman who was now slowly circling the room in his arms.

"Hold me, hold me..." Jeff realized he was whispering the words, and Angela's arms tightened around his neck. Their feet were shuffling back and forth, barely moving. They were concentrating more on the gentle sway of their bodies rubbing, arousing, than the intricacy of their dance steps.

He bent his head and she was waiting for him, her lips slightly parted and totally irresistible. Their kiss was urgent and impatient, bringing them both to the level of

excitement they had been enjoying several minutes earlier. His hands slid under the knitted band of her sweater
and the form-fitted turtleneck until his fingers touched
the smoothness of her skin. His hands spread wide as
they moved up her spine until they reached the barrier of
her bra. His fingers fumbled slightly as he released the
hooks, whether from anticipation or lack of experience, he didn't know. There had been women in his life
since Angela, but they had been different. What he had
had with them was sex, even though he had hoped for
something more.

But his memories of Angela had always gotten in the
way. Either he was thinking of how fantastic it had been
between them or he was reminded of how much she had
hurt him. It was obvious he didn't understand women at
all, so to avoid being hurt again, he had guarded his
personal feelings with the fervency of a confirmed
bachelor.

In spite of his resolve and good intentions, seeing
Angela again had made him forget his obsessive cau-
tion. It had been foolhardy to think they could live together under the same roof for two weeks without the
old feelings being rekindled . . . assuming those feelings
had really existed.

The way his heart was pounding, sending his blood
racing in wild ecstasy through his limbs, assured him his
memory hadn't been faulty. Angela still had the ability
to make him ache with longing at the slightest touch.

The years fell away. They were the only two people in
the whole world, and nothing outside the cabin walls was
important.

"Thrill me, thrill me . . ." Jeff lifted her sweater and
turtleneck and she helped him pull them off and toss
them aside. Her bra fell, too, freeing for his heated gaze

her perfectly formed breasts. One of his hands moved to cup the precious weight, holding it tenderly as if it were a fragile treasure.

"Angie," he murmured, bending to capture her lips in an increasingly demanding kiss. "How can you be even more beautiful than I remember?"

"I wish that were true." Her laugh was languid and distracted. "No woman is better looking when she's thirty-nine than when she was twenty-one."

He shrugged as if his opinion was irrefutable. "You are," he repeated positively.

Her cheeks were flushed as she replied, "I'm glad you think so. You don't look too bad yourself." Her fingers loosened the buttons of his shirt and pushed it off his shoulders, leaving only a white T-shirt covering the expanse of his chest and the bulge of his shoulders. "Mm, nice," she murmured, running her hands over the soft cotton covering.

He would have loved to stand there staring at her forever, but afraid that she might be chilled in the rapidly cooling room, he led her to the fireplace. "I'll be right back," he promised, and in only a few seconds returned from one of the bedrooms with two thick comforters and a king-size pillow. After draping one comforter around her bare shoulders, he spread the other on the floor in front of the hearth, then turned to toss a couple more logs on the fire.

When he looked, she was watching him, an affectionate smile playing along her lips. If he had doubted she was telling the truth about her fondness for him before, the glow in her eyes reassured him. Knowing that she *had* cared for him was like a heavy weight being lifted off his chest. And knowing that she still cared for him was wildly exciting. He dared not hope for or even think about this being a step in resuming their affair. At the moment he didn't want to consider the possibility that this would be a one-night stand.

His life had undergone many changes. He had grown more mellow and less predatory. But in all the years since he had met Angela, the one thing that had remained the same was his attraction to her.

"Are you any warmer?" he asked, his eyes sweeping over her.

As if reading his mind, she swung the blanket open and flashed him a seductive grin. "A little. But I wouldn't mind sharing my blanket if you'll share your body heat."

"Kiss me, kiss me..." It was an offer he couldn't refuse. He stripped off his T-shirt before joining her. As if neither of them could wait any longer, their hands bumped and tangled with each other as they unfastened and removed the rest of their clothes. All the while his lips were pressing kisses on her eyelids, her neck and her mouth, swallowing her words of endearment and encouragement. By the time they had reached their socks, they were lying on the comforter, their legs entwined and their bodies pressing together.

His hands roamed freely over her, reacquainting themselves with every curve and valley. Her fingers tickled down the hair-dusted line in the middle of his stomach to the sensitive area below. As soon as she touched him, stroking him to full arousal, he moaned and rolled her onto her back. His lips wandered lower, savoring the sweet taste of her breasts. His tongue circled their proud, pouty tips before he drew one swollen nipple into his mouth.

Her body arched upward and her fingernails dug into his buttocks, urging even greater intimacies. His lips returned to hers as he followed her persuasive directives. Centering himself between her legs, he felt her warmth surrounding him, pulling him deeper, calling him home.

A LOG BROKE IN TWO, falling with a rumble and a pop off the grate. Jeff knew he should put a few more logs in before the fire burned itself out, but he couldn't summon enough energy to get up and accomplish the simple task.

"You know, I was wrong," he murmured, his face buried in the tumbled mass of her dark hair.

"About what?" she asked. Her words were followed by a relaxed, satisfied yawn.

"About you and me."

He could tell he had gotten her attention when she pulled away far enough to look into his eyes to try to gauge the seriousness of his remark. She didn't voice a question, but the arch of her black eyebrows showed she was waiting for him to complete his observation.

Deciding not to keep her in suspense, he caressed her with a gentle, contented smile and said, "I thought I remembered how good it was with you." He reached out and brushed a thick lock of hair from her face before adding huskily, "But it's even better!"

Pleased with his comment, she snuggled closer against him. "Yes, it is," she whispered, her breath soft against his neck.

They must have dozed because the next thing he knew his back was freezing and, except for the limited light cast by the glowing coals, the room was in total darkness. Knowing it could no longer be put off, he regretfully disentangled their arms and legs and forced himself away from her delightful warmth.

Working quickly, he rebuilt the fire, rearranging the coals and waiting until their sparks caught the dry aspen logs.

He didn't realize Angela was awake until he felt her lips gently pressing against his shoulder.

"I wondered how badly it would scar," she said, as her finger lightly outlined the faint, jagged marks.

"I was lucky not to have lost my arm. If I hadn't had such excellent medical care, I would have had more than a little scar."

"It was a bad wound, and you didn't make it easy for me to try to keep you in bed so it would heal."

He twisted around until she was cradled in his arms. "You won't have any trouble keeping me in bed now," he growled playfully before scooting to their snug nest.

They made love again, giggling and romping under the comforter until their passion grew too hot, and they kicked the cover aside. They decided not to move to his bedroom, but to stay on the floor by the fire.

However, when the morning sun woke them, their bones and muscles were protesting from the abuse.

"Does this mean we're too old for slumber parties?" Angela asked as she stretched.

Jeff rose to a squatting position and gathered her and her comforter cocoon into his arms. Without seeming to make an effort, he stood and carried her to his bedroom. "When a person gets older, he gets smarter. Or at least he should. And I say it's time to move this slumber party to a mattress."

They burrowed under a pile of blankets and fell asleep, wrapped in each other's arms. The sun had warmed the room to an almost bearable temperature by the time they woke again. Jeff, with a blanket wrapped around him, braved the chill and built a new fire. Angela waited as long as she could, but soon nature's call could not be ignored, and she, too, had to leave the warmth of the bed.

Hastily she exchanged the blankets for her jeans and sweater before making a run to the little house outside.

"I never realized the value of indoor plumbing until I was in the Army," she stated through chattering teeth when she returned. "I suppose men can tolerate that sort of thing, but for women, it's pure torture."

"It sounds as if you could use a cup of coffee," Jeff commented with an indulgent grin. "It's made from fresh spring water. You won't taste anything like this back in Boston."

She took the cup and wrapped both hands around it, trying to use some of its warmth to thaw out her fingers. Gingerly she sipped the dark liquid. "It *is* good. Now all I need is a hot shower and a toothbrush."

"I can provide you with the latter." He reached into an overhead cabinet and pulled out a large metal first aid kit. He flipped open the lid and picked up a toothbrush still wrapped in its original box.

Angela looked at the half dozen toothbrushes remaining and couldn't resist commenting, "Do you entertain that often here?"

His grin widened. "No, I've never *entertained* here. I kept forgetting to bring a toothbrush with me, so one day when I was at the grocery story, I bought enough to last me a few years." He took one for himself before handing her the toothpaste and setting the kit on the countertop.

"Okay, so you don't entertain here. But surely you don't go for days without a shower."

"Of course not. I couldn't stand smelling myself after spending a day working with the sheep or pushing the dirt around to make a new road or a dam. Occasionally, I've been crazy enough to jump into the pond in the horse pasture, but even in the heat of the summer that water is pretty cold. A couple of summers ago I rigged up a solar shower in the backyard, and it works great. Unfortunately, it wouldn't work too well at this time of year.''

He finished his coffee and stepped close to her. Wrapping his arms around her, he nibbled on the soft skin below her ear and murmured, ''I don't mind that you smell like perfume and passion and wood smoke. It's a sexy combination.''

She tilted her head, offering him more area to nuzzle. ''You're not exactly an impartial judge.''

''I'm a severe critic. I've never told another woman that she smelled good.'' The truth was, Angela's perfume was the only artificial feminine fragrance he had ever given more than passing notice.

''The commercials used to promise that 'Wind Song stays on your mind.''' She chuckled. ''I never realized that would be so literally true.''

He wrapped her in a gentle hug and gave her a long, sweet good morning kiss on the lips. ''That wasn't all that stayed on my mind,'' he confessed, an appreciative twinkle lighting his eyes as he realized she had dressed so quickly she hadn't bothered with her bra.

But instead of letting their libidos rekindle, he stepped away. ''What time is your flight tomorrow afternoon?'' he asked with studied nonchalance.

''Five forty-five.'' She took another sip of her coffee and her soft brown eyes peered at him over the rim of the cup. He wished he could read the thoughts that were hidden in their unfathomable depths. He desperately needed a clue to what she was feeling.

"Were you planning on driving to Denver today or tomorrow morning?"

"I think I'd rather go tomorrow morning. It took us about five hours, didn't it?"

"Yes, but you should allow yourself a little extra time in case the road through Glenwood Canyon is closed for construction. And you have to turn in your rental car."

Their words were so restrained, so neutral. They were discussing the matter of her leaving as if it meant nothing to either of them. Jeff wasn't certain how she felt, but already he was stricken by how lonely life would be without her.

It was funny, because a month ago he had considered his life to be full and satisfying. The ranch was doing well and he had turned a substantial profit every year. He funneled it into the business and into paying off the small house where he lived when he wasn't staying at the cabin. He'd made many friends in the area and had as active a social life as he wanted. But that was before Angie had shown him just how much fuller his days and nights could be.

He wanted to ask her to stay longer, but he hesitated. Yesterday his ego had received a positive boost. However, it was still too fragile to chance her rejection. He would be very busy with the lambs next week as he prepared them for their release into the big pasture. There wouldn't be another chance for a getaway like this one, not even for a night.

And she had never seemed to show any regret that her visit was temporary. Much too often for his taste, she talked of her brownstone in Boston, her clinic and her busy, busy life. She hadn't actually been marking the days off on the calendar that was posted in his kitchen, but he knew she was as aware of their passage as he was.

He might as well not consider any other possibilities. Tomorrow Angie would be leaving—again.

"Well, then, we'd better see if we can find something for breakfast so we can head back before noon." He opened the cabinets and studied their contents.

She nodded, picked up the toothbrush, toothpaste and a canteen and stepped out the back door to finish her minimal morning toilet.

"Spaghetti, beef stew or chicken noodle soup?" Jeff called to her after reviewing the meager contents of the cabinets. "Or we could eat the sandwiches we brought. I believe they've thawed out by now."

"It's a tough choice," she answered with an unenthusiastic glance at the two stale sandwiches that had been abandoned yesterday. "But I suppose I'd prefer the chicken noodle soup. Let me finish getting dressed and I'll help."

The soup was ready by the time she came out of the bedroom, once again covered in demure layers. They had both worked up quite an appetite last night, so they dug into their soup with enough gusto that it didn't matter that chicken and noodles weren't usually considered breakfast food.

Almost in silence, they washed and dried the dishes and replaced everything in the cabinets. Jeff turned off the propane bottle and made certain the fire was out in the fireplace. Finally, when all the chores were finished, they looked around the room, each deep in thought.

Angela was committing every detail to memory. She knew that once she was in Boston, this experience would seem like a dream. Jeff had been the consummate lover, tender and attentive to her needs, yet so aroused he had barely been able to hold back until she was satisfied. He had seemed to succeed in putting his responsibilities and worries about his sheep behind him, as well as any thoughts about Craig and her current boyfriend. The fact that neither she nor Jeff appeared to have given even a fleeting thought to anyone else certainly indicated something.

But Angela didn't want to think about that right now. She would have plenty of time on the flight home. Perhaps then she would be able to figure out why she couldn't feel for Richard what she felt for Jeff, especially since Richard suited her requirements perfectly. He was a successful businessman, her partner in the clinic and a respected veterinarian. He was strikingly handsome and socially popular, and he came from one of the best families in Boston. And he wasn't upset that she couldn't have children. In fact, he didn't want any.

Jeff, on the other hand, was totally opposite. While he was relatively successful, he lived from day to day, year to year, flock to flock. If he had just one bad season, it would take him years to work his way back. He was no less handsome than Richard, although Jeff's looks were rugged and outdoorsy as compared to Richard's always perfectly groomed and urbane appearance. She had never spent the night with Richard and couldn't even summon a picture of him with his hair tousled and his jaw and chin shadowed with a day-old beard, like Jeff's were this morning.

And, although they hadn't discussed it, Angela suspected Jeff would eventually want children.

She shook her head as if to push out those errant thoughts and get back to reality. Once she got away from this ranch—and Jeff—she would be able to think clearly again.

"Ready?" Jeff asked after they had put on their coats, boots, hats and gloves.

Angela felt an unexpected sting of tears and ducked her head as she walked through the door.

They followed their path to the shed and Jeff pushed their snowmobiles onto the driveway before they climbed on them. When he didn't immediately turn on the engine she looked at him and found he was studying her with a disturbing intensity.

"I've got one more place I want to show you before we go," he said, breaking the silence. Without waiting for her response, he turned the key and the machine roared to life. Angela followed suit and trailed behind him far enough so she wouldn't be covered in the snow that was spraying up from his runners.

They passed through a large pasture, but instead of following the fence line, Jeff turned up the mountain. Weaving around rocks and trees, he didn't stop until they topped the last ridge and the land leveled out. He drove to the center of a clearing and turned off the engine. Angela drove next to him and stopped.

He held out his hand and helped her off the snowmobile. Instead of letting go, he threaded his fingers through hers and led her to a spot with such unerring direction that she knew it was very familiar to him. He stopped several feet from the edge of a steep decline.

Angela stood next to him and followed his gaze as it drifted over the panorama below them. To the south, the jagged, snow-covered peaks of the San Juans dominated the skyline. The mountains to the north and east were slightly less impressive, but still magnificent, while the landscape to the west settled into gentler hilly formations. And, in the winter-barren valley between the mountain on which the ranch was located and the eastern range, miniscule sparkles of windows and windshields reflecting the sun's rays showed where the town of Montrose was located.

"This is my special place," he explained, a note of reverence in his voice. "I love to come up here and look around. I feel as if I'm on top of the world . . . literally. I can almost believe I'm all alone, just me against the elements, and nothing that happens down there will affect me."

The statement could have sounded like a power trip. But Angela sensed a loneliness deep in Jeff's heart. In spite of the hundreds of creatures and Doch Thu's family who were all dependent on him, Jeff had no one to go home to each night, no one with whom he could share his plans and dreams.

Angela reminded herself that she was in a similar situation. She had an office and clinic staff of four, and although her creatures were constantly changing, there was always a considerable number to occupy her time. But there was no one she cared about enough to share her plans and dreams with. Richard and her parents didn't know about her anguish over being unable to bear children, or her guilt over giving up nursing, or the mixture of pride and horror she carried from her involvement in the war. No one understood her feelings about Vietnam. No one knew the truth about Craig. No one would understand that, either. Not unless they had been there and lived the experience.

Everyone thought she was so strong and capable. They thought she was in total control of her life, which was partially true. Until she had left the reunion with Jeff, she had known what she would be doing at almost any given moment of any given day. Her schedule was tight and well organized. She had thought that by making her life predictable, she would make it safe. But now

she could see that what she had done was make it boring.

"I have a place back home I go to where I can sit and
think," she said, trying to remind herself how much she
was missing the city. "I can't actually be alone there
since it's a public park, but I can *pretend* I'm alone."
She forced her mind's eye away from the natural beauty
of the Rockies and visualized the emerald green grass of
the Common and the colorful flower borders that were
planted each spring next to the maze of sidewalks. "I
like to walk through the rose garden and smell the
blooms. I've never seen so many colors, and the flowers
are huge. Then I go down to the lake, sit under the lacy
branches of a weeping willow and watch the swan boats.
In the spring, ducks and swans swim by, followed by
their little babies, and it's very calming."

Jeff was still holding her hand, but a wall had suddenly sprung up between them. Angela could have
kicked herself for mentioning Boston, a subtle reminder that she didn't belong here on this mountain with
Jeff. It occurred to her that she thought of home every
time Jeff touched her emotions or made her realize her
life wasn't as perfect as it seemed.

With her free hand, she pulled off her stocking cap
and ran her fingers through her hair. It was more of a
restless gesture than vanity. At the moment, she wished
she could be unaffected by the man who was standing
beside her, able to see things in perspective. Of course
she didn't belong out here in the West, on top of a
mountain, staying in a cabin that had no bathroom and
no electricity. Of course she couldn't be happy with a life
so simple and yet so hard. Of course she couldn't fall in
love with a man like Jeff.

But who was this man? The man she had known in Vietnam had been nicknamed Hawk, and he had lived up to his name through his sharply honed instincts and clever aggression techniques. He had been dangerous, frightening, unpredictable and unstable.

The man she'd grown to know during the past two weeks was none of those things. A guardian angel, Lady Luck or whoever else might be looking over those who are unwilling or unable to look after themselves, had stuck with him through the bad times and given him something to live for. The new Jeff was settled, focused and pleased with his success. At some point, he had shed his reckless attitude and replaced it with responsibility. She would have trusted the old Jeff with her life and her body, but not her heart. She still had no doubt he would be able to protect her life and satisfy her body, but her heart's defenses had weakened through the years. Whether she wanted to admit it or not, she hadn't been able to stop it from falling in love with him then, and her resistance was no better now.

A shrill scream pierced the air, and Angela's gaze jerked up until she found the source of the sound. A large brown bird soared across the sky, gliding on long, outstretched wings on a thermal layer of air. "That's not an eagle, is it?" she asked.

"Same family, wrong species. That's a hawk, but there are plenty of eagles around here. We lose a few lambs to them every year."

"You're kidding," she responded skeptically. "I know eagles are big, but I never would have thought they could carry an animal the size of a lamb."

"Believe me, they can. I've seen it with my own eyes several times. When the lambs are still very young and small, an eagle can swoop down, pick one up in his talons and fly off with him. There's not much we can do since eagles are an endangered species. But I wish they would stick to eating rabbits, prairie dogs and mice.''

The hawk screamed again. There was a higher, more piercing sound as another hawk joined him.

"That's the female," Jeff explained. "They look almost exactly alike, except for size. The females are usually stronger and bigger than the males."

Angela and Jeff watched in silence, mesmerized by the birds as they kept flying upward, circling, occasionally passing close enough to each other to grab a mouthful of feathers in their hooked beaks. When they were so high they had almost flown out of sight, there was another exchange of screams and whistles, then the two hawks crashed into one another.

"Look, they're trying to kill each other!" Angela cried as the birds began plummeting toward the earth.

Jeff chuckled. "Maybe so, but it's out of passion and not anger."

"You mean . . . ?"

He leaned over and whispered with suggestive emphasis, "They're making love. They mate in midair, then free-fall until their coupling is complete. They're risking their lives for a few seconds of passion . . . but what a way to go."

The hawks were tumbling over and over until, less than a hundred feet from the ground, they separated and with apparent ease, spread their wings and lifted themselves to the heavens.

Angela realized she had been holding her breath, which now exited in a relieved whoosh. "Whew, that was close. I didn't think they would pull up in time."

"Eagles and crows also mate like that, and I've never seen one hit the ground yet. They seem to know just how high to go before joining, and how long they can stay together before letting go."

The drama and peril of the moment had left her heart pounding, almost as if she had been falling with the hawks. She turned her gaze to Jeff and saw he was studying her, that blend of pain and longing once again in his eyes.

"I've known people who handle their own love lives much the same way," he commented casually.

But Angela was reminded of his plaintive question last night when he had wanted to know why she had chosen Craig over him. Now she understood that, in his eyes, she had strung him along until someone better came along. Even though he had never pressed her for a commitment, he thought she had deserted him, taking him to the heights of passion, then flying away before they hit the ground.

"Maybe those people panicked when the fall got too dangerous." She followed his lead, keeping the subject nonspecific, but the conversation couldn't have been clearer if they had been naming names.

"Maybe those people should have trusted each other." His fingers tightened around hers, lifting to press her gloved hand against the roughness of his unshaven cheek.

"But it was too dangerous. What if they misjudged it and it didn't work out?"

"Hawks usually mate for life."

Angela felt the tears well up in her eyes. "But what if one of them dies and the other is left to fly alone?"

Jeff turned his head until his lips were against the back of her hand. His words were muffled and suspiciously husky as he spoke. "If they were meant to be together forever, it would be worth the risk."

Chapter Eleven

"Only Love Can Break A Heart" —Gene Pitney

"I'm going to the sheep pasture and check on things. Unless there's a problem, I won't stay long." Jeff replaced his snow boots with rubber boots as he spoke. "As soon as I get back, why don't we go out to dinner?"

Angela removed her boots, then unzipped the insulated overalls he'd loaned her and stepped out of them. "That sounds good. I'm starving," she agreed. "I'll probably still be in the bathtub when you get back."

He glanced at her as he stood in the doorway. One dark eyebrow was lifted in roguish delight. "Then I'll make it a point to hurry. I wouldn't want to miss that. Save me a place."

Her smile was both flirtatious and shy. The very thought of him joining her in the tub was enough to send tingles of anticipation streaking through her; yet the mention of their intimacy made her blush like a schoolgirl.

After he left, she unpacked enough clothes for the evening while the tub was filling. Her suitcase and garment bag sitting by the door were a constant reminder of how soon she would be leaving. Confused by what she was feeling, she returned the garment bag to the closet and shoved the suitcase inside, out of sight...but not out of mind.

She tried to relax as the warm water enveloped her body. Leaning her head back until it rested on the curved porcelain rim of the tub, Angela shut her eyes and tried to blank out her thoughts. Tomorrow she would be in her own house, in her own tub, alone in her own bed.

It wasn't the fact that she would be alone that bothered her. She had long ago learned to be comfortable with her own company. It was the only time someone wasn't expecting something from her. But she was not happy at the prospect that Jeff would never share that bed with her.

And it was more than the pleasure he gave her. The very reason she had avoided pressing him for a commitment eighteen years ago was one of the reasons he appealed to her now. The lady he chose would know he would always be there when she needed him. Jeff didn't need to be taken care of. Not only could he handle his own life, but he would take care of his woman, too.

Angela sighed. It would be nice for a change to be the one that was being taken care of instead of the person shouldering all the responsibility.

She was drying off when she heard the telephone ring. At first she didn't make an attempt to answer it, but when it continued for nine, ten, then eleven rings, she wrapped the towel around her body and ran into the living room. Thinking it might be Jeff calling from a pay phone to tell her he would be delayed or their plans had changed, she was delighted at his thoughtfulness and answered with a cheery, "Hello."

"Angela? Is that you?" a voice on the other end of the line questioned.

A disappointed breath slipped out too quickly to repress, "Hello, Richard. Yes, it's me."

"You sound so different. I didn't interrupt anything, did I?" he asked, making no attempt to hide his suspicions.

"Don't be silly. I'm here alone. I was just getting out of the bathtub when the phone rang."

"Oh." There was a moment of silence before he went on to comment peevishly, "I haven't heard from you since you arrived there. I was beginning to wonder if you had forgotten about me . . . and the clinic."

Angela had never noticed the annoying whine that had crept into his voice. "I was busy. We've been out at the sheep pens from dawn to midnight, and then we fall into bed too exhausted to even eat dinner."

"Into bed? Is that one bed or two?"

"Richard!" she snapped. She dared not try to explain the sleeping arrangements for fear she would sound like she was protesting too much. Besides, she reasoned, she didn't owe Richard a blow-by-blow account of her visit, particularly last night, which would, of course, be the details Richard would be most interested in hearing.

"Sorry. It's just that I miss you and can't wait for you to come home."

She opened her mouth to tell him that she was anxious to go home, but the words couldn't, in all honesty, be said. The truth was, she didn't want to leave Jeff. Returning to Boston and Richard, the clinic, the payroll and the bills, the traffic and the smog held no appeal at all for her.

"What time does your plane arrive tomorrow?"

A sense of panic rose in her throat, cutting off her answer. She didn't want to be on that plane.

"Do you want me to pick you up?"

Her chest constricted. No, she didn't want Richard to pick her up. She wanted Jeff to tell her he loved her and ask her to stay.

"I've got tickets for the symphony. We could eat at that new French restaurant after the performance. I've heard the chef's escargot are magnificent and his—"

"No!" The word came out stronger and louder than she had expected, so she took a deep breath and repeated it a little more gently. "No thanks, Richard."

His sigh expressed his aggravation. "Well, I really wanted to eat there, but if you'd prefer someplace else, I guess I could change my plans. I'll just cancel the reservation and—"

"No, Richard. I don't want you to change your plans," she hurriedly interrupted. "In fact, I'm not sure about my own plans. Look, I'm dripping on the floor. I'll call you later and let you know about my flight."

"But, Angela—"

"Bye, Richard." She replaced the receiver in its cradle with a clatter and pulled her hand away as if she had just touched a hot stove. Why had she done that? Now she would have to call him back and give him her flight information. Even worse, she had hung up without asking how the animals at the clinic were doing. Usually very conscientious, especially about her patients, she was horrified that she hadn't given them even a passing thought.

"Was that him?"

Angela whirled around, one hand clenching the towel together over her breasts and the other hand over her mouth as if to stifle a scream of alarm. She hadn't heard Jeff's truck and his sudden presence startled her. "How long have you been standing there?" she asked, realizing, too late, that it sounded as if she had said something she hoped he hadn't heard. There was that little statement about her plans being indefinite, but perhaps he wouldn't realize how much he had to do with her indecision.

"Not long," Jeff answered shortly. "I heard conversation and thought . . . Well, I suppose he's anxious for you to get back."

She shrugged noncommittally. It was an awkward situation because she sensed Jeff didn't really want to hear that Richard was impatiently waiting for her return, and yet she was hesitant to admit that she wasn't ready to leave until she knew whether or not that change of plans would please Jeff. "I'm supposed to call him later with my flight number and arrival time."

"Why didn't you give it to him now?"

She looked down at her almost nude body. "Because I didn't have my ticket on me at the moment," she retorted, then instantly regretted that she had let him goad her. She lifted her gaze to the frosty blue eyes that seemed to have noticed, for the first time since entering the room, that the towel was barely covering her vital areas.

"I'm sorry," he muttered, forcing his attention to her face. "You don't owe me any explanations."

"Actually, I think I do. At least about Richard."

He shook his head. "He won't ever find out about last night if you don't tell him."

"That's not it at all." She wished they could be having this conversation under more dignified circumstances. Being wrapped in a towel with her wet hair falling around her face, she was definitely at a disadvantage. She tried to adjust the towel, but when the bottom threatened to gape open at a dangerously revealing spot, she left well enough alone.

In spite of the cool temperature, beads of perspiration had appeared on Jeff's forehead. "If you're through in the bathroom, I think I'll take my turn now." It was obvious he, too, was trying to ignore the volatility of the situation.

Impulsively, she stepped forward and stopped him. "No, wait. I *want* you to know this." Nervously, she moistened her lips as she thought of the best way to say what she wanted to say without giving too much away. "I lied to you about Richard," she finally admitted.

His stance stiffened slightly. "Oh?" he prompted.

"Yes, I sort of made you believe that Richard and I were seriously dating." She forced herself to keep her gaze from flitting away from the steadiness of his. "The truth is, Richard and I *have* been dating. I can't speak for his intentions, but as far as I'm concerned, there's nothing between us other than our business relationship. Certainly no intimacies."

Relief flooded his eyes, washing away their harsh glitter. "You didn't have to tell me that."

"I know. But I didn't want you to think there's something there when there isn't."

His mouth softened as one corner lifted in a perceptive grin. "I'm glad there isn't. I don't like to trespass on other people's property."

"It didn't stop you last night," she reminded him with a twinkle lightening her dark eyes.

He took a step forward and hooked his finger over the top of her towel. With a gentle pull, it fell open and curled around her as it slid to the floor. "It wouldn't have stopped me now, either. Not where you're concerned. I let someone steal you from me once before without a struggle. I figured Richard could fight his own battles."

He combed his fingers through her hair, lifting the damp strands off her neck as he lowered his lips. The prickle of his still unshaven face against her tender skin was electrifying. Her arms circled his waist, steadying her suddenly shaky knees.

"How hungry are you?" he murmured as he nibbled the soft flesh of her ear lobe.

"Hungry for what?" she breathed. "Food or you?"

His hands trembled as he gathered her into his arms. Not waiting for an answer, he carried her into his bedroom and placed her on top of the black and gray geometrically patterned comforter. Before she had time to miss his embrace he had removed his clothes and joined her on the bed.

Lying side by side, they let their eyes caress each other. Angela's fingers followed her gaze, rippling over his rib cage, tangling in the dark curls of hair that circled his belly button, stroking the inside of his thighs. But it was difficult for her to concentrate on the perfection of his form when his fingers had slipped along her thighs and into her warmth. The tickle deep in the pit of her stomach tightened to a restless throb, aching for relief—relief only Jeff could give.

No man had ever brought her such pleasure. Craig's lovemaking had been gentle and sweet, but there had been none of the wild exploding passion she felt with Jeff. And no other man had even tempted her.

"Angie," he breathed, whispering her name as he moved over her.

As Jeff's mouth closed on hers, she moaned from a satisfaction so complete she wondered how she could have been so foolish as to ignore her love for him those many years ago. And she wondered how she could make him love her enough to ask her to stay.

Oh, how she wanted to hear him say he loved her. She doubted it was a word he used often or loosely. Considering his lack of affection for his parents, Angela wondered if he had ever experienced love—not physical love, but emotional love, the type that bonded a relationship and encouraged a lasting commitment.

The sensuous friction of his body inside her forced the more serious thoughts away for the time being. At the moment, Angela's ability to hold onto any coherent thought was replaced by a mindless desire for release. Her breath grew ragged and shallow as the tempo increased. She writhed beneath Jeff, encouraging him, exciting him. As the explosions ripped through her, she clung to him, her fingernails biting into his skin, branding him as belonging to her.

She listened, anxiously hoping to hear a declaration of affection, but only heard him cry her name one more time as he plunged deeper, then hung on the edge of ecstasy before spilling over. She felt his heat fill her, but she also felt the heat of tears on her cheeks, tears because he was still withholding the most valuable part of himself—his love.

The callused pad of his thumb brushed beneath her eyes, followed by a tender kiss on her lids. She opened her eyes and saw him studying her with a frown of concern wrinkling his tanned brow.

"What's wrong, Angie? Was it that bad for you?" he asked, his voice still husky and breathless.

"It was wonderful," she rushed to assure him. "Really it was."

"Then what is it?" He stroked the silken strands of her almost dry hair.

"It's just that . . ." She hesitated, trying to think of a way of telling him how much she wanted to stay without putting him in the awkward position of trying to appear happy about her change of plans. "I wasn't planning on anything like this to happen. . . ."

A look of awareness washed over his expression. "Of course. I should have thought of that and provided some sort of protection."

His smile was unapologetic as he added, "I wasn't expecting this to happen today, either. I suppose I have an excuse for being irresponsible at the cabin." Again he bent to brush her lips in a sweet kiss. "But when I saw you standing there with that towel barely covering your beautiful breasts and your legs stretching for miles . . ."

"That's quite an exaggeration, considering I'm only five foot two." She managed a weak chuckle.

"Five foot two of the sexiest woman I've ever met." His gaze swept her petite nude form with open appreciation. "But I'm getting off the subject. What I was trying to say was, you bewitched me until I wasn't thinking clearly or I would have used something."

She detected a softening in his expression as he went on to say, "I don't want you to worry about anything. It wouldn't be so bad if we made a baby, would it? I wouldn't mind, and I would take good care of both of you."

Angela turned her head away, hoping he wouldn't notice the fresh trickle of tears his unintentionally painful words had brought on.

But his perceptive gaze missed nothing, and with his hand cupping her damp cheek, he rolled her head until he could look into her eyes. "I know I'm not too experienced with children, but if I could learn to run a ranch, I think I could learn how to take care of a baby." There was a moment of heavy silence before he asked, "Is the thought of my child that distasteful?"

She could barely see him through the blur of tears pooling in her eyes. "Of course it isn't. I'd love to be the one to give you a child." She squeezed her eyes shut in a defense mechanism to block his expectant look from her conscience. This was one more reason he wouldn't want her hanging around any longer than necessary. But she couldn't go any further in developing a relationship between them without telling him the truth. "But a child is something I would never be able to give you. Without going too deeply into the medical whys and why nots, I can't have children." As she spoke, her voice gradually dropped to a level slightly above a whisper.

Only a fraction of a second passed before he exclaimed, "Well, that's no big deal. I didn't have the best role models to go by anyway, so I probably wouldn't be such a terrific father."

"Oh, no, don't say that. You'll be a wonderful father. You're sensitive and intelligent enough to have learned from whatever happened to you when you were growing up." As she spoke, she forced herself to open her eyes and meet his gaze. She was searching for any sign of disappointment or falseness in his response.

He shrugged with apparent indifference. "I'm too old to be thinking about such things anyway. As you pointed out before, I wouldn't want to have to use my cane for a baseball bat."

They were both silent for several minutes, each lost in thought. Angela wished she could believe him, but she knew how heartbroken she had been when told of her infertility. She hadn't known until a couple of years after her marriage when a visit to a specialist had confirmed it was her fault and not Craig's. Already Craig's illness was becoming evident and she had desperately wanted a child to fill the emptiness. Even though she knew having a baby wasn't a cure for unhappiness, she would have done anything at that point.

And she would do anything now to be able to have Jeff's baby. She wanted it more than she had ever wanted Craig's. But it was a waste of time and emotion to wish for something that would never be.

Jeff wrapped his arms around her, pulling her close in a comforting hug. "I suppose we should get up and get dressed," he commented at last. "That chicken noodle soup wore off about five hours ago."

For the moment, the subject was closed. She and Jeff took a quick shower together and she dried her hair while he was shaving. He had told her to dress casually, so she put on a pair of designer jeans, a white silk blouse and her rose pink blazer. When she returned to the living room, her heart sped up as she saw him. His dark hair, still wet from the shower, looked almost black as it obeyed, at least temporarily, his casual styling. The blue and gray patterned wool sweater brought out the varied shades of blue in his eyes.

He greeted her with a lingering kiss as if he hadn't seen her in days instead of mere minutes. *I love you, I love you,* kept running through her mind. *Tell me you love me, please.* She tried to send him the message, hoping he would intercept it and obey. Instead he took her arm and said, "We'd better leave. Montrose shuts down pretty early and I don't want to get to the restaurant after it closes."

The parking lot at the barn-shaped barbecue restaurant was crowded with pickup trucks and Jeeps, making Angela believe it must either be a popular meeting place for the local ranchers or a good place to eat. It turned out to be both.

There wasn't an empty table, but after greeting several groups of people, Jeff accepted the invitation of a couple to share their table.

"Angela, this is Max and Ina, some very good friends of mine. They moved here a few years ago from a small town in Arkansas," Jeff said before turning and completing the introductions. "This is Angela. She was my nurse in Vietnam. We bumped into each other at a veterans' reunion, and she agreed to come out here and help me with the lambing."

"You suckered her in, huh?" Ina laughed. "She must not have known how much hard work was involved."

"I tried to tell her. Honestly. But she was overwhelmed by my charm," Jeff joked.

The waitress arrived with the menus and they ordered their meal, all while keeping up a running conversation with the other couple. Angela was immediately comfortable with them and was soon telling them stories about her pampered patients and their hypochondriac owners while Max and Ina told her about their experiences in the sheriff's department from which they had both recently retired.

The food was delicious and they all cleaned their plates, then ordered thick slices of homemade pie for dessert.

"For the first time since I arrived, I'm too full to move," Angela moaned.

"Are you trying to say that I'm not a good cook?" Jeff asked with an injured look.

"I don't think she was *trying* to say that," Max pointed out wryly. "I think she came right out and said it."

"It's not that what I've been eating hasn't been good," Angela hurried to explain. "It's just that I haven't seemed to be eating very often or with any regularity. I'll bet I've lost ten pounds in two weeks."

"It's a heck of a way to diet, isn't it?" Ina chuckled. "Max puts me to work irrigating the alfalfa fields every summer and the same thing happens to me." Since she was a tiny woman, too, it was easy to see she truly understood Angela's problem.

"Maybe you should try feeding your hired help," Max suggested with a mischievous twinkle in his pale blue eyes.

"Hired help! But he hasn't been paying me anything." Angela pretended to be shocked at the thought that she'd been missing out on a salary.

"Oh, then it's okay if he starves you," Max responded.

Almost everyone else had left the restaurant when the four people finally finished. Jeff and Max walked to the cash register to pay their bills while Angela and Ina went into the ladies' room to freshen up and wash all traces of barbecue sauce off their fingers.

"Jeff's a really nice guy, isn't he?" Ina asked when the two women were alone.

Angela sensed the older woman was trying to test the seriousness of Angela's involvement. It was touching that Jeff had a protector looking out for his interests, and the thought occurred to Angela that even though Jeff might not realize it, Max and Ina seemed to be filling the positions of his absentee parents.

"Yes, he is," Angela answered cautiously. "But he works so hard. It's too bad he couldn't afford to hire someone to help him with all the chores."

"He's been working like that ever since we've known him. It's a case of him being land rich and cash poor."

"What do you mean?"

"His place in the mountains is worth plenty of money, but unless he wants to sell part of it, he has to depend on his sheep for income."

"I didn't realize the land around here was that valuable."

"It wasn't until a few years ago when some actors and other rich folks saw how pretty it is here. Several large ranches have been sold to them for a ridiculous price, which in turn has driven up the prices for everyone else. A fashion designer bought thousands of acres and redid all the houses and outbuildings on the place just like they would have looked a hundred years ago. Then an actor hauled in forty thousand aluminum cans and thirty-five hundred old tires to make a house that's supposed to be very energy efficient." Ina smoothed her black hair in its single neat braid, which hung well past her shoulders. "I suppose they liked the slower pace and the friendly people. Max and I sure did. We came for a visit and never wanted to go back to Arkansas."

"I can understand that," Angela admitted with a trace of wistfulness. "I'm supposed to leave tomorrow, but I don't want to go back to the city."

Ina was obviously delighted by that news. "I'll bet Jeff is happy to hear that."

"He doesn't know." Now that she had begun to tell her feelings to Ina, Angela went on, "He's busy, and I don't want to be a burden to him."

"A burden! By the look in his eyes, he'll be devastated after you've gone."

"But I thought he had a girlfriend here in town."

"He dates, but as far as I know, he's never been even close to getting serious with anyone."

"I don't think he wants to fall in love."

Ina smiled. "I think it's too late. I'd be willing to bet my last dollar that that man is in love with you."

"I wish that was true." Angela tried to reapply her lipstick, but her hand was shaking too much. "More than anything I want him to love me."

"Would you be willing to give up your life in Boston if he did?"

It was an honest question that deserved an honest answer. "I don't know. I haven't thought that far ahead. If I knew what Jeff was feeling, it would make my decision easier." She shook her head. "He hasn't led me on . . . and he hasn't asked me to stay."

"Honey," Ina said, leveling a conspiratorial look at Angela. "Whether or not that man knows it, he's in love with you. He's a fine man, honest, hardworking and gentle. He needs a woman like you to make his life complete. If I was you, I would make him admit it. And I sure wouldn't leave if I loved him."

Chapter Twelve

"Kiss An Angel Good Morning" —Charley Pride

On the way to Jeff's house Angela thought about Ina's advice. She ran several conversations through her mind, but rejected them all. Surely there was some way to let Jeff know how she felt without leaving herself vulnerable to his rejection. She was all too aware that a man's passions in bed were not necessarily long lasting once they were exposed to the harsh light of day. While she desperately wanted to know if there was a possibility that Jeff might love her, she was afraid to press the issue. Now that she had realized how much she cared about him, it would crush her if he could never reciprocate her love.

Angela recognized her dilemma. She and Jeff had changed roles. It was she who could have her heart broken. And it was she who now needed a second chance.

Eighteen years ago when she so callously informed Jeff of her impending marriage to Craig, she had given little thought to Jeff's feelings. Just because he hadn't whispered words of love in her ear didn't mean he couldn't be hurt by her rejection. Whatever feelings he might have had for her then had surely been shattered. He hadn't come right out and said it, but the implication was that he had been hurt when she chose Craig over him.

Angela was ashamed that she had been thinking only of herself and her welfare when she made her choice. Coolly and logically she had considered each man's positive and negative attributes, and Jeff's column had come up glaringly negative because of his uncertain future.

How drastically she had been proven wrong. Craig had done nothing with his life. He had come home a near-invalid, but his injuries had turned out to be more mental than physical. And Jeff had found happiness and peace in the mountains of Colorado. His personality had changed. The devil-may-care attitude had been replaced by an acceptance of responsibility. He was calm and predictable, except where his emotions were concerned. His emotions were turning out to be a well-kept secret.

Pepper met them at the door, his hairy tail thumping merrily against their legs. Clearly distracted, Jeff barely paused to rub the dog's ears as he held the door open for Angela.

In the kitchen the dog headed straight for his food dish to see if anything had been added or removed since he last looked, while Jeff and Angela hesitated on opposite sides of the small room. They exchanged thoughtful glances. Neither seemed ready to discuss sleeping arrangements or travel plans.

"Do you want me to wake you up in the morning when I leave?" Jeff asked, breaking the silence at last.

"I . . . I suppose so. I might as well get an early start."

Another long moment passed, their gazes locked and their expressions closed.

"I've had a wonderful time," Angela told him. "I learned a lot about sheep and ranching. I might even write a story about it for one of the veterinary journals."

He shrugged out of his jacket and hung it on the back of a chair. "You were a lot of help. I have to admit that I never thought you'd make it. But you did great. Thanks."

"Thanks for putting up with me."

His sensuous lips twisted into the little half grin she found so appealing. "It was my pleasure," he confessed wryly.

He isn't going to ask me to stay. The realization devastated her.

She's going to walk out of my life forever, and I can't stop her. Jeff's mind scrambled for a reason she shouldn't get on that plane tomorrow. The lambing was almost over and he didn't need her help with the docking and castration that would keep him busy for the next week. He definitely needed her in his bed, but that was not an acceptable argument for extending her vacation. He cursed silently. There was only one reason for her not to leave, and that was because she *wanted* to stay.

It wasn't enough that he wanted her to—it had to be her decision, just as it had been her choice to leave before. But this time, he wanted the ending to be different.

How could she make love with such passionate abandon and not care enough about him to want to be with him? She was not the type of woman to sleep around. Once he had wanted to believe that she could be. He had tried to convince himself that her morals were loose and she was available to the man of the moment. But always, deep inside, he had known that wasn't true.

At least her enthusiasm had repaired some of the damage to his self-confidence. When she had so abruptly tossed him aside, he'd been afraid he hadn't satisfied her. She'd seemed to find as much pleasure in their rainy afternoon trysts as he had. But she'd been able to walk away without a backward glance. She hadn't appeared to have any regrets or feel any loss. It made him wonder if he'd ever understood her.

Now they had one more night—less than twelve hours. At least this time he had enough notice to store some memories—the memories that would have to last the rest of his life.

He thrust the coffeepot under the faucet and turned on the water. "Do you want a cup of coffee?" he asked, desperate to stretch their waking time together.

She started to nod, then moved her head in a negative shake that sent the blunt-cut ends of her silky hair brushing against her neck. How he loved the feel of her hair against his skin.

"No, I supposed I'd better not or I won't get any sleep at all." She took a step toward the living room, then paused and looked at him again, hesitantly, breathlessly, as if she had something else to say.

He waited.

So did she.

Neither spoke.

The water overflowed the coffeepot and Jeff reached to turn off the faucet. The action must have broken the spell because Angela sighed and began to walk away. She took a couple of steps, then once again stopped and turned to face him.

"Angie, please don't go..."

"I don't want to leave..."

They began talking at the same instant and both halted as soon as they realized the other person was speaking.

"What did you say?"

"What did you mean?"

Once more they spoke simultaneously, then stopped.

The tension was as palpable as a heartbeat, bouncing from wall to wall, pushing Jeff and Angela closer together. In two long strides he had crossed to her. She met him halfway.

"Angie, is there any way you could stay a little longer? Another month maybe? Or a couple of weeks? Even a few more days?"

Her black eyelashes fluttered over her eyes, hiding their expression not in a coquettish manner but in confusion. "Do you still need help with the lambs?"

"Yes...no...That's not why." He raked his fingers through his hair with nervous roughness. This was so important. He had to give it one last shot. He couldn't just let her slip away again. "Angie..." Her name left his mouth in an anxious breath. "I can't ask you to give up your fancy life in the city and your clinic in exchange for living way out in the middle of nowhere with a struggling sheep rancher. But maybe if you stayed here a little longer, you might begin to like it. And then...well, we'll take it one step at a time..."

Her eyes were wide and dark, as startled as the eyes of a wild deer frozen in the headlights of a car as she looked up at him. "It wouldn't be such a sacrifice," she answered softly. "I've been trying all evening to think of an excuse to miss that plane tomorrow."

The air left his lungs in a relieved whoosh. He hadn't realized he had been holding his breath.

"Really?" He tried to react with a calmness he wasn't feeling, but he had to get her to confirm what he hoped he had just heard. "You wouldn't mind staying a while longer?"

Her smile was genuine and as relieved as his. She wrapped her arms around his waist and rested her head on his chest with the familiarity of a person who had come home at last. "I thought you'd never ask."

ANGELA LEANED into the feed bin and scooped beans into a bucket. Then she carried two full buckets to the row of lambing pens. Pushing aside an anxious ewe's head, Angela poured dried pinto beans into the wooden box that was attached to a post. Then she moved to the next pen.

Straightening, she stretched her tired back muscles. All but about a dozen ewes had had their lambs, and most of Angela's time was spent carrying feed and water to pens and corrals. In the morning the sheep were fed beans, in the evening they were fed corn, and a constant supply of alfalfa hay was kept in the pens for munching between meals. When the feeding was done, the animals had to be watered. Beginning with the first pen, Angela would go down the rows. By the time she finished, the process had to be started all over again.

But soon the pens would be empty and all the sheep would be in the small corrals, waiting to be paint branded and clipped, or in the large pastures where they had access to free-flowing streams. And in only two more weeks, if the snow melt in the mountains continued as expected, the entire flock would be transported to the ranch where Doch Thu and his family would move for the summer.

Jeff had explained how the sheep were then almost wholly in Doch Thu's care until September, when the lambs were sold and shipped away. During the summer the small trailer that reminded Angela of a Gypsy caravan was pulled up to the ranch and parked for the Vietnamese family to live in. Each morning the sheep would be herded to nearby areas where they would feed until almost nightfall when they would be brought to camp for the night. Lambert and the two border collies kept guard while the shepherds slept. When all the grass around the camp had been eaten down, the trailer would be moved to a new location until all accessible areas of the three-thousand-acre ranch had been grazed. Then the rotation would begin again.

Angela wasn't sure how she would fit into that schedule. As Jeff had suggested, they were taking it slowly and letting things happen naturally.

For the moment, her life in Boston had been put in limbo. There were dozens of loose ends she would have to tie up should anything permanent develop between her and Jeff. But for now, she had turned over the management of the clinic to Richard, who hadn't been very enthusiastic about her news, and her mother was checking Angela's mail and forwarding anything that needed immediate attention.

She had turned in her rental car and cashed in the return portion of her airline ticket. Jeff gave her an old Jeep to use. Not that she and Jeff spent very much time apart. From early morning, when they took turns making breakfast, until late at night when they returned from the sheep pens, from a meal in town or a shopping excursion, they were together almost every waking moment . . . and every sleeping moment, as well.

At his suggestion, when Angela unpacked her suitcase, she had placed her things in an empty drawer in Jeff's dresser and hung her clothes next to his in the closet. Somehow that minor event seemed like a major step toward establishing their future together. And the bed in the spare room was left empty while she slept in his arms, an arrangement that suited them both.

A sudden tug on her jeans made her realize she had been daydreaming and had not moved in several moments. Looking down, Angela brushed away the tiny wet nose that was nibbling at the denim hem of her pants leg.

"What's the matter, Louie?" she asked, squatting to scratch the pesky little lamb's fuzzy chin. "Are you hungry, or just wanting some attention?" She rubbed her fingers over his mouth and he sucked them in greedily. "Okay, okay, so you're hungry. Let me see if anyone has any extra milk."

Angela opened the gate to one of the pens and stepped inside. The ewe rolled her eyes wildly and tried to butt Angela, but the woman was ready for the sheep and grabbed her around the neck.

"Calm down, big mama." Angela kept her voice low and soothing while she felt the ewe's milk bag to see how full it was. The sheep's lamb was lying on a bed of straw in the corner, obviously full and satisfied. "Good. You've got plenty of milk."

Angela pushed the gate open and called, "Louie, Louie, come and get it." As young as it was, the bum lamb knew exactly what was about to happen and trotted inside the pen. "Okay, big mama, now be a good girl and let Louie eat. He's not lucky enough to have a mother who loves him like your baby is."

The ewe wasn't enthusiastic about the dinner guest, but Angela's choke hold on her didn't allow for much of a protest as the unwelcome visitor nudged the ewe's full udder and began to suckle. His long, unclipped tail whipped back and forth, showing his delight at the delicious meal, and his whole body wiggled as he pushed and swallowed. Dribbles of milk leaked out of the corners of his mouth in his eagerness to get his fill.

Angela had grown quite attached to the baby since his mother had abandoned him two days earlier. Jeff had shown her how to take advantage of the ewes who produced too much milk so Angela wouldn't have to spend all her extra time bottle feeding Louie. But at night there was no way to avoid the bottle. She took him home and let him sleep on a blanket on the back porch, setting her alarm every four hours for his feedings.

Jeff told her there were usually a half dozen bum lambs, but they were lucky this year to have only one. The babies had no chance of survival unless a ewe who had lost her lamb could be convinced one of the bum lambs was her baby. To trick her, Jeff would skin her dead baby and wrap the hide around the bum lamb like a sweater so the ewe would recognize the smell. Fortunately for Jeff, but unfortunately for Louie, they had lost no lambs this year.

Angela remembered Jeff's story of how he had adopted all the bum lambs he could until he built up his flock. When she saw the tiny black and white spotted baby, she knew this was her first lamb, the beginning of her own flock. When she expressed her interest to Jeff, he had indulgently given her Louie. It wasn't until she was already attached to the lamb that he broke the unpleasant news that the male lambs were always sold, especially the spotted ones. All of his rams were expensive purebreds or proven crossbreds he had purchased from outside ranchers to avoid interbreeding and improve the bloodlines of his stock.

Refusing to be discouraged about the inauspicious beginning of her flock, Angela continued to watch over her baby with motherlike zeal, and Louie returned the affection by chewing on her clothes and following her everywhere she went.

"You're a noisy little boy, aren't you?" Angela continued her gentle patter until he stepped away. Looking at her with his bright clear eyes, he opened his wet mouth and uttered an appreciative bleat that she interpreted as thank you. "You're welcome, Louie. Now I've got to get back to work before Jeff comes over here and finds me goofing off with you." She released the ewe and led Louie out the gate, then poured the rest of the beans into the ewe's feed box. After emptying the other bucket she returned to fill the buckets again.

The bin where the beans were stored was just taller than waist high. It had a flat lid that she had propped open with metal rods so she could lean into the bin and fill the buckets. But the bin was almost empty, so every scoop was getting more difficult to collect.

Angela stood on her tiptoes, stretching... stretching. The bucket barely reached the beans. One more inch. If only she was one inch taller or her arms were one inch longer, she could reach. Her stomach pressed against the rim and she leaned forward, balancing on the edge for a split second. Gravity pulled rank, and as there was more of her body inside than out, she slipped. The slick sides of the bin offered her nothing to grab to stop her fall. With a total lack of grace, her legs flipped up and she tumbled head first onto the not very soft cushion of beans.

For a moment she didn't move, but lay flat on her back gazing up at the swirls of clouds scuttling across the unbelievably blue sky. The thought occurred to her that she had forgotten how blue a sky could be after living in the city for so long. Even on clear days, the Boston sky was more watery gray with just a hint of blue rather than the deep, rich color above her now.

Another thought occurred to her, and that was if someone had told her two months ago that she would be lying at the bottom of a bean storage bin and admiring the beauty of the Colorado sky, she would have told them they were completely crazy. Yet, here she was, surrounded by four metal walls, pebble-like pintos and . . . a face staring down at her.

"Taking a little rest, are we?"

She giggled, an automatically immature response for the silliness of her predicament. Patting the beans beside her, she gave him a flirtatious wink and suggested, "Why don't you join me?"

His eyes twinkled and he hoisted himself over the edge. "I've heard of rolling in the hay, but I've never heard of frolicking in the beans."

The bin was much too short for his six foot frame, so he had to keep his legs bent as he lay down next to her.

"What are we looking at?"

"The sky. Isn't it gorgeous?"

He turned his head so his gaze rested on her profile. "Hmm, yes it *is* beautiful."

She realized he wasn't paying attention to the clouds and looked at him. Their faces were only inches apart, too close to see each other clearly, but close enough that she could feel the warmth of his breath.

"Do you like it here?" he asked.

She intentionally misunderstood him to pay him back for not taking her sky-watching seriously. "Here, as in the bean bin?"

He rolled over until he was straddling her legs and peering into her eyes. "No, here as in Montrose . . . with me," he growled with good-humored persistence.

Angela looped her arms around his neck and smiled at him. "I'm having a wonderful time in Montrose . . . with you."

His mouth lowered to hers until their lips met in a tender yet undeniably passionate kiss. For several minutes they took advantage of the unexpected privacy to participate in a little serious necking. His hand soon found its way under her sweater. Lifting the elastic band of her bra, he freed her breasts to his caress. Beneath his work-roughened fingers, her nipples hardened anxiously. Lifting his lips from hers, Jeff let his gaze stroke the soft, full mounds.

"They're perfect," he murmured.

Angela shrugged off his compliment because she had always wished for a more generous bosom. She remembered her embarrassment when everyone had been throwing away their bras and no one had noticed that she hadn't really needed to wear one. As she matured, she had developed a respectable chest, but not one that would ever make a centerfold in a men's magazine.

"Let me be the judge," he reassured her, correctly interpreting her self-deprecating gesture. His tongue moistened one rosy tip before he drew it into his mouth. She gasped as the always surprisingly intense sensation coiled in the pit of her stomach, tightening with each gentle tug of his lips. "Just the right size," he murmured before repeating the treatment on her other breast. Her body squirmed beneath him, pressing against his masculine hardness in a primeval reaction to his almost unbearable stimulation.

Reluctantly, he moved away, pulled her bra in place and primly lowered her sweater. "We'll finish this later," he promised, his breath as ragged as hers. "The truck delivering more beans will be here any minute and I'd hate to have them find us in the middle of something that delivery men shouldn't witness."

At the moment, she would have been willing to chance discovery. But she could understand his reasoning and accepted it with the knowledge he would more than make up for the interruption once they were home. *Home.* How easily the word slipped through her mind.

Jeff stood and climbed easily out of the bin. Angela scrambled to her feet, slipping and sliding on the beans. She braced her hands on the edge and was going to hoist herself up until she could raise one leg high enough to get some leverage. But Jeff, his large hands almost spanning her waist, lifted her as effortlessly as if she was one of the newborn lambs.

"See, you fit in my hands," he commented. "All of you."

He dropped another quick kiss on her lips before adding, "And you taste like beans."

She responded by a punch to the ribs. "If your feed containers weren't so tall . . ."

"Or if my workers weren't so short . . ."

"Petite."

He smiled, a sexy, lopsided smile. "Perfect," he repeated.

A warm, liquid feeling spread through her body . . . a feeling of happiness. And a feeling that she belonged. Not *to* this man, but *with* this man.

Louie butted against her legs, insisting on his share of attention. Jeff bent down and picked up the long-legged baby.

"So how did you know I was in the bin?" she asked Jeff as they walked toward the water pump to wash the bean dust off their arms and faces.

"I just happened to glance around when your legs were sticking straight up into the air." He chuckled. "Then when I arrived here, Louie was standing next to the bin, looking up as if he had just lost his best friend."

"Well, at least someone cared," she joked as she rubbed her face against the lamb's soft black and white body, letting the tight curls tickle her cheek. She knew she was blatantly fishing. In spite of all the closeness they had shared during the past few weeks, Jeff still hadn't admitted how he felt about her. And with each passing day, she needed more desperately to hear it.

"Of course he cared," Jeff responded lightly. "You're his meal ticket. If you leave, he'll be lamb chops before the plane takes off the ground."

Angela's eyes widened. She was horrified at the thought. "Lamb chops! You wouldn't." She wrapped her arms around Louie and tried to pull him out of Jeff's arms.

"Then I guess you'll just have to stay forever...to protect Louie."

Angela stopped struggling and lifted her gaze to meet Jeff's. It was there, hiding behind the teasing, behind the desire in his eyes. She could see it; he loved her. But why couldn't he say it?

Slowly she nodded. She would have to stay. But she was determined to make him speak the words. For now, she would have to be patient . . . and play his game until they both felt comfortable with what love would entail.

"I'll stay," she informed him, then added with a teasing twinkle, "for Louie."

Chapter Thirteen

"I Should Have Known Better" —*The Beatles*

"Damn!" Jeff cursed. "It's snowing."

Angela forced her eyes open and tried to bring the digital numbers on the clock into focus. It was only 4:00 a.m. No wonder she hadn't heard the alarm go off; she and Jeff usually didn't wake up until six.

Striding into the bedroom from the kitchen, he jerked open dresser drawers, grabbed the clothes he needed, then pulled them on as he walked across the bedroom.

"What are you doing up?" she managed to ask.

"I went into the kitchen for a drink of water and saw it's snowing outside. Damn," he repeated, "those weather forecasters never know what's going on. I listened to two stations last night and neither of them predicted snow. This was supposed to be a little cold snap with no moisture at all."

Angela's mind was sluggish from sleep, but it registered that Jeff was extremely upset. Throwing the covers aside, she followed his lead, dressing as quickly and warmly as he had. She had no idea what he planned on doing, but she wanted to be prepared. Taking only enough time to brush her teeth and comb the tangles out of her hair, she went to find him.

He was in the kitchen, pulling on his rubber boots.

"Oh, good, you're dressed," he said as soon as he noticed her. "I'll need all the extra hands I can get this morning. We don't have time for breakfast. We can make some coffee in the sheepherder's wagon. After we get everything covered, or if the snow stops, I'll take you out to breakfast."

It proved to be an unfulfilled promise. By the time they arrived at the pens, there was more than an inch of snow on the ground and there was no sign it was going to let up anytime soon. Doch Thu and his son were struggling with heavy tarpaulins, trying to spread them over the birthing pens.

Jeff leaped out of the truck as soon as the engine stopped and ran to help them, leaving Angela to trail along behind.

After that first awkward encounter, she had succeeded in avoiding Doch Thu. It was one part of Jeff's life that she could not accept. She thought she had been able to put Vietnam behind her. If she could make it through a week without thinking about it, she was pleased. A month made her ecstatic. A year would have been a dream come true. But with the surge of Vietnam movies and television shows, it had become almost impossible.

That didn't lessen her resolve, however. It became a matter of principle to separate herself from that era so completely that she could believe she hadn't been there.

Being around Jeff could have made that impossible. But he had changed so much since then. The devil-may-care warrior had been replaced by a sensitive gentleman. He made it easy for her to ignore the part he had played in the war and the circumstances under which they had met.

Except for the fact that almost two thousand miles separated their homes, she and Jeff could have met at the grocery store or a gym. Well, maybe not a gym, since she couldn't visualize Jeff working out on a stationary bike or hopping through an aerobics class. Not when he had enough exercise doing daily chores. Nor could she see him taking part in the singles' bar scene.

Angela must not associate Jeff with Vietnam, particularly because of the way her husband had died. She had witnessed the devastating effects of post-traumatic stress disorder once, and she knew she couldn't survive a second round. It was a fight she couldn't win, even though she had given it her best shot. And it was a fight she would avoid at all costs.

Angela watched the men for several minutes until she figured out how they were unrolling the tarps over the tops and down the backs of the pens to form a protective barrier against the wind and snow. She knew she couldn't hope to pick up a thick canvas roll, but she could tie knots.

The problem was that meant she would be working beside Doch Thu. While Jeff and the older man's son lifted and positioned the heavy tarps, Doch Thu was on his knees in the drifting snow, tying the corners to the bottom of the posts.

Angela gritted her teeth. This was for the benefit of Jeff's sheep. Even with her lack of experience, she could see the necessity of keeping the lambs out of the wet snow and cold winds. Their woolly coats were still too thin and short to offer much natural protection, and there wasn't a barn or shed that would hold the entire flock, which had tripled in size since lambing began.

She had to put aside her personal prejudices. Resolutely, she sloshed through the snow to a tarp. She grabbed a piece of rope and threaded it through a metal eye in the tarp, tied a knot, then wrapped the other end of the rope around a post and pulled. When as much slack as possible had been taken out, she tied a knot, then moved around Doch Thu to the next eye. She didn't speak to the elderly man, and tried not to glance in his direction as they moved down the row.

The snowflakes were huge and very wet, which Jeff had told her was typical for a spring storm. Several inches fell in a very short time. No matter how tight Angela and Doch Thu pulled the canvas, the snow quickly accumulated on it and began to make it sag dangerously low. If the tarps dumped their loads of snow inside the pens, it would defeat the purpose of their hard work.

Angela noticed a particularly overloaded pocket and tried to shake the snow off. But the weight was too much for her to lift, so she entered the pen and tried to push upward with her back. She strained and shoved, but couldn't make the heavy snow shift.

Over the sound of the howling wind, she heard the gate open. Her awkward position kept her from seeing who had joined her in the pen. Together she and her helper were able to push against the sagging material until the snow tumbled harmlessly off.

"Thanks," Angela said, her breath coming out in staccato puffs that hung in the frigid air. She turned to look into the slightly flat face with its narrow, slanting eyes, and she felt her heart do an involuntary leap of fear. It was at that moment that she realized there was more to her feelings for Doch Thu than dislike. He frightened her. He reminded her of hundreds of similar faces she had seen in her worst nightmares.

But the war was over, she told herself. He wasn't the enemy. Whatever his background, he was devoted to Jeff. He worked long hours and gave excellent care to the sheep.

Grudgingly, she admitted that Jeff wouldn't be doing so well without Doch Thu's help. The Vietnamese man could be home right now with his wife, eating breakfast or sleeping. His shift was over. He had no obligation to stay longer. But he was here.

"Thanks," she repeated, more sincerely this time. "I couldn't have done it without you."

The old man's weathered face broke into a grin. He nodded several times as he responded in broken but understandable English. "You work very hard. You do good job. I just help you a little."

"You helped me a lot. And you help Jeff a lot."

He continued nodding. "I like Mr. Jeff. He very good man."

Angela discovered she was nodding in rhythm with him. She smiled and forced her head to be still so he wouldn't think she was mocking him. "We'd better get back to work. They're getting ahead of us."

As he fastened the gate behind them, she noticed that he wasn't wearing any gloves. His fingers were red and chapped from the cold, but he hadn't uttered a word of complaint. Reaching into the pocket of the jacket she had borrowed from Jeff, she pulled out an extra pair of heavy cotton gloves she had put in there in case her gloves got soaked.

"Here, you can use these," she said, holding them out to Doch Thu.

He hesitated, his eyes watching her expression. "Yes, yes, thank you very much. I did not bring my gloves last night because it was not cold.'' Again, he nodded and grinned. ''It very, very cold now, though.''

Ironically, the cold had broken the ice between them. By the end of the morning, Angela's attitude toward Doch Thu was beginning to gradually thaw. They completed their tasks as quickly as possible, securing the tarps over the pens. Then Doch Thu took the dogs out to herd the sheep in the pasture together against a rock windbreak.

Angela stood for a moment and watched the dogs work the sheep. She could barely make out the figures through the lacy curtain of falling snow. The dogs were black and white shadows darting and circling while the old man followed behind the flock.

''I see you and Doch Thu are on speaking terms now.'' Even through the padding of her sweater and a heavy coat, she could feel Jeff's warmth as he slipped his arms around her waist and pulled her against him, letting his body protect her from the chilling elements.

''He's very loyal to you,'' Angela commented as she snuggled closer to Jeff. ''He never quite came out and asked, but I think he wanted to know what my intentions are.''

Jeff leaned over and rubbed his cold nose against her neck, causing her to squeal and jump away. ''So what *are* your intentions?''

''Right now, they're to get something warm and filling into my stomach and get some feeling back into my fingers and toes.''

His eyebrows lifted wolfishly. ''I can take care of both those things. Let's go hop in the bean bin.''

''Actually, I was thinking more about a cup of coffee and a warm fire.''

"Oh, that," he said, his lips curved into a teasing grin. "Why didn't you say so earlier? There's a fresh pot of coffee and a wood-burning stove going at full blast inside the camp wagon."

"Then why are we standing out here in the snow?" she asked incredulously.

"Because you look so beautiful with snow in your hair and hanging from your eyelashes . . . not to mention the pink flush of your cheeks."

"That's frostbite, you crazy man!" She laughed. "No wonder you were so warm. I'll bet you've already spent a few minutes by that fire and sampled some of that coffee."

"Just one cup," he admitted, then dodged as she scooped up a snowball and threw it at him. He packed a fistful of snow and blasted a quick return shot at her. She ducked and ran toward the trailer, stopping only long enough to fire a volley at him before she jumped inside and shut the door behind her.

"Let me in," he called as he knocked on the door.

"Are you unarmed?"

"Not entirely. But I'll leave my snowballs outside," he assured her wryly.

She opened the door. "I'll take my chances with your other weapons."

He tossed his gloves onto a small table and advanced on her with his fingers outstretched. "How about being caressed by icy fingers?"

She shivered at the thought and retreated to the far end of the room, which was only a few steps away. With the backs of her legs pressed against the edge of the bed, she was convinced he would make good his promise. But before he touched her, a knock on the door halted them both in their tracks.

Jeff passed her an amused, disappointed look and shrugged. "We've got company." He turned and opened the door, then stood aside so Doch Thu and his son could enter.

Angela poured four cups of coffee and handed one to each of the men before sipping from her own. The stove had filled the limited space with welcome heat that soon became almost stifling.

"The sheep have settled in the pasture. The dogs are with them." Doch Thu looked at Jeff and waited for his approval.

"That's good. I think the snow's letting up, so they should be okay out there. You and Dohn have been here all night. Angela and I can handle it from here on out, so why don't you two go home and get some sleep," Jeff suggested. "I really appreciate you and Dohn staying to help. I hate to think how many lambs we would have lost if we hadn't gotten those tarps spread and tied down so quickly."

Doch Thu nodded and smiled. "I am pleased to help you. I hope the sheep will be okay."

"So do I," Jeff agreed. "But we can't do anything else until the storm stops."

Doch Thu and Dohn left, the sound of their truck muffled by the fluffy snow. There was only the slightest whisper as the fat flakes hit the windows and melted against the sweating glass.

"How did you meet Doch Thu?" Angela asked, her head tilted thoughtfully. She sat at the table, took her boots off and propped her sock-covered feet on a piece of split aspen wood in front of the stove. She suspected there was more to the story of Doch Thu's presence at Jeff's ranch than the usual boss-employee relationship. "You knew him from Vietnam, didn't you?"

"Yes, I met him near the end of my second tour." Jeff pulled out another chair and stretched his feet toward the fire. Keeping his gaze focused on the crackling flames behind the metal grill, he told his story. "He lived with his wife, two sons and a daughter on a small farm outside the village of Khe Sanh. They hid me from a Communist patrol while I was on a mission near the Laos border. They saved my life, and I promised to do whatever I could to help them. But by the time I got to Da Nang the cease-fire agreement had finally been approved and before I knew it, I was on the last troop flight out of the country."

Jeff refilled his cup and leaned forward, staring into the swirling black liquid. His voice was filled with regret and sadness as he continued. "It was twelve years before I could get back over there, before they would let Americans in. One of Doch Thu's sons and his daughter had been killed by the NVA when they took over the area the year after I left. But Doch Thu's wife had given birth to another son. It took quite a bit of doing, but they were finally able to sneak out of the country. They contacted me after they were free and I helped them get visas. George had died in 1986, so I really needed their help."

Jeff smiled. "Doch Thu and his family had never even seen a sheep, much less taken care of one. They were fascinated by their wool—and their stupidity. Apparently, even the water buffalo they use to till their paddies were more intelligent than a sheep. We all learned a lot that first year, but they never made the same mistake twice. And now I trust them with my flock all summer. They watch them as carefully as if those sheep were their own."

Angela looked around the compact shepherd's wagon. A stainless steel sink, a two-burner propane stove and refrigerator lined one wall, and the wood-burning stove and dining table took up the opposite wall. A double bed built on a set of drawers stretched across the front, with the door at the back. "This isn't a bad setup for one person, or maybe two. But how do Doch Thu and his whole family live in here?"

"They don't all stay at the ranch at the same time. Doch Thu and one of his sons stays. His wife will come up for a visit once or twice a week, and he'll go down to their house in Montrose for a break while his sons go up with the sheep. They work out a schedule they can live with, and I let them arrange it to suit them."

"What do you do all summer?" Angela asked.

"That's when I get all my work done on the ranch. For the past four years I've been building the cabin. I finished it last summer, and now I need to build a new barn and dig out a couple more ponds. There's always road maintenance and fences to be repaired."

He glanced outside. It was still snowing. "Well, I guess we'd better go back out there and make sure all the sheep have plenty to eat. They'll need the fuel to keep warm."

By the time Jeff and Angela had provided the morning ration of beans and alfalfa, they were wet and cold. The pregnant ewes were in the birthing pens with Louie, who got an extra thick cushion of alfalfa to snuggle in after Angela found him a wet nurse for his lunch.

"You warm up while I check on the dogs and the sheep in the big pasture," Jeff suggested. He brought another armload of wood inside before he left, and Angela fed the fire, then rummaged through the cabinets to see what she could fix for lunch. Settling on a can of chili and crackers, she had the meal ready by the time he returned.

Even though he had been wearing a stocking cap, his hair was wet and plastered to his forehead. While he sat by the fire, warming up and eating the chili, Angela stood behind him and dried his hair.

"Mmm, that feels good," he moaned as she put aside the towel and let her fingers massage the muscles at the base of his neck and across his shoulders. "When I think of all the time I've spent in this trailer..."

Her fingers tightened.

"With just Pepper for company." He finished his sentence quickly. He twisted his head so he could look at her, his smile suspiciously smug. He asked, "Do I detect a little jealousy?"

"Jealous? Me?" she answered innocently. "Of course not. What you did with other women in the past is not my business..." Her voice trailed off as her hands slid inside his coat and over the curve of his chest.

"What about other women in my future?" he prompted, waiting for her reaction.

Angela tried not to let her emotions show, but she could tell by his pleased expression that she wasn't too successful at hiding her discomfort at the thought. However, until she knew what the future might hold for them, she dared not be too possessive. "I hope you won't begin including those women in your activities until I've left," was as neutral a comment as she could make.

His response was quick and abrupt as he stood and turned, pulling her into his arms. Burying his face in her hair, he muttered, "I don't even want to think about when you'll be gone. Angela, we need to talk..."

She leaned back and placed her fingers over his mouth to silence him. "Not yet," she cautioned. "One day at a time for now. Remember?"

"But . . ."

Her arms circled his neck, her fingers burying themselves in the thickness of his hair as she pulled his head down. Stretching up to touch her lips lightly to his, she whispered, "Not now. Not here. Let's take advantage of being snowed in, all alone with nothing but a bed and a fire. We can talk about tomorrow tomorrow."

"Sooner or later tomorrow's going to get here, you know."

She pushed his coat off his shoulders and let her hands slide under his sweater. "I know." The tip of her tongue traced the masculine curves of his lips before teasing them open. "I don't want to think about leaving you," she murmured, her words swallowed by his answering kiss.

But as they undressed each other, both were thinking that sooner or later the subject would have to be discussed. Would Angela be able to give up her family, her home, her business, her life in Boston? Would Jeff be able to adjust his life-style to include a woman? Could he accept not having children? Could either commit the rest of their lives? Was there any such thing as a permanent relationship?

Neither of them had a family background that showed permanence or harmony. How could they hope to succeed when their parents, who had been raised in a more conservative era, had not been able to? But how could Angela consider giving up her roots in Boston for anything less than a total commitment?

The bed was cozy and comfortable, and the continued snowfall shut them off from the rest of civilization.

Jeff and Angela made love as if they had all the time in the world, even though they both knew they didn't.

THE SNOW STOPPED FALLING early in the afternoon, but the sky was still heavy with thick gray clouds that brought an early nightfall. The day seemed to pass slowly. But Jeff and Angela weren't complaining. Except for making the rounds of the pens, checking on the lambs and the pregnant ewes and pushing the accumulated snow off the tarps, they spent the day wrapped in each other's arms, making love or listening to the radio. They didn't do much talking because there was one subject that was sure to come up and neither wanted to disrupt the mood.

Doch Thu and Dohn arrived at eight in the evening, rested and ready to handle the night shift. Angela and Jeff picked up a bucket of fried chicken on the way home and put together an impromptu meal after taking turns in the bathtub. They carried their plates into the living room and sat in front of the television to catch the news even though Jeff continued his tirade against the weather forecasters.

As usual, the moment they had arrived with Louie, Pepper had taken over supervision of the lamb. The dog never let Louie out of his sight, lying for hours with his head on his paws, watching the lamb's every movement. As soon as Louie would take a step toward the kitchen, Pepper would spring into action, blocking the doorway and herding the confused little lamb into the covered porch and utility room.

"I think Pepper's going to miss that lamb more than you do once Louie joins the flock," Jeff commented. He was sprawled across one end of the couch, leaning against the cushions with his legs lying intimately next to hers as she reclined on the opposite end of the couch. "That dog tolerates humans, but he really loves sheep. I don't think his blindness bothers him as much as not being able to work with the flock does."

"How do they bond with the sheep like that? Dogs are natural predators of sheep."

"When they're still puppies, before their predatory instincts kick in, we put them in a small pen with a ewe. As the dogs outgrow their surrogate mothers, they become very protective of the sheep instead of wanting to kill them. And we try not to make pets of the puppies because they need to be closer to the sheep than they are to humans. Of course, that works against them when they get too old or disabled to stay with the flock." Jeff looked fondly at the elderly border collie who was vigilantly watching his charge. "Even though I raised him and took him with me everywhere while we were both learning how to be sheepherders, he never lets me forget that I'm his second choice. And if you think it's humiliating to be tossed aside by a woman who chooses another man, just think how much worse it is to know your dog would prefer spending his time with a bunch of smelly sheep. So much for the man's best friend theory."

He spoke lightly, but Angela could hear the hurt beneath his joking words. When she chose Craig over him, there must have been a deep wound, much deeper and more complex than she had imagined. She reached out and took his hand in hers. "Jeff, I'm so sorry. I didn't look at it from your viewpoint at all. I know it's not a very good excuse, but I was confused and burned out. I was desperate to escape from the pain and sadness.

When I was with you, I wanted you more than anything in the world. But every day when I was working my shift in the hospital, Craig would beg me to marry him and let him take care of me. He was offering me security and a return to the life I had known before. I had to get away from the rain, the heat, the bugs, the Vietnamese, the blood . . . and especially the memories. Craig could give me all that.

"But you," she continued, her expressive eyes begging for his understanding, "you offered me nothing. Nothing but a few afternoons of temporary escape. You weren't going home. For all I knew, you might never go home. And I was too young to be a widow."

"You're a widow now. Was it any easier when you were five years older?" There was a bitter edge to his voice that he couldn't quite temper.

"No, it was a thousand times more difficult because I had to live through the five years before it." She could barely speak around the lump that had risen in her throat, a reaction to her guilt about Jeff and Craig. She hadn't been honest with either of them, and her selfishness had cost them all their happiness. "Craig told me he loved me and I believed him." A wistful sigh emphasized her feelings. "It was what I *wanted* to hear."

"Would it have made any difference if I had told you I loved you?" he asked parenthetically.

She was silent for a few moments as she considered how different the outcome might have been. But finally she admitted, "No, probably not. I had lived with the danger and the turmoil for too many months. I was ready for a calm, predictable, safe life. You couldn't give me that then."

Now it was his turn to let the silence stretch. When he spoke, he leveled a piercing look at her that demanded the truth. "Did you love him?"

How could she answer that? "There are different types of love," she said, hedging the issue.

"But did you love Craig?"

"There were lots of things about him that I loved," she replied. "I felt comfortable with him. He had a terrific sense of humor and he was very nonthreatening, sort of like a brother."

Jeff rubbed his hand across his forehead as if soothing away a headache. "So what you're saying is that you wanted a brother more than a lover?"

"I wanted both, but they didn't come in the same package. So I had to choose."

"Love didn't matter?"

"Love was such an overused word in the sixties and seventies. It was too free and easy, and it meant nothing."

"What about now?" he asked, almost casually. "Are you looking for love or are you still holding out for security?"

She wished she knew the answer to that. The one thing she had learned from her marriage to Craig was that marriage was not as simple as it seemed. Just because someone offered security didn't mean they could provide it. And she suspected the same would be true of love.

How long did love last? Was it as temporary as what her parents had had or as stressful as what she and Craig had felt? Were love and security equal on the scale of importance in a relationship? As she grew older, she had made her own security, but she had never found true love—except with Jeff. How could she give up love now that she realized what a rare and special treasure it was?

When she opened her mouth to tell him all these considerations, she was interrupted by the ring of the telephone.

Chapter Fourteen

"If You Leave Me Now" —Chicago

She wished he wouldn't answer it. They were so close to the truth. She felt certain if they could keep on the subject for just a few more minutes, he would tell her his feelings, she would tell him hers, and they would be able to decide whether or not there was a foundation on which something could be built.

But the phone didn't ring very often at Jeff's house, and all his calls were important.

Jeff, too, seemed to regret having to interrupt the discussion. But after only a few seconds of hesitation, he swung his legs off the couch and walked to the wall phone in the kitchen.

Between the voices on the television and her distraction, only a few words of the conversation drifted to her ears.

"Bones...positive identification...Michael Delaney...next week...Da Nang...Marines...engineer battalion...land mines...children...hospital...Yes, I'll let you know."

When he returned, Angela could see he was distracted. She waited for him to tell her about the telephone call or to pick up their discussion. But he did neither. He sat on the couch, then glanced at his watch and jumped to his feet. Pacing with uncharacteristic nervousness, he seemed to barely notice her existence.

Finally, she stood, stretched, then picked up the dinner dishes. "I'll do the dishes, then I think I'll go on to bed," she informed him, sensing he needed some time alone. She was curious but not angry at his sudden change of mood. However, she did resent the intrusion at a crucial moment. But since she could do nothing to retrieve that moment, she decided to give herself a few extra hours of sleep to catch up on what she had lost that morning.

Jeff didn't try to dissuade her, so she carried the dishes into the kitchen and filled the sink with soapy water. After the dishes were done, she fed Louie, gave some scraps to Pepper, then turned out the lights and walked through the living room.

The television was still on, but Jeff wasn't paying any attention to it. Instead, he sat with a pad of paper and a phone book in his lap, and was writing some sort of list.

"Good night, Jeff," she called, not really expecting him to hear her.

But he leaped to his feet, as if too restless to remain seated long, and circled the couch. Wrapping his arms around her, he gave her an unexpectedly energetic hug.

"Good night, Angie. I don't know how long I'll be, so don't wait up." He dropped an almost chaste kiss on her forehead. Then, as abruptly as he had embraced her, he stepped away and returned to the couch, immediately picking up the pad of paper and resuming the list.

The bed felt strangely empty, even though she had spent twelve years sleeping alone. She traded pillows so she could breathe in Jeff's musky, masculine scent and pretend he was lying next to her. It was a poor substitute.

It was time for her to face her feelings and admit that she loved him enough to leave her life in Boston. If he loved her, too, then they shouldn't throw it all away because they were afraid of a lack of permanency.

Of course, it might be quite a challenge to wrench the words from Jeff. There was a chance that it wasn't that he didn't *want* to tell her he loved her, but that he *couldn't* actually say the words. If his childhood had been as awful as he had led her to believe, then words of endearment wouldn't come easily to his lips. There was a possibility that he had never spoken the word *love* to anyone.

Well, it was time he faced his feelings, too. If he loved her, she would *make* him tell her, just like the words of their favorite song. She wasn't quite sure how to accomplish this feat, but if there was a way, she would find it. It was time Jeff loved someone and accepted her love in return—as long as that someone was Angela.

Relieved that she had reached a decision of sorts, Angela snuggled deeper into Jeff's pillow and let sleep overtake her, hoping her subconscious would work out the details of her mission. After all she and Jeff had shared during the past few weeks, she couldn't believe Jeff didn't love her at least a little. Soon she would make him say how much. Tomorrow was the day for the truth.

The sun shining in her eyes woke her. She sat up, immediately awake. Someone had turned off the alarm, and she had overslept. It was almost eight o'clock. Jeff must have thought she needed her sleep after yesterday's storm, and had probably left without her. Leisurely, since there was no need to hurry, she dressed, taking special care with her makeup and hair and planning a special menu for dinner that evening. As soon as they finished eating, they would have time to have that serious discussion they had been putting off.

The smell of coffee drew her like a magnet to the kitchen, reminding her of Jeff's thoughtfulness. When she entered the room, she slid to a stop.

"What are you doing here?" she asked bluntly, startled to see Jeff sitting at the kitchen table with a spray of papers in front of him. He was not out with the sheep, as she had expected. And he was dressed as if he had no plans to go to the pens. He was wearing slacks and a sports shirt. With his dark hair neatly combed he looked like a businessman on his way to the office—and completely unlike the man Angela knew. Then she noticed the suitcase. "Are we going somewhere?"

"I am," he answered, abandoning his paperwork to get up and pour her a cup of coffee. "I realize the timing isn't very convenient, but I won't be gone but a week."

"Gone? Where?"

"Vietnam."

He could not have shocked her more if he had said the moon. For her, the two places were equally unthinkable.

Her thoughts must have been evident in her expression. Jeff pulled out a chair and gently urged her to sit. "I suppose this is something that would have come up sooner or later, so we might as well talk about it now," he confessed with a notable lack of enthusiasm, probably because he suspected how she would respond.

"I make three or four trips a year to Vietnam, sometimes with our government's blessing, but usually without."

Angela slumped in her chair and stared at him as if he was speaking in a foreign language that she didn't understand. "Why on earth would you want to go there?"

"I don't *want* to go. I hate it there. It reminds me of the screams of men dying. I never take a step into the jungle without smelling the stench of terror and breaking out into a cold sweat."

"Then why go?"

"Because no one else will," he answered simply, even though his reasons were much more complicated.

"What do you do?"

"I've made some valuable contacts through the years. I've been able to recover the remains of American servicemen who have been listed as missing in action. I've followed several leads to find POWs, but the only live soldier I've found and brought home was Bo."

"*You're* the one who found Bo Dayton?"

"It was a case of mistaken identity, but it turned out okay. You see, I went over there because my sources had seen a man who fit the description of Melora's brother, Michael. It turned out that Bo had been injured when his plane crashed, causing him to lose his memory. Two old women took him in, hid him from the NVA and used him to work their fields. He didn't remember the world beyond the jungle's edge, so he didn't know to escape. Melora took him to the States and helped him adjust to the changes that had occurred while he was MIA."

"But where do you fit into all this?" Angela inquired, not able to put all the pieces of the puzzle together. "How did you get involved?"

"My first trip was to help Doch Thu and his family. I learned a lot about government red tape and bureaucratic blindness. Then a friend of mine wanted to try to find his buddy who he thought was a POW, so I used my

contacts and found the guy's grave. Because of the re-
percussions and an implied admission of some sort of
guilt, the NVA had been reluctant to tell the whole truth
about the casualties. A persistent individual who is willing to grease a few palms and go in the back door seems
to have better luck than a government agency pussy-
footing through diplomacy and protocol.''

"But isn't it dangerous?"

He shrugged. "It can be. But I have a great group of
guys that help. And no one knows what I'm doing other
than them, the people I've helped—and now you."

"If the Vietnamese government caught you, you could
be considered a spy and probably executed." The pieces
were beginning to fit, but their picture was a frightening
one. "And since no one knows you're there, you could
disappear forever on one of these missions. Does that
about sum it up?"

"I'm careful."

"Yeah, right." She snorted. "I've zipped up body
bags on men who were *careful*. And I thought you'd
changed." She rubbed her throbbing temples, trying to
discourage a headache that was beginning to pound.
"But you're the same old reckless war-horse, rearing to
get into the action and play GI Joe. You've been hiding
behind the respectability and serenity of a sheep rancher,
when all the time you haven't let it go at all."

"I can't ignore the possibilities. If there's something
I can do to help a family find out if their loved one is
dead or alive, then I'll do it. As long as there's a chance
I'll find some live POWs, then I have to take the risk.
Just look at Bo. He could have lived the rest of his life
working in a rice paddy like an ox."

Angela stood up so abruptly her chair tumbled backward, hitting the wooden floor with a clatter. "Well, I

guess that sort of answers any questions I might have had about our future.''

"Angie, surely you can understand—''

"I understand all right. Vietnam's in your blood. That bullet didn't kill you, but that darn war will get you yet." She straightened her shoulders and stated with firm resolve, "And I won't stick around to see it happen."

"Does that mean you're leaving?"

"It means that if you leave today, I won't be here when you come back."

He heaved a pained sign and roughly raked his fingers through his hair. "I have to go."

"I can't stay," she cried, unable to stop the tears that had sprung to her eyes. "I've seen it happen before. I thought I could stop it, or at least help ease the pain. But I couldn't . . . I couldn't." She covered her face with her hands.

"You did all you could," he soothed, wrapping his arms around her and cradling her head against his chest.

"It wasn't enough. He couldn't get over it. It broke him and left him an emotional invalid."

"Who? Are you talking about Craig?"

"He didn't die from his wounds," she said, sobbing. "But Vietnam killed him. The war killed him. He wasn't strong and brave. They drafted him, handed him a gun and made him kill or be killed."

"At least Craig had you," Jeff whispered.

But instead of calming her, that only increased her anguish. "I couldn't help him. In fact, I might have made it worse." She sniffled and was silent for a moment before adding, "I think he knew all along that I was in love with you. I tried to love him. I really did. But he must have known. Why else would he tell me you had died?"

"You loved me?"

"I didn't want to. I tried to forget you," she admitted. "I learned my lesson about acting on impulse when I spent two years in Vietnam, and I wanted to return to an orderly, peaceful world. I thought Craig was what I needed. And I thought I was what he needed. If only I had tried harder to love him. If only I could have given him a child. If only I could have made his life happier, then maybe he wouldn't have..." Her voice choked and she was unable to finish the sentence.

"He wouldn't have what?" Jeff prompted gently.

She had never admitted it to a person outside her family and Craig's. It had caused her immeasurable pain, and she hadn't wanted anyone to know about Craig's weakness and her failure. But Jeff should know. Maybe it would prove to him how damaging it could be to hold on to that part of his past. It took more strength than she could have imagined to speak the words. "Craig committed suicide."

It was evident her announcement caught Jeff by surprise. For several minutes, he simply held her, stroking her hair and letting the news sink in. When he finally spoke, there was a hint of a quaver in his voice. "You shouldn't hold yourself responsible for what Craig did to himself."

"I've tried to tell myself that. But I keep thinking of all the things I could have done differently."

"It wasn't your fault."

"I wasn't the one who pulled the trigger. But I should have seen how deep his emotional wounds were. He couldn't let it go. It consumed him. It destroyed him. And as I was holding his head in my lap, waiting for the ambulance to arrive, I vowed I'd put as much distance between me and that war as possible. I shouldn't have gone to the reunion. And I shouldn't have come here with you. I was so startled and relieved to see you alive and well that I wasn't thinking clearly.''

"But you stayed."

She sighed, unable to deny that she had certainly been thinking clearly when she decided to stay...as clearly as one can think when she's in love.

"I'm not Craig," he reminded her pointedly. "I've gotten through the post-trauma stress and I'm not suicidal. I can take care of myself."

Angela pushed away. "Sure, I've heard that before, too."

"No, I don't think you have. You only let yourself get involved with people who are dependent on you. I'll bet both your parents ran to you with their problems during their divorce and that Richard couldn't have gotten that clinic going on his own. You have a generous, nurturing spirit and you've been programmed to be strong and responsible. Those are admirable traits, and that's why you were such a terrific nurse. But maybe it's time you let someone take care of you for a change."

She stared at him, denial rising in her throat. But his words had struck a chord of truth. Had she always chosen men who needed her so they wouldn't leave her like her father had left her mother? Did she feel she should be the strong one in the relationship so she could retain control? Had it been her recognition that Jeff was strong and independent enough to live without her that had frightened her the most?

"I *have* changed," Jeff explained. "I'm happy with my life and I know I'm not a failure. But I can't ignore cries for help."

"What about my cries for help?" she implored. "I don't want you to go. I hate that place. It swallows people up, body and soul."

"It's not the same as you remember. When I was crawling on my belly through those jungles, I never noticed how beautiful it can be. You can hear the birds and monkeys instead of the chattering of M-16s or the scream of mortars."

"You make it sound like a tropical paradise."

"No, it's definitely not that," he agreed. "But it's not hell anymore, either."

Angela shook her head, refusing to accept the rosy picture he was trying to paint. "It will always be hell to me," she stated flatly.

A smile flickered across his features. "Then I suppose you'll just have to go with me to see for yourself."

Angela was horrified at the suggestion. "Absolutely not. The day the plane lifted off the Saigon runway, I vowed not to set foot in Vietnam again, and I knew I would never want to visit any Far Eastern nation that might remotely remind me of it."

"You've changed, too," Jeff reminded her. "You didn't think you'd ever be able to accept Doch Thu, but you found out he's not a villain. He's just a man whose country suffered through violent military conflict for years. He lost members of his family, his farm, his home, everything. If you could go back to Vietnam and look at it objectively without helicopters filled with wounded soldiers landing or the smell of napalm lingering in the air, maybe your opinion about Vietnam would change."

"I don't want it to change."

There was a knowing glint in his eyes as he challenged, "You'll never be able to let it go until you face it one more time. The longer you let it grow and fester in your mind, the nastier and more horrible it gets."

"That's not true," she protested hotly. "I *have* let it go. I threw Vietnam away when I tossed my uniform in the garbage."

"Then why can't you go back? If it didn't matter, you would be able to walk down the same old streets and see the people without breaking into a cold sweat."

At the thought of returning, she was struck with a shortness of breath and a tremor of her heart that she couldn't ignore.

"It was hard for me the first time," he admitted. "But it was a sort of catharsis that set free all the resentment and pain I had been holding inside. I still can't go into a jungle without a small anxiety attack, but it's not any worse than riding the New York subway."

"I don't know . . ."

He must have sensed she was weakening. "Is your passport up to date?"

"Yes, I went to Europe last summer, but . . ."

"Since this is a cooperative effort between our government and theirs, getting a visa for you shouldn't be a problem. Oh, by the way, Bo's going with us. I talked to him earlier, and he and Melora are trying to make arrangements to meet us in San Francisco in two days."

"Exactly what will you be doing in Vietnam?"

He cleared his throat and shifted his weight from one foot to the other, obviously hesitant to tell her. "Maybe you've heard about the trips that have been made to dig up and defuse old land mines. Well, there've been a lot of children hurt lately in an area northwest of Da Nang, an area I happen to be very familiar with."

"Oh, terrific! Why don't you just gargle some arsenic and juggle chain saws while you're at it?" She sputtered in dismay. "Now I know why you want me along...you need someone to carry the plastic bag home." It was even worse than she had expected. She had been lulled into thinking the mission wouldn't be dangerous because the government was sponsoring it.

He dismissed her concerns with a casual lift of his broad shoulders. "The mine field will be the easy part. My men know what they're doing. The tricky part will be getting the remains of a man we think might be Melora's brother home for inspection. Like I said before, the Vietnamese like to time these things to suit their purposes, and if it's not advantageous for them to release the bones, they won't. So I'm going to have to smuggle them out of the country." He frowned at a new thought. "On the other hand, maybe it would be better if you didn't go. I wouldn't want them to think you had anything to do with it if I should get caught."

Angela threw up her hands in resignation. "One minute you're telling me not to worry, and the next you're talking about getting caught. Of course, now I can go back to Boston and not worry about your little junket into the jungle."

She didn't want to go to Vietnam. She didn't want to change her opinion of the country or its people. But she loved Jeff, and she respected his concern for others.

She didn't want to go, but she didn't want to let Jeff leave without her. She *couldn't* let him. He would be in danger from the moment his plane landed in Da Nang until it returned to San Francisco. She knew it wasn't logical, but she believed that her presence would somehow protect him and bring him back safely. He had called her his angel of mercy. And at least once more, he would need all the help and support she could give him.

"I'll probably hate you and myself for doing this, but I'm going with you. You make the arrangements and I'll pack my suitcase."

Chapter Fifteen

"The Eagle and The Hawk" —John Denver

"I wish I could go." Melora's expression was clearly envious. "Angela, please take care of my husband. Make sure he doesn't get hit on the head and forget where he lives again."

"I don't have to go," Bo responded. "I wouldn't be disappointed to miss this trip. I'm sure Hawk will be going to Vietnam some other time. But I doubt if my wife will be having twins again any time soon."

"Twins!" Angela repeated. "I still can't believe you're going to have twins. You two may have gotten a late start, but you're sure making up for it."

"We couldn't believe it, either," Bo exclaimed with obvious pride. "But because of Melora's age—"

"Watch it buster," his wife cautioned good-naturedly.

"Uh...because we don't want to take any chances with these babies, the doctor has recommended that Melora stick close to home and stay off her feet as much as possible. She wants me to go, but paying a personal visit to the two old sisters who saved me is not as important as my babies. Hawk knows where they live. He can give them some money for me and see how they've been getting along."

"Absolutely not. I won't let you miss this chance to go." Melora shook her head so emphatically that several dark red strands of hair slipped free of her French braid. "The doctor said I'd have to take it easy, not that I'd have to be treated like an invalid. I believe I can get along by myself for a couple of weeks. Besides," she said, reaching up to caress her husband's cheek, "this is your trip. You've learned so much about your past and the world since you were last in Vietnam. You really need to go back, to put it all into perspective."

"I hate leaving you alone."

"I won't be alone. My mother and grandparents are only a few minutes away. And I promise I won't be taking any chances." Melora smiled as she rested a hand over her slightly bulging stomach. "I want these babies as much as you do."

Bo hesitated, clearly torn between the responsibility he felt toward his family and his wife's logical arguments in favor of the trip.

"I could stay with you, Melora," Angela offered. "I've delivered enough twins lately to feel I could handle any situation."

Melora laughed but refused the offer. "No, you are *all* going. I won't object if you promise to think about me and feel sorry that I missed the trip. But I absolutely refuse for any of you to worry about me while you're gone. After all, I've still got more than five months to go. There'll be plenty of time for Bo to fuss over me when he gets back."

And Angela didn't doubt that he would. Bo and Melora were so obviously in love. It was as if they were on a different level than the rest of the world. An exchanged glance, a lingering touch, a shared smile—the couple communicated in a language that was solely theirs.

Angela looked at Jeff and saw he was watching her. The glances they exchanged were hesitant, questioning, always wary. There were such strong emotions just below the surface, emotions they weren't certain how to handle.

In a way, it would be nice if she and Jeff could have met with none of the pain, the doubts, even the passion between them. In their time together at Jeff's house and on his ranch they had found new facets in each of their personalities. If their major problem was trying to coordinate their different life-styles so they could be together, they might be able to find a solution. But they had the ghost of Craig hovering over their shoulders, the hurt Jeff had felt, the doubt she had felt. The obstacles seemed insurmountable.

"Now don't forget to take lots of pictures," Melora reminded them as they were preparing to board the plane. "My editor says the text to my book is ready to be typeset, but she'd like to include some photographs of Vietnam now."

"Melora's too modest to tell you, but there was quite a battle between three publishers for the rights to her book. It'll be out around Christmas, and they're already bidding on paperback rights," Bo informed the group. "They expect it to be a best-seller, even though it's nonfiction."

"I can't wait to read it," Angela said. "From all Jeff's told me about it, your book sounds like it will be the definitive study of the war's effects on the soldiers and their families."

The line moved forward, and Bo gave Melora a kiss goodbye and a final unnecessary reminder that he expected her to keep her promise about taking good care of herself while he was gone. Melora took his nagging with good humor and waved to them until they could no longer see her standing by the terminal gate.

It was a long flight. They had a day and a half lay-over in Hong Kong, where they did a little sightseeing and shopping before flying to Bangkok, then to Ho Chi Minh City. They spent the night in the city that had once been called Saigon before boarding a plane that appeared to be held together by spit and rubber bands for the short flight to Da Nang.

As they sputtered along, Angela focused her attention on the landscape in an attempt to keep her mind from considering the reliability of their aircraft. Land so green it looked like emerald velvet stretched below her. Low-growing hedgerows divided the fields into asymmetrical patterns. On one side of the plane, in the distance, Angela could see the South China Sea, sparkling in the sunlight, and on the other side she caught glimpses of the jungle, the palm trees looking like delicate lace. The contrast of the lush, dark, verdant countryside against the deep blue of the water was striking and, Angela was forced to admit, incredibly beautiful. She had barely noticed the scenery before. And she definitely didn't remember the beauty.

They tried to find her EVAC base, but apparently it had been bombed out of existence. All signs of military habitation had been replaced by a village that had sprouted up in its place. But Angela could remember the layout of the buildings and tents with picture-perfect clarity. She could visualize herself running from the hospital to the officers' club while the pounding rain drenched her to the skin. She remembered the row of open-topped shower stalls several yards from the nurses' quarters, and the curling barbed wire fence that protected the perimeter of the base.

But with the quonset hut hospital gone, the memories of what had gone on inside it weren't clear. The helicopter pad where the wounded had been loaded onto waiting gurneys was now a cluster of brightly colored awnings, probably a marketplace. The secluded area looked peaceful and quiet. It revealed none of the bustle and trauma of its previous occupants.

The plane circled the Marble Mountains before easing into the Da Nang airport. "I didn't realize those mountains were so rugged. They sort of remind me of the Rockies," she commented to Jeff who was sitting next to her.

"Yes, they do. A kind of miniature version without all the snow," Jeff agreed. As the plane began to land, he added, "Look how much the city has grown. It seems to have really spread out in the past few years."

They found the hotel where everyone on the mission was to meet, and Jeff and Angela settled into their room. Bo was in the room across the hall. The accommodations were not deluxe, but they weren't uncomfortable.

Jeff took them to the restaurant where Bo had had his first meal after leaving the jungle. He and Bo discussed how much Bo had learned about himself and the world since that dinner, and Angela listened, fascinated by the story of Bo's rescue.

The next morning, Bo wanted Jeff to take him into the jungle to the Vietnamese sisters' farm. Not willing to be left behind, Angela rode with them in a borrowed Jeep.

It was a rough trip once they left the main road. Narrow ruts led the way deep into the mass of trees and twisted vines. During all her months in Vietnam, Angela had never had to go into the jungle, so this was a new and slightly unnerving experience. The jungle was wild and exotic, with eerie animal noises and the constant annoyance of insects that seemed to follow the Jeep in a hungry cloud. A heavy dose of repellent kept all but the most tenacious bugs from biting, but she could feel them hitting her skin and getting tangled in her hair.

The claustrophobic feeling of the foliage closing around them and the sense that they were being watched made her uncomfortable. When she expressed her unease to Jeff and Bo, they nodded.

"I can see its beauty, but I'll never again be able to walk through a jungle without expecting to be ambushed," Jeff admitted. "I suppose a person who has been mugged in a dark alley would feel the same way about being on a city street at night."

"It's sort of pretty in an overgrown, natural way, but I can see how the NVA could hide in here, invisible and deadly dangerous to our soldiers," Bo commented. "I remember staring at the twisted, tangled vines and trees while I was working in the paddies and wondering how any human could possibly survive in there. Little did I know that there was a whole world on the other side."

Angela turned to him. Her forehead was creased with a perplexed frown as she said, "I can understand why you would want to go back and see the place where you were held prisoner for so many years. But what I can't quite figure out is why you'd want to reward the old women for their awful treatment of you."

Bo gave her a patient smile. "I know it sounds strange, but while the sisters didn't exactly treat me like a guest, they didn't turn me over to the VC, either. I realize their motives were self-serving, but they *did* save my life. Granted, I slept in the barn and ate inadequate portions of fish and rice, but those two old ladies didn't live much better than that. I have no idea what their beds were like, but I know their meals were the same as mine.''

''I remember how you were worried they wouldn't survive without your help,'' Jeff said.

Bo shrugged. ''I'm not sure they have. There were no men left in their family. Most of the men in the area were either killed or badly wounded. The sisters are very old. But it takes very little money to live here, so I hope my contribution will make the rest of their lives comfortable enough so they don't have to worry.''

Angela shook her head, not quite understanding his motivations. Bo had been treated like a beast of burden, working long days in the rice paddies and sleeping on a pile of straw in the barn. Melora had told her it had taken him weeks to adapt to sleeping on a bed, and months for his undernourished body to gain weight.

Instead of hiding the Jeep in the thick underbrush, as Hawk and Melora had done when they had been on their rescue mission, they drove right up to the door. The mud shack with its thatched roof looked much the same as it had a year ago, Bo said. The fence of saplings had leafed out, providing an attractive, if not very substantial barrier to keep the animals from wandering into the front yard. But Angela knew saplings were planted to protect a house's occupants from evil spirits as was the spiritual belief of the Vietnamese natives, rather than to keep livestock out.

Angela stayed close to Jeff and Bo as they approached the house. She noticed Jeff slip a pistol into the pocket of his lightweight jacket as a precaution against the unknown.

A flock of scrawny chickens scattered in noisy confusion as the three people rounded the corner of the house and scanned the field, looking for the women. They were easy to spot. One was slowly following the lumbering water buffalo through ankle-deep water. The other woman was bent over the plants, chopping weeds with a short-handled hoe. Bright green blades of rice grew thickly in curving rows.

It wasn't until the buffalo rounded the end of one row and headed toward the house that the women noticed the visitors. There was a rapid, high-pitched conversation between the sisters. Jeff and Bo were able to understand only a few words of it.

"They're frightened," Jeff said. "Bo, maybe you could say something to them."

Bo took a few steps closer to the women and called to them in French. They stared at him in apparent shock, then resumed their staccato chatter. Cautiously, they approached him, studying him from the top of his golden blond hair to the soles of his leather boots.

Smiles revealed yellowed, crooked teeth in their wrinkled, weathered faces. They circled Bo, reaching out to touch him almost gingerly, followed by bursts of Vietnamese and girlish giggles. It was evident they were delighted to see him, not at all the reaction of jailers to an escaped POW.

Jeff leaned closer to Angela and whispered, "They said they were worried he had been killed by wild animals, and they are glad that he is alive and looking well."

Whenever they talked to Bo, they spoke in French, and he answered in the same language as he took a substantial roll of Vietnamese dongs out of his pocket and held it out to them. At first they seemed hesitant to accept it, shaking their heads in confusion, apparently concerned with what might be expected of them in return. But finally Bo was able to convince them it was for them to use any way they wanted, with no strings attached, and he pressed the money into one of the women's small, callused hands.

Angela looked around her, noting how much work would be involved in keeping the farm operational. She couldn't imagine how two very tiny, elderly women could do all the manual labor. She was surprised that they had survived without a man's help. Just handling the placid but hostile-looking water buffalo must have been quite an accomplishment for someone who weighed only a fraction as much as the huge, heavy beast.

She began to understand why Bo felt a responsibility to these old ladies, even a kinship of sorts.

There were tears in the women's eyes when Bo turned to leave. They sneaked shy looks at the other two Americans who stood patiently waiting for their friend. Angela smiled and nodded, bobbing her head as Doch Thu did when he was talking to her. They seemed to accept the gesture of friendship and bobbed their heads in response.

"They said the crop hasn't done too well this year," Bo said when the Jeep was bouncing down the rutted path away from the farm. "Maybe now all they'll have to worry about is their garden. And they won't have to fool with that buffalo."

"I've never understood how people tame those buffaloes and make them do what they want them to." Angela brushed her hair out of her eyes, holding it off her face with one hand as the breeze tried to pull it free.

"They have their bad days," Bo agreed. "Sometimes that guy and I would have a battle of wills. He would decide he didn't want to move, and I was equally determined to convince him he had to. It was a good thing I was smarter than he, because I sure couldn't have forced him to do anything he didn't want to do.''

"Don't they believe the buffaloes have souls?" Angela asked. When Bo nodded, she remarked, "I'll bet they treated him better than they treated you."

"It used to annoy me that I had to share the barn with him." He chuckled wryly at the memory. "He wasn't the best-smelling roommate. Buffaloes are considered to be prized possessions, because not too many people have one, so I can understand why they would want to take good care of him."

That night, as Angela and Jeff were getting ready for bed, she admitted to him, "It *has* changed quite a bit since I was here. It's very different without the tanks and the planes."

"It's too bad everyone can only remember the fighting and the dying. Vietnam is a beautiful country and most of the people are very warm and friendly. They were as devastated by the loss of the war as we were." Jeff sat on the bed, a towel around his neck, his hair still wet from a shower. "The first time I came back, the streets were filled with Amerasian children who were cast out by their own people, and crippled Vietnamese veterans who no longer could work. It was very sad."

Angela had been sitting with her back against the headboard, but she moved forward to wrap her arms around Jeff's waist. Resting her head against his shoulder, his scar beneath her cheek, she sighed. "I don't suppose I ever considered their hardships or their losses. There were no winners, were there? We all lost our innocence, our naiveté."

He took her into his arms and cradled her tenderly. "Some people lost more than others." He rubbed his cheek against her hair.

"We were too young to be here then. We should have been home, going to the beach and riding around in our Mustangs listening to the radio without a care in the world."

"I'd probably be stuck in a blue-collar, dead-end job in Pittsburgh and hating every minute of it."

"And I'd probably be married to a doctor and living in a mansion in Boston."

"We would never have met."

She twisted in his arms until she could look into his face. "And that would have been a real loss," she whispered, her voice husky with emotion.

His eyes shimmered with longing, but there was also desperation in their blue depths. "I don't want to lose you again, Angie. I'm not a rich doctor, and the best I can offer you is a cabin I built with my own hands. What can I do to make you stay?"

Her arms twined around his neck and she leaned forward until her lips met his. He lay back, pulling her with him as they kissed with all the passion of lovers anxiously trying to make every moment count. His hands gripped her waist and he lifted her, letting his lips move down the graceful column of her neck until the roundness of her breast filled his mouth. Her fingers dug into the thin bedspread on each side of his head as he nibbled and tantalized her nipples. Her hips positioned themselves over him and he pushed inside, letting his maleness swell within her until every movement caused a provocative friction that made her cry out her impatience.

He guided her motion, steadying her and forcing her to wait until the throbbing ache within her could stand no more. The explosion of passion rippled through her, carrying her almost beyond consciousness with its sweet devastation. As she drifted through the misty fog of ecstasy, she could feel him thrusting deeper until, with a ragged moan, he poured his heat into her.

For several minutes, they lay in each other's arms, gasping for breath and waiting until their heartbeats slowed. Angela was sprawled across his chest, and she murmured against the curve of his neck, "An indoor bathroom and electricity might do it."

"Might do what?" he asked, still dazed from the violence of their lovemaking.

"Might make me stay."

In a smooth movement, he reversed their positions until he was on top. "I'm serious about this. Don't joke," he cautioned gruffly.

"I'm not joking," she assured him. "I know we have a lot of things to work out, but I'm willing to give it a try."

"What about my trips here? Can you live with them?"

Angela drew in a deep, shaky breath. "I'm not sure, but I can try."

"Does this mean you'll marry me?"

She glanced up at him. "Is that a proposal?"

"Would you accept it if it was?"

There were mentally circling each other, waiting for a bolt of wisdom to reveal the solution to their doubts and fears.

"Maybe we should live together for a while first," she suggested. "I want you to be sure you won't resent me because I can't give you children. A man needs an heir, someone to carry on the family name. Who will you teach to take your place? Who will you pass the ranch to when you die?''

His thumb stroked the curve of her cheekbone, then trailed across the full curve of her lower lip. ''Someone will come along, just as I did and just as George Randall did before me. And as for my family name, I couldn't care less.''

Angela frowned. ''Jeff, what happened during your childhood to make you dislike your parents so much? I know you don't want to talk about it, but I wish you would share it with me so I could understand.''

It was obvious he didn't want to think about it, much less talk about it. But as if he accepted that she should know more about his past if she was considering becoming a part of his future, he said, ''There's not much to tell, actually. I was unfortunate enough to have parents who should never have had children. My father was an alcoholic. I guess he would be called a mean drunk. He would stumble into the house and beat the hell out of the first person he saw. My mother took it for a while, then she left. I was only about eight or nine at the time, but I remember how devastated I was that my mother would leave me behind.''

No wonder Jeff had viewed her marriage as an abandonment. His mother had set the pattern of desertion, and Angela had unwittingly followed, reopening an old wound. ''Oh, Jeff, I'm so sorry. That must have been awful for you.''

He shrugged, but there was hurt in his eyes. ''I got over it. As soon as I could figure out a way to live on my own, I left home, too. When I was fifteen, I lied about my age and got a job and a room near the school. I don't know how I did it, or even why I kept trying, but I made it through high school. The day after I graduated, I shipped out to basic training. Six months later I was on my way to Vietnam.''

"And you never heard from your mother again.''

"No. For all I know, she could be dead.''

"And your father?''

He shook his head stiffly. "I don't know, and I don't care. He never thought I'd amount to anything, and I wouldn't give him the benefit of knowing how my life has turned out.''

She wrapped her arms around Jeff, and hugged him as tight as she could. "It doesn't matter anymore. You've proven him wrong. You're a wonderful man and you've made something of your life. Against all odds, you survived *and* succeeded.''

He returned her hug with an almost painful desperation. She knew he would be devastated if she should leave again. She snuggled closer, loving the feeling that she had found what she had always been looking for—a man who needed her, but who was strong enough so she could lean on him, too. He would take care of her but not smother her, and she could help him without having him drain all her energy.

"Now about that bathroom,'' she said, a peaceful smile smoothing away the emptiness that had been in her heart for so long.

THE NEXT MORNING, they met with the men Jeff had contacted for the mission. Several members of the local government were also present, and after an hour of conversation, the Vietnamese officials gave their approval to the plan.

Angela tried not to think how dangerous the mission would be. Jeff had assured her that with the sensitive equipment they would be using and the maps the Marine Corps provided, the risk should be minimal. Several of the men had been in the engineer battalion that planted the mines. But Angela was afraid that now, when she and Jeff were so close to developing some sort of future together, something awful would happen and he would be taken away from her. It would be a tragic poetic justice if she should lose him after she had passed him by once before to marry another man. Angela would be the one who was left alone.

"Angie, I want you to meet a couple of buddies of mine," Jeff said as he led her over to two men who were dressed in baggy camouflage fatigues. "The guy with the receding hairline is Gopher, and the other one is Lucky. Guys, this is Angela Greene. She was a nurse, stationed in Da Nang when I was there."

Gopher gave Jeff a withering look, apparently in reference to his thinning hair, but when he looked at Angela, he smiled broadly. "Is this her? Is this the woman you cried in your beer about for a whole year?"

Jeff didn't answer, but there was a sudden flush of color high on his cheekbones.

Gopher held his hand out to Angela. "It's nice to meet you at last. I figured you'd be a beauty, and I was right."

Lucky, too, extended his hand and greeted her warmly. But she barely had time to exchange a few words of conversation with them before Jeff announced it was time to hit the road.

Risking teasing from his friends, Jeff took an extra moment to give Angela a long, lingering kiss before he climbed into the Jeep next to Bo, with Gopher and Lucky in the back. Noting her worried look, he flashed her his crooked grin and said, "Don't worry, Angie. Nothing's going to happen to me. I promise."

She tried to return his smile, but she knew it was weak. She wished she shared his confidence, but she couldn't. A heavy ache pulled at her heart and she clutched her hand to her chest in an effort to relieve the pain. "I love you, Jeff. Please come back," she called, but she knew her words were lost in the roar of the Jeep's engine.

Chapter Sixteen

"Forever and Ever, Amen" —*Randy Travis*

Angela was too restless to sit in her hotel room and wait for Jeff to return. She wished she could shrug off the premonition of tragedy that hung over her, but she couldn't. Knowing that she'd better find something to occupy her mind for the next eight to ten hours or she'd go crazy with worry, Angela decided to check out the marketplace.

The sun was shining brightly, heating the humid air to an almost unbearable temperature. Angela was glad she had pulled her hair into a clip that kept it away from her face. But determined tendrils still managed to curl around her neck, sticking wetly to her skin.

In a country where bicycles outnumbered cars by more than one hundred to one, the noise of the streets was much different than what she was used to back in Boston. Instead of horns and screeching tires, there was the whir of spoked wheels and the constant chatter of the Vietnamese dialect mixed with barking dogs and the sound of sandaled feet slapping against the pavement.

Angela wandered along the street, looking into the people's faces, noticing, for the first time, that each was different. They were not a faceless mass of humanity, bent on the killing and maiming of Americans. She saw the sweet smiles of the children and heard their laughter. Beautiful young women with long, straight black hair, their slender, petite bodies completely covered by ankle-length slitted dresses worn over black trousers, walked from shop to shop, woven baskets hanging from their arms. Beggars and crippled soldiers slouched against the buildings, holding out their hats, hoping to collect enough money to buy a meal. Old men with wispy white beards sat on park benches, watching the city pass them by.

But all of them, old and young, wealthy and poor, had the same haunted look in their eyes, as if they had seen it all and expected the worst. Angela couldn't imagine how awful it would be to live in a country that had been devastated by war for so long. The Vietnamese had lost their land, their homes, their families, their businesses. At least the GIs had America to return to when their tour was over. Even though some people hadn't welcomed them, at least they had family and friends waiting.

Angela was standing in front of the Da Nang Civic Hospital, and impulsively decided to go inside. During the war, she had heard horror stories about the local medical facilities. Since she had a few hours to kill, she thought she would see if there had been any improvement.

Rows of wooden benches lined the walls, and people were sitting or lying on the hard slats as they stoically waited their turn. A nurse dressed in a white robe, her head covered by a flowing cowl, moved from patient to patient, asking questions and taking notes. A few minutes later a doctor hurried in. He and the nurse conducted a rapid conversation. He glanced at her notes, then pointed to the most seriously ill people.

It wasn't until he had stepped closer that Angela recognized him. "Khiu Xi, is it really you?" she asked in amazement. The last time she had seen him, he was just a skinny little kid hanging around the hospital, always willing to run errands. Khiu had been a favorite with the doctors and nurses. Even Angela had had a degree of fondness for the gangly, eager-to-please boy.

"Yes, Lieutenant," he said, a delighted smile greeting her. "I am Khiu, but I cannot believe it is you, here, in my hospital."

"Your hospital? Are you in charge here?"

He nodded, then looked around at the chipped tile floor and the strips of peeled paint that left ragged bare spots on the plaster walls. "It is not very nice and there is a great shortage of supplies. But it is better than dying in the street, is it not? Would you like me to show you around?"

Angela started to point out there were patients waiting, but remembering Oriental hospitality, she knew she would be gravely insulting her host if she declined his invitation. "Yes, I'd like to see your facilities."

She followed him through the large, overcrowded rooms, trying not to show the shock she was feeling at the sight of two or three patients sharing a bed. Each intravenous bottle fed several tubes that were stuck in the patients' arms, some without tape to hold them steady and keep them from pulling out or painfully jerking the skin.

"I know we do not have all of the nice facilities you had at your hospital. We do not have enough money to buy all the antibiotics and other medicines we need." He shrugged. "But we have to make do."

The nice facilities they had! Angela couldn't believe anyone would consider the facilities at the EVAC as *nice*.

Compared to Stateside hospitals, the base facility had been barely adequate. Their equipment had been out-of-date and unpredictable, and there was always a shortage of supplies. But at least they could count on new shipments on a semiregular basis. Occasionally, they had had to improvise, but even at the worst of times, they hadn't had to take the dangerous shortcuts this hospital was taking.

"How many doctors and nurses are on your staff?" she asked as they walked down the hall.

"There is only one other doctor besides myself. After the war, I went to medical school in Hong Kong. There were many of my countrymen at the school, but most did not come back here to practice. I was glad to return to help my people. But the nurses do not have your skills or your knowledge. They cannot handle the situations you and the other Army nurses did. I used to watch all of you and admire how any of you could take care of an emergency almost as well as the doctors. If only we had someone to train our nurses, we could save so many lives."

Angela was humbled by his observations. It triggered memories. Khiu had always been in the background, watching and apparently learning. He bombarded them with questions, and when they had the time, they answered him. He made it a point never to be in the way, and he became such a constant presence that they often forgot he was around until he spoke up.

Little Khiu had grown up and taken advantage of all he had seen. But he couldn't do it alone.

A whimper of pain caught Angela's attention, and she stopped next to one of the pallets on the floor. A woman, very young and very beautiful, lay there, her well-rounded stomach clearly announcing her advanced pregnancy. Her skin was paler than that of most of the people around her, and her eyes were large and only slightly slanted. Probably American blood ran through her veins. She peered at Angela, silently pleading for relief. Her hand was pressed tightly against her mouth to muffle her cries.

"Khiu, have you checked this woman? She appears to be in an advanced state of labor."

"I have no time right now. There are many, many others to care for." He bent and spoke softly to the woman, and she smiled weakly. Doctor Khiu stood and turned to Angela. "And now I must go. It was very good to see you again. I thank you for being patient with me when I was but a small boy. It helped me much."

He bowed silently, then headed toward the waiting area. The woman shifted on the hard, uncomfortable pallet, and another cry escaped her covered mouth. Angela stared at the doctor's retreating back for several seconds before she called after him. "Doctor, maybe I could help. I know this is very unconventional, but I wouldn't mind assisting in the delivery."

"I am the only doctor here right now," he answered. "I will try to make it back to her in time to deliver her baby, but I cannot promise. But, yes, we would very much appreciate your help with Liah. It is her first child and I think she is a little frightened."

A little frightened! Terror radiated from Liah's liquid brown eyes. Angela thought "a little frightened" was a huge understatement. Doctor Khiu had already disappeared around the corner, leaving Angela alone with her decision. *What on earth do you think you're doing?* she asked herself as she rolled up her sleeves and knelt next to the woman. *You haven't practiced nursing for seventeen years.* Lacking a stethoscope, Angela placed her ear on Liah's distended stomach. She could hear the baby's heartbeat faintly echoing inside the woman's womb. And she could feel Liah's muscles contracting as the baby began its journey into the cold, cruel world.

Angela smoothed Liah's silky black hair from her perspiration-moistened face. "You don't have to do this alone, Liah. I'll help you." She stood and flagged down a passing nurse. Assuming the no-nonsense voice she used in critical situations, Angela asked the nurse to help move Liah onto a bed in a more private area. And she gave her coerced helper a list of the basic items she would need for the delivery.

The nurse obeyed with only the slightest hesitation, leading Angela and Liah to a corner of one of the wards where a tattered but serviceable Chinese-patterned screen provided a modicum of privacy. The nurse left Angela and Liah, but soon returned with most of the things Angela had requested.

The crown of the baby's head was already visible when Angela finally finished minimal preparations. She was glad she didn't have time to consider what she was doing or she would have probably chickened out. She had joked with Melora about delivering her babies because of the experience with the ewes and the lambs, but animal births and human births were too different to be compared.

"Push, Liah, push," she instructed and the nurse interpreted the command. Liah tried to keep quiet, but her cries couldn't be stifled. "It's okay to scream," Angela assured her soothingly. "It'll all be over in a few minutes and you'll have a beautiful little baby to take home." The contractions eased and Angela showed Liah how to breathe to help her muscles relax until it all began again.

She lost track of the time, but it was a relatively quick and easy birth. The baby's head finally appeared, then his body slid into Angela's waiting arms. She was shaken by the magnitude of the moment. Working from long-buried memories, she clipped the baby's umbilical cord and helped him catch his first terrified breath of air. Angela looked into the wet, pasty face. His eyes were squeezed tightly shut and his mouth was wide as he screamed his disapproval, and she smiled. He appeared to be healthy and normal. What parent could ask for more?

Reluctantly she handed the baby to the nurse so Angela could complete the post-delivery details. "He's a strong, handsome boy," she informed Liah. "I'm sure your husband will be very proud." When the nurse translated that sentiment to the new mother, a volley of conversation followed, but since Angela didn't understand any but the most basic words of Vietnamese, she didn't pay any attention. She made sure Liah was comfortable.

Exhausted, but pleased by her contribution, Angela washed up in the small scrub room. It wasn't until it was all over that she realized how shaky her knees had become. Limply, she sat on a chair and let her head rest in the palms of her trembling hands. It had felt wonderful to be back in the action, helping another human being. But it struck her with incredible clarity that she had no desire to return to nursing full time.

There had always been a little guilt that she had given up a worthwhile occupation. She wouldn't mind helping to teach these nurses how to handle simple situations. But she realized her life was no less meaningful because she didn't care to handle human patients anymore.

The thought began to grow in her mind that she could pass on her knowledge to these desperate people. And she was certain she could find others to help her. Maybe her old friend Dr. John Stone would be willing to come back for a mission of mercy such as this. It would coordinate so well with Jeff's work here that he would surely approve of her idea. For several minutes she sat, making plans and growing more enthusiastic.

She left the scrub room and went to the ward to say goodbye to Liah. As she walked to the corner of the room and rounded the screen, she stopped in her tracks. The bed was empty. Liah was nowhere in sight.

The nurse had removed the sheet and was spreading a relatively clean one across the thin mattress.

"Where is Liah? She shouldn't be up so soon." Angela was concerned that the young woman had been allowed to move around.

"She is gone," the nurse informed her in halting English.

"Gone? Where? I must get her back into bed."

"No, she is gone from the hospital."

"Even if Liah was ready, the baby certainly shouldn't have been allowed to leave yet. He hasn't been properly cleaned up. And I wanted to check him to see if all his vital signs were normal."

"Oh, but she did not take the baby. He is still here."

Angela shook her head, assuming she and the nurse were having a problem understanding each other. "Surely she wouldn't leave her baby behind."

"A lot of women like Liah do this," the nurse explained, as if deserting a child was a natural occurrence. "She has no husband and the baby's father is also half American. The baby was not wanted. Liah cannot take care of him all alone, and he will keep her from finding an acceptable husband."

Angela knew how difficult it was for Amerasian children to be accepted by Vietnamese society. Being neither Oriental nor American, the children had been rejected by both cultures. The first generation of Amerasian children had grown up not fitting in anywhere. They were now in their late teens to mid-twenties, and still they were having trouble finding their place. Apparently, Liah had had a relationship with another Amerasian, making her baby twice cursed. The poor infant didn't have a chance.

"What will happen to him?" Angela asked the nurse as they moved the screen aside.

"He will be taken to an orphanage in a few days."

"Is it likely that someone will adopt him?"

The old lady shook her head. "Oh, no. There are many, many children in the orphanage. No one can afford to take them home. But they are quite happy there. The sisters give them lessons."

Angela straightened to her full height, which was only a fraction of an inch taller than the Vietnamese woman. An idea was forming in her mind, an idea even more impulsive and crazy than her decision to deliver Liah's child. "Well, we'll see about that. Do you have any idea where Doctor Khiu is right now?"

JEFF WAS EXHAUSTED. It had been a nerve-racking day. Even with the maps and the locating equipment, it had been a very tense group of men who had scoured a huge field north of Da Nang, searching for long-buried land mines. Time and erosion had caused the mines to work their way up to the surface. The mines were in various stages of decomposition, and they would explode with the smallest impetus. The men had had to move slowly and carefully.

But eventually, more than one hundred mines had been located and destroyed, and the area had been clean before the men left. Jeff, Bo, Gopher and Lucky had made a detour to pack the remains of three skeletons believed to be American soldiers into the boxes that had held the equipment they used to find the mines. Hidden in the boxes, the pieces of bones would travel to the U.S. without discovery. The equipment had already been cleared by the Vietnamese government for an expedient return.

In Jeff's pocket was a dirty, frayed badge attached to a piece of drab green cotton that had been found with the bones. The name DELANEY was sewn on the badge. It might identify one of the men whose remains were being returned. And Jeff and Bo had mixed hopes that that particular Delaney would be Melora's brother. She had searched for him for so long, it would be a relief to finally know his fate. On the other hand, it would end all possibilities that her brother was still alive and would, someday, somehow be discovered and sent home.

Jeff was dirty, sweaty and hungry. He was also anxious to see Angela. He realized he had blown his chance to press her for a commitment to marry him. She had given him the perfect opportunity, but he had been surprised. When his mind was not preoccupied with his mission, he had given it much more thought and decided he would not settle for a vague response. It was time Angela told him her true feelings. And it was time he told her his.

He knew it wouldn't be easy to voice the word "love." It was not a normal part of his vocabulary. No one had ever told him he was loved. And he had never said he loved anyone. But, for the first time in his life, he knew what the word meant, and he could no longer hold his emotions inside. Whether or not she returned his love, he had to tell Angela and chance her rejection.

And so his hand shook as it closed around the doorknob of their hotel room. He hated to think of how lonely he had been without her. But so much had happened between them since the reunion. They were being given a second chance, and Jeff felt confident that this time they could make it.

The thin, reedy cry of a baby sounded as if it was coming from beyond the door, but Jeff knew that wasn't possible. When he opened the door and the volume of the cry increased, Jeff automatically checked the room key against the number on the door to make certain he hadn't somehow let himself into the wrong room. The numbers were the same.

"Angie," he said when he saw her leaning over the bed, her back to him. "I'm back. Everything went just fine. We..." His words trailed off as she turned and approached him. His gaze flickered briefly across her uncertain but ecstatic expression before it lowered to the tiny bundle in her arms.

Dark brown fuzz covered the top of the baby's head, and large, slightly slanted dark blue eyes squinted up at the two adults. Incredibly small fingers curled around Angela's. Round pink cheeks, a mere dot of a nose, and a circle of lips still posed as if they had just been suckling completed a face that was so adorable and precious that Jeff's breath caught in his throat.

"I wasn't gone that long," he managed to say at last. "You were certainly busy today."

The story spilled from Angela's lips, her excitement evident in the way her warm brown eyes softened every time she looked at the sleeping infant. "I just couldn't let him go to the orphanage. I delivered him. I was the first person to hold him in my arms. I couldn't let them just lose him in the crowd of unwanted children. Because someone *does* want him." She searched Jeff's eyes with a serious look. "*I* want him. But I want you, too. If you don't think you can accept him, then I'll put him up for adoption once we get to the States."

She took a step closer and smiled at him with an affection so sincere Jeff couldn't help but believe it. "I've been doing a lot of thinking about us—you and me. I love you, Jeff. Now I know you're not comfortable with that word, and you might not even feel as strongly about me as I do about you, but I want you to know that I love you. I always have and I always will." Angela breathed a wistful, anxious sigh. "I'll admit that I resisted it. I didn't want to love you because it meant I would have to give up all that was familiar to me. After spending time in Vietnam, I just wanted to fall back into a comfortable rut and live the rest of my life without any conflicts.

"Of course, it didn't turn out that way. I was devastated when I thought you were dead. But I'm not going to be so foolish again. You might risk your life on these little missions of goodwill, but I'd rather spend the rest of my days and nights with you than without you."

Jeff felt the air rush out of his lungs in a relieved chuckle. "You and I must have been on the same wavelength today because I've been rehearsing my speech all afternoon. Angie, I can guarantee that I've never said this to another person before, but I love you. I don't want us to waste any more time. I think we should get married right away, especially now that we're parents."

"Really, Jeff? Is this what you want, or are you humoring me?"

He smiled at the tiny gift in her arms. "I've never thought I wanted to be a father because I wasn't sure I would know how to love a child. But I don't see that this little guy would be all that difficult to love." Jeff's smile was suddenly replaced by a frown. "How much trouble do you think it'll be to get him home? I don't want him living over here until he's two or three before the paperwork comes through. In fact, I just happen to know someone here in town that could come up with some very authentic documentation."

"No, we don't have to do that. You see, the doctor at the Da Nang hospital is an old acquaintance of mine. He was more than willing to issue a birth certificate in my name to give this baby a good home. And I've promised to come back to help teach his hospital staff. I know it's not quite legal to falsify an official document, but under the circumstances, I think it's justifiable. This baby's coloring is similar to mine, and he is half American, so his features shouldn't be too Asian to be unbelievable."

Jeff reached out and stroked the baby's soft cheek with one of his large, tanned fingers. Already he felt stirrings of an emotional bond with the infant. "Do you think it would be too late to list me as the father?" he asked, his voice revealing the depth of his feelings on the issue.

Angela relaxed as if she finally believed his declarations of acceptance. "I was hoping you'd say that. Of course it isn't too late . . . Daddy."

Daddy. He would never have thought that one little word would touch him so much. Jeff Hawkins, cold, efficient soldier, unemotional man that he had thought he was, felt his eyes fill with tears. Boy, would his buddies laugh if they could see him now. But he didn't really care that they might think he had gone soft. There was a time for planting and a time for sowing; a time for living and a time for dying; a time for loving and a time for hating. This was Jeff's time to love and be loved.

A knock on the door interrupted his thoughts. Reluctant to leave his fiancée and their baby for even a moment, Jeff called for the person to come in.

"I'm starving. What time are we going to dinner?" Bo asked as he stepped into the room.

"You're always starving." Jeff laughed. "We'll go to dinner in a minute. But first, I want you to be the first to meet my son and hear the news that Angie and I will be getting married as soon as possible."

Bo barely blinked an eye. "Melora's going to be furious that she missed this." He walked closer and stared at the soundly sleeping baby. "Can I hold him? I'd better get in practice. My turn will be here soon enough."

Angela transferred the infant into Bo's arms, then greeted Jeff with a belated but adoring kiss. He hugged her tightly, so happy he felt as if his heart might burst in his chest.

"What do you think about the name Randall, after your friend George?" she asked. "I thought it might be fitting to let life come full circle."

Jeff's smile held all the tenderness and love in his soul. "I think that's just perfect."

The Hawk and his mate had found peace and happiness at last.

RELIVE THE MEMORIES....

From New York's immigrant experience to San Francisco's great quake of 1906. From the muddy trenches of World War I's western front to the speakeasies of the Roaring Twenties, to the lost fortunes and indomitable spirit of the Thirties . . . **A CENTURY OF AMERICAN ROMANCE** takes you on a nostalgic journey through the twentieth century.

Glimpse the lives and loves of American men and women from the turn of the century to the dawn of the year 2000. Revel in the romance of a time gone by. And sneak a peek at romance in an exciting future.

Watch for all the **A CENTURY OF AMERICAN ROMANCE** titles coming to you one per month in Harlequin American Romance.

Don't miss a day of **A CENTURY OF AMERICAN ROMANCE**.

The women . . . the men . . . the passions . . . the memories . . .

PASSPORT TO ROMANCE VACATION SWEEPSTAKES

OFFICIAL RULES

SWEEPSTAKES RULES AND REGULATIONS. NO PURCHASE NECESSARY.

HOW TO ENTER:

1. To enter, complete this official entry form and return with your invoice in the envelope provided, or print your name, address, telephone number and age on a plain piece of paper and mail to: Passport to Romance, P.O. Box #1397, Buffalo, N.Y. 14269-1397 No mechanically reproduced entries accepted.
2. All entries must be received by the Contest Closing Date, midnight, December 31, 1990 to be eligible.
3. Prizes: There will be ten (10) Grand Prizes awarded, each consisting of a choice of a trip for two people to: i) London, England (approximate retail value $5,050 U.S.); ii) England, Wales and Scotland (approximate retail value $6,400 U.S.); iii) Caribbean Cruise (approximate retail value $7,300 U.S.); iv) Hawaii (approximate retail value $9,550 U.S.); v) Greek Island Cruise in the Mediterranean (approximate retail value $12,250 U.S.); vi) France (approximate retail value $7,300 U.S.).
4. Any winner may choose to receive any trip or a cash alternative prize of $5,000.00 U.S in lieu of the trip.
5. Odds of winning depend on number of entries received.
6. A random draw will be made by Nielsen Promotion Services, an independent judging organization on January 29, 1991, in Buffalo, N.Y., at 11:30 a.m. from all eligible entries received on or before the Contest Closing Date. Any Canadian entrants who are selected must correctly answer a time-limited, mathematical skill-testing question in order to win. Quebec residents may submit any litigation respecting the conduct and awarding of a prize in this contest to the Régie des loteries et courses du Quebec.
7. Full contest rules may be obtained by sending a stamped, self-addressed envelope to: "Passport to Romance Rules Request", P.O. Box 9998, Saint John, New Brunswick, E2L 4N4.
8. Payment of taxes other than air and hotel taxes is the sole responsibility of the winner
9. Void where prohibited by law.

PASSPORT TO ROMANCE VACATION SWEEPSTAKES

OFFICIAL RULES

SWEEPSTAKES RULES AND REGULATIONS. NO PURCHASE NECESSARY.

HOW TO ENTER:

1. To enter, complete this official entry form and return with your invoice in the envelope provided, or print your name, address, telephone number and age on a plain piece of paper and mail to: Passport to Romance, P.O. Box #1397, Buffalo, N.Y. 14269-1397 No mechanically reproduced entries accepted.
2. All entries must be received by the Contest Closing Date, midnight, December 31, 1990 to be eligible.
3. Prizes: There will be ten (10) Grand Prizes awarded, each consisting of a choice of a trip for two people to: i) London, England (approximate retail value $5,050 U.S.); ii) England, Wales and Scotland (approximate retail value $6,400 U.S.); iii) Caribbean Cruise (approximate retail value $7,300 U.S.); iv) Hawaii (approximate retail value $9,550 U.S.); v) Greek Island Cruise in the Mediterranean (approximate retail value $12,250 U.S.); vi) France (approximate retail value $7,300 U.S.).
4. Any winner may choose to receive any trip or a cash alternative prize of $5,000.00 U.S in lieu of the trip.
5. Odds of winning depend on number of entries received.
6. A random draw will be made by Nielsen Promotion Services, an independent judging organization on January 29, 1991, in Buffalo, N.Y., at 11:30 a.m. from all eligible entries received on or before the Contest Closing Date. Any Canadian entrants who are selected must correctly answer a time-limited, mathematical skill-testing question in order to win. Quebec residents may submit any litigation respecting the conduct and awarding of a prize in this contest to the Régie des loteries et courses du Quebec.
7. Full contest rules may be obtained by sending a stamped, self-addressed envelope to: "Passport to Romance Rules Request", P.O. Box 9998, Saint John, New Brunswick, E2L 4N4
8. Payment of taxes other than air and hotel taxes is the sole responsibility of the winner
9. Void where prohibited by law.

PASSPORT **WIN** 1 of 10 Vacations SEE INSIDE TO ROMANCE

VACATION SWEEPSTAKES

MONTH 3 ENTRY

Official Entry Form

Yes, enter me in the drawing for one of ten Vacations-for-Two! If I'm a winner, I'll get my choice of any of the six different destinations being offered — and I won't have to decide until after I'm notified!

Return entries with invoice in envelope provided along with Daily Travel Allowance Voucher. Each book in your shipment has two entry forms — and the more you enter, the better your chance of winning!

Name

Address Apt.

City State/Prov. Zip/Postal Code

Daytime phone number Area Code

☐ I am enclosing a Daily Travel Allowance Voucher in the amount of $ Write in amount revealed beneath scratch-off

© 1990 HARLEQUIN ENTERPRISES LTD.

PASSPORT **WIN** 1 of 10 Vacations SEE INSIDE TO ROMANCE

VACATION SWEEPSTAKES

MONTH 3 ENTRY

Official Entry Form

Yes, enter me in the drawing for one of ten Vacations-for-Two! If I'm a winner, I'll get my choice of any of the six different destinations being offered — and I won't have to decide until after I'm notified!

Return entries with invoice in envelope provided along with Daily Travel Allowance Voucher. Each book in your shipment has two entry forms — and the more you enter, the better your chance of winning!

Name

Address Apt.

City State/Prov. Zip/Postal Code

Daytime phone number Area Code

☐ I am enclosing a Daily Travel Allowance Voucher in the amount of $ Write in amount revealed beneath scratch-off

CPS-THREE